CHAPTER ONE

February 14, 1924

'A duel?' Swift's scepticism was patent even through the hiss and crackle of the telephone line. 'Pistols at dawn in this day and age?'

'Yes, Swift,' I replied, trying to get a word in. 'And Lady Bancroft has asked us for help.'

'We're not private investigators for hire, Lennox, we're professional consultants to Scotland Yard,' he reminded me tersely.

'Which is why I telephoned Scotland Yard and asked DCI Billings what he thought,' I replied with as much patience as I could muster.

The receiver hummed in my ear for a moment as he absorbed that piece of news. 'Billings wouldn't support any attempt to absolve a murderer, assuming that's what her ladyship is after.'

'No, and he said we should take over the investigation,' I told him. I'd have told him that already if he'd actually taken the time to listen. Billings had taken to calling us in

1

when blue blood was spilled. *Detectives to the toffs*, as he termed it. 'We need to find out why they had the duel. It may not be murder at all.'

'Two men took shots at each other. What else could it be?' Swift asked tartly. He was in London, having decided on a romantic weekend break with his lovely wife, Florence. It didn't seem to have improved his tendency to tetchiness.

'Some sort of ridiculous theatre between two swains that went wrong,' I replied dryly. 'It's Valentine's Day, it was probably over a lady's favour.'

'I know it's Valentine's Day, Lennox, I was hoping to spend it with my wife. Who were the idiots involved?'

'Charles Flyte and Bernard Wilmslow.'

'Do you know either of them?'

'Not personally, but I know their reputations. Wilmslow was argumentative and unpopular,' I said. 'You must have heard of Flyte, he's frequently in the papers.'

'Charles Flyte, the heir to the mercantile shipping fortune?'

'One of the heirs, yes. Wilmslow's the one who's dead. Flyte is still laid up at Bancroft Hall. He took a bullet to the shoulder according to Lady Bancroft. I'm going over shortly to ask him what the devil he thought he was playing at.'

Greggs entered the hall. I cast an eye in his direction. He had donned a blue and white striped apron over his butlering togs and was wielding a feather duster, which he now aimed at the grandfather clock. It was the maids' job to dust, and they had been in only a couple of days ago so I knew what he was up to – eavesdropping, as usual.

Saint Valentine's Day Murder

Karen Baugh
MENUHIN

ISBN: 979-8-3038008-0-9

First paperback and ebook edition.

June and Chris German,
and all the family

'Lennox, are you listening?' Swift's voice in my ear.

'What?'

'I asked if there were any witnesses?'

'No idea. Probably. Persi said Lady Bancroft's some sort of matchmaker.' Despite having lived in the Cotswolds all of my life, apart from school and the war, my wife of just over a year seemed to know far more of what went on than I ever did.

'A romantic matchmaker, I assume,' Swift said.

'Well she's hardly manufacturing Swan Vestas,' I replied dryly. 'Apparently she invites eligible singles for the weekend and lays on some sort of bash with the hope of igniting a few sparks.'

'Eligible toffs, you mean.'

'Yes, Swift…' I was going to say more but my butler was reaching up with the feather duster, one arm extended, one leg raised, tummy straining against his waistcoat, absurdly reminiscent of a portly cherub. 'Greggs, what on earth are you doing?'

He dropped his arm and feigned innocence. 'I am dusting, sir. There are cobwebs.'

'No, there aren't.'

'Lennox?' Swift's voice sounded from the receiver.

I lifted it back to my ear. 'Swift, I'll take Fossett with me and let you know if there's anything worth investigating.'

'What? Did you say Fossett?' A sudden buzz on the line grew louder.

'Yes, speak later,' I shouted back, then put the damn receiver back on the hook because it was really quite annoying.

'Constable Fossett, sir?' Greggs stopped wafting the feather duster and raised his brows.

'Yes, he can take notes or something; there's nothing in Ashton Steeple to occupy him. And Greggs,' I warned him, 'you had better not spread any of this about the vicinity.'

'Such a thing would never cross my mind, sir,' he replied huffily. 'And Bancroft Hall is too far distant for anyone local to be familiar with the household.'

'It's not that far away,' I said, shoving my hands in my pockets.

'Bancroft is in the next county, sir,' he reminded me. 'I have heard that Lady Rose Bancroft holds an annual ball each Valentine's Day for the younger set. The intention being to allow introductions between the… erm…' His cheeks turned pink as he fumbled for the word.

'Sexes,' I provided.

'I had intended to say "gentry", sir.'

'I know all this Greggs, I've just explained it to Swift.'

'Very well, sir,' he huffed.

Persi came in; she was already dressed in a long camel coat over a burgundy wool frock and was pulling on her gloves. Fogg, my little golden spaniel, came with her, tail aloft and wagging with excitement. 'Ready?'

'No. I haven't called Fossett yet.'

'I sent Tommy over to fetch him,' she said.

'When?'

'After you spoke to Lady Bancroft. Tommy came home for lunch, and to fetch his homework, which he said he'd forgotten.'

Tommy was our boot boy, and Cook's orphaned nephew. 'A likely story.'

'Yes,' she agreed. 'They are studying poetry, and today was Elizabeth Barrett Browning. He was supposed to write a paragraph to describe "How Do I Love Thee" but declared it too soppy to be worth comment.'

'He's got a point,' I said in the lad's defence.

She looked up at me, a smile playing on her lips, her blue eyes sparkling. 'A duel sounds much more intriguing, and I'd love to visit Bancroft. I've heard it's an old medieval hall house.' Persi was an archaeologist and specialised in human remains, although anything historic intrigued her. A hall house was a Nobleman's seat that had started life as a huge barn-like building where feasting, drinking and general merry-making was indulged. And fighting of course. 'And you'll need a hand,' she continued, 'especially as you haven't got Swift to organise things.'

'I could also be of assistance, sir,' Greggs offered, hope in his eyes.

'No, you couldn't,' I told him.

'Very well, sir.' He let the feather duster droop, his phiz falling with it.

'What would you do if you did come, Greggs?' I asked. 'I'm simply going to question the blighter who shot the other chap. It's hardly likely to detain us for long.'

'As you say, sir.' An air of martyrdom was descending.

'You have your own Valentine's shindig to go to, don't you?' I said, in an attempt to mollify the old fellow. 'I heard Lady Clementine was having some sort of get together this evening.' Lady Clementine was the owner of Ashton Hall and a colourful addition to the village. A feisty older lady who had any number of elderly beaus dancing attendance on her.

'It is a soiree, sir,' he informed me loftily. 'Cocktails, supper, and possibly some dancing. I am helping her ladyship in the organisation.'

'Right, there you go then, more than enough to keep you occupied. Now where's my coat?'

'It is in the boot room, sir.' He put the feather duster on the hall table with a sigh. 'I will be but a moment.'

'Poor Greggs, perhaps we should take him,' Persi said, pushing blonde strands under a blue silk scarf she'd fixed over her hair.

'You know he only wants some piece of gossip to entertain the ladies with tonight.'

'What's wrong with that? Ladies like to be entertained,' she countered, then gave up when I frowned. 'Do you know where the Bancroft estate is?'

'Warwickshire. Somewhere off the Stratford road. Have you seen my flying helmet?'

'On your desk in the library; your goggles are there too,' she said. 'There's some sort of ancient mystery about Bancroft Hall. Lady Clementine mentioned it when we were discussing local history, but didn't know what it was.'

'That's the nature of mysteries,' I said as I crossed to my library. I found my helmet on top of the pile of correspondence I'd been ignoring. I pulled it over my head, fixed the strap under my chin, then donned the goggles and returned to the hall. Greggs had fetched my great coat, which I'd taken to wearing over my thick winter tweeds because the weather had been freezing since before Christmas.

Today, the sun had finally emerged after a heavy frost and hazy morning. I'd intended to spend a couple of hours after lunch fishing in my lake with my dog for company. There was very little chance of catching anything, but I'd been looking forward to an afternoon of crisp country air amid the tranquil beauty of water and woods.

'Did you pick up the new notebook I bought you?' Persi asked.

'No need, it's just a ridiculous spat gone wrong. Fossett can take notes if we need any.' I shrugged into the coat then headed for the front door. 'I'll bring the Bentley round.'

By the time the car spluttered into life and I'd motored her from the coach house to the turning circle, Fossett had arrived and was waiting with Persi and Fogg by the front porch. Fossett was in full police uniform, the badge on his helmet polished and shining, a leather satchel hanging from his shoulder.

'Hop in,' I ordered as I yanked on the handbrake.

'I've brought a map, Major Lennox,' Fossett said the moment he could be heard above the engine.

'Fine.' I pulled out the choke to give her more fuel. The Bentley had always been temperamental and threatened to cut out altogether in the cold.

Persi climbed into the passenger seat. Fossett and Foggy hopped in the back as I revved the engine in readiness for the off. Greggs came out of the door and held up a hand, then puffed over to the car.

'What?' I said.

'Sir, Tommy is late for school. Could you possibly drop him off?'

'What? Greggs, this is supposed to be some sort of emergency. Where is he?'

'Coming now, sir.'

'Why isn't he taking his bicycle?'

'He has lent it to Laura Elliott, sir.'

'Who?'

'The daughter of Farmer Eliott from Sandy Hill Farm, sir,' Greggs replied. 'I believe hers has broken a spoke.'

'Hello, sir.' Tommy raced out of the house, hair unkempt, school tie flying over his shoulder. 'Fancy anyone fightin' a duel. I'd have used swords, that's proper fightin' that is. I bet it was just some soppy romantic stuff and they was showing off. Serves 'em right they got shot…' Tommy had an inveterate enthusiasm for absolutely everything, except poetry, apparently.

'Why did you lend Laura Elliott your bicycle? She could have used one of her brothers' bikes,' I asked him from over my shoulder.

'He's soft on her,' Fossett said above the noise of wind and engine.

'No, I'm not,' Tommy objected. 'It's about bein' chival-rous, like Ivanhoe. I've been readin' about him. I got it out your library, sir, after Lady Persi said it was alright. *Ivanhoe* is supposed to be a romance, but it's not, it's a proper book, with knights an' battles an' people gettin' killed. We should be readin' them sort of books in school, not stupid poetry.'

He carried on in the same vein until we dropped him off at school.

Forty minutes later, after Fossett and Persi's unhelpful directions through the maze of country lanes, I steered the car between wide-open gates and entered the Bancroft estate.

I slowed down at the lodge house, expecting to speak to a gatekeeper, but the place was shuttered up and looked to have been for quite some time, so I opened up the car and let her rip down the long and winding drive. The house remained hidden by a series of shallow hills until I sailed over a low rise to find it in the hollow of a pretty vale.

Built of rugged Cotswold stone with a jumble of steep slate roofs, myriad smoking chimneys, and numerous lead-paned windows glinting in the sunshine, it appeared to have almost grown from the ground it stood in.

A square tower stood in one corner with a blackened platform atop it. Formal gardens spread around the house, enclosed by a low wall and surrounded by meadows. Arcs of thorny brambles and hedges of holly and hawthorn straggled between stands of winter-bare trees following the contours of the land. It spoke of a landscape rooted in history, too old for the passing fads and fashions of more recent centuries.

I stopped the car in front of the columned porch just as the door opened with a loud creak. An elderly chap gazed at us in some surprise. 'May I enquire if you are Major Lennox, sir?'

'I am,' I replied, pulling off goggles and helmet.

'I…we were expecting…*ahem.* I understood a police inspector would also be attending, sir…' he said then halted in confusion. Slightly stooped, with white hair, his lean features lined with age. He was togged in a neatly pressed butlering outfit that was faded and dulled.

Foggy bounced from the car to run around yipping loudly, then raced past the old man into the house. He looked around, then back at me. 'Would that be your dog, sir?'

'Yes, he's Mr Fogg, and this is my wife, Lady Persi, and that's Constable Fossett,' I said as they came to join me.

The sight of Fossett in uniform seemed to reassure him. 'I am Redfern, sir, butler and factotum to Lady Bancroft. Her ladyship is expecting you.'

'Jolly good,' I replied. 'But I'd like to interview the injured man, Charles Flyte, first.'

'Ah, indeed, sir,' Redfern said. 'Doctor Frazer had to remove the ball from Mr Flyte's shoulder, it was considered a matter of urgency. As a consequence Mr Flyte is in bed and heavily sedated. He is unable to answer any questions at the moment, I'm afraid,' he intoned. 'However, Lady Bancroft has stated that she would very much like to talk to you.' He bowed and stepped back to allow entry into the huge hall.

'Fine,' I sighed, waiting for my wife to enter before me.

'Gosh, it's quite marvellous,' Persi said as she crossed the stone-flagged floor and stopped to stand and stare.

'Oooh, this is a proper old house, this is.' Fossett looked

about with wide eyes. 'And there's a real suit of armour. It's old isn't it? The oldest I've ever seen anyway.' He went over to a battered suit next to a blazing log fire.

'The armour was worn by the first Lord Bancroft at the battle of Agincourt in 1415,' Redfern said, his narrow chest swelling with pride.

'It never was?' Fossett's eyes rounded, then he put out a hand. 'Can I touch it?'

'You may, sir,' Redfern allowed.

'And he really looked out of these eye holes at all them French knights fightin' the battle? And watching the archers fire their longbows.' Fossett peered into the narrow slits formed in the heavy metal helmet.

'He did, sir,' Redfern said. 'The first Lord Bancroft was a renowned warrior. He fought valiantly alongside King Henry the Fifth himself. The King ennobled his Lordship after the battle was won.'

Their voices echoed up to the high ceiling above. The wall above the fireplace held three pairs of crossed lances, a half dozen shields and a couple of tattered flags. One in faded red and gold bore the English coat of arms, the other in green and grey depicted a stag's head on a silver chevron shield. Both were battered and torn, long threads hanging from ragged cuts, and stained with dark patches of blood, mud or whatnot.

Despite the display of weaponry the place held a feminine air. Embroidered cushions plumped on upright Elizabethan chairs. Persian rugs in red, gold, and blue. Graceful plants in delicately painted pots. An oval table supporting a painted vase of flowers and a small brass bell. High up on the wall between two stone mullioned windows hung a huge tapestry.

To our right an ancient oak staircase rose upwards in shallow steps. To our left, a minstrel gallery supported on massive posts jutted about fifteen feet into the hall. Blackened with age, it was even older than the staircase.

'May I take your coats, sir? Milady?' Redfern offered.

'Is this the original medieval hall?' Persi asked as we handed over our damp togs.

'Indeed, milady, it is termed the Great Hall,' he said as he laid our coats over his arm. 'Although the ceiling has been lowered to allow floors to be added above,' Redfern explained. 'Bancroft was a feudal manor predating Agincourt. After the first Lord was ennobled, he had the banqueting hall modified and extended after returning from France. The fireplace was installed, it was very modern for the times.' He indicated the monumental stone hearth. 'The minstrel gallery was at its present height and is entirely original.' He led Persi over to it and they both paused to gaze up at the carved and painted boards forming the underside of the structure.

'Hello.' A woman stalked in from one of the passages; tall and slim with gleaming black hair, her black dress almost moulded to her body. She radiated an air of unassailable self-confidence. 'I see the police have arrived.' She eyed Fossett with an appraising glance. 'Hardly impressive. Lady Bancroft said they promised to send Scotland Yard.'

'They did,' I said. 'It's me.'

She turned to focus dark eyes in my direction, looked

me up and down, then allowed a cool smile to curl her cherry-red lips. 'Well, I rather think you'll do,' she drawled. 'I assume you're going to drill us and make a thorough search. You can start with me if you like.'

I'd usually become a babbling idiot when confronted by an attractive woman, but marriage had stiffened my sinews. 'My wife's in charge of searches,' I replied, nodding in Persi's direction, who was still staring at the underside of the minstrel gallery.

The woman's smile turned frigid then vanished altogether. 'Oh, for heaven's sake,' she said, then stalked off, a cloud of expensive perfume trailing in her wake.

'Who was that?' Fossett asked Redfern.

'Miss Barbara Boden, one of the guests,' Redfern replied, his enthusiasm suddenly draining. 'May I show you to the drawing room, sir?' He didn't wait for an answer and we all traipsed up the broad staircase. I kept an eye out for my dog but he must have gone off somewhere, the kitchens probably. Redfern led along a wide passage, carpeted in shades of green and gold. Paintings of country landscapes, stately mansions, horses, coaches, and a few foreign places, lined the pale green walls. There were radiators too, large cast iron ones, and they were warm. I stopped to feel one. It was a surprise to find in so old a house, but then the modern world did occasionally throw up some improvements over the past. Cars, for instance, and aeroplanes.

We arrived at a pair of tall double doors; Redfern deftly swung one side open. 'Major Heathcliff Lennox, Lady Persi Lennox, and Constable Fossett,' he announced.

CHAPTER TWO

Two elderly women sat in wine-red chairs upholstered in tufted velvet. They were placed either side of a merrily burning fire and had colourful knitted blankets wrapped about their knees. An array of sofas and armchairs were ranged before them in the usual drawing room fashion.

The plumper of the two pushed her blanket aside and struggled to her feet. 'Sir Heathcliff! Oh, I am so relieved you have arrived.' She advanced on me.

'It's Major Lennox.' I bowed in polite manner. 'Lady Bancroft, I presume?'

'I am Lady Rose Bancroft, yes.' She smiled; a short lady, dressed extravagantly in plum-coloured faille with puff sleeves and frills of lace around her neck. 'And this is Miss Mary Lovelace.'

'Delighted,' I uttered as Lady Rose Bancroft continued effusively.

'We've been beside ourselves, haven't we, Mary?' She waved a dimpled hand toward the thin lady still seated, blinking up at us. 'Dreadful, simply dreadful! And Lady Persi?' She peered around me. 'Oh, a perfect English rose,' she rattled on as Persi tried to greet her. 'So pretty, and the major, a most well-built man. What a splendid couple you make. We are thrilled you are here, aren't we, Mary?'

'Of, yes, yes, we are.' Mary nodded, her faded blue eyes trying to focus in a face creased and careworn. 'Most pleased.' She wore an old-fashioned frock of grey crepe, buttoned to the neck.

'Is there another one?' she asked, looking about.

'Constable Fossett.' Redfern indicated him standing behind me.

'Ah, yes, very good,' she replied. 'And the inspector?'

'No, milady,' Redfern replied.

'Oh. Well, never mind, I'm sure we can manage. Please, do join us, and your young constable, Major Lennox.' Lady Rose Bancroft eyed Fossett again. 'Redfern, we need tea,' she declared, then added, 'and cake. This is an occasion for cake! Although I believe any occasion is worthy of cake, haha.' She laughed with a slight touch of hysteria.

'Certainly, milady. I will arrange a tray,' Redfern said with a stiff bow, and left, closing the door quietly behind him.

'Where would you like us to sit, Lady Bancroft?' I asked politely.

'Oh, anywhere, anywhere, and it is Lady Rose. We are not formal.' She waved at the collection of comfortably padded chairs and sofas surrounding them, then sank down into the chair she had vacated and pulled the knitted blanket back across her knees. 'Lady Persi can sit next to me, she will need to keep warm. Such a cold winter it has been. Would you care for a blanket, Lady Persi? Dear Mary knits them. So clever of her.'

'It's not necessary, thank you, it's wonderfully warm in the house,' Persi assured with a smile and went to sit on a yellow sofa. I took a large wing chair opposite and Fossett remained standing with hands behind his back in a proper policeman's pose.

Comfort suffused the handsomely proportioned room. The walls were painted in traditional regency yellow and adorned with numerous portraits and gilt-framed mirrors. It was typical of many old mansions I'd been in, although more homely than most, with gilded nicknacks in china cabinets and decorative lamps on small end tables set among the seating.

'You telephoned, Lady Rose,' I began.

'I did, Major Lennox,' she replied, raising a hand to pat her thick white hair. 'I spoke to Doctor Frazer. We had to call him.' She lowered her voice. 'Wilmslow's death… and…and the injury to Charles Flyte. Such a shock. Then Constable Kibble came from the village. Kibble called Stratford-upon-Avon, and a van full of policemen arrived. They were very suspicious, and then most disparaging when we explained that it was really not as serious as they took it to be. I told them it was caused by a flare of hot tempers and merely an unfortunate accident.'

'Was it?' I raised a sceptical brow.

'It must have been,' she replied, her blue eyes intent. 'They had fallen out. I explained this to the police officers. They were here all morning, going over the grounds, and through poor Bernard Wilmslow's room. They wanted to interrogate Charles, but Dr Frazer was removing the ball from his shoulder, so they could not. We were convinced they were determined to make more of it than it actually was, and of course rumours are already beginning to fly. It was only a duel, a matter of settling a dispute in a time-honoured way. Neither would have intended to kill. The situation was fraying our nerves, but Redfern came to the rescue; he informed us of your new venture, Major Lennox. He said you had begun working with a police inspector from Scotland Yard, and you could both be counted upon to proceed in the most discreet manner. Once the Stratford police had departed, I called you. I was certain you and your Scotland Yard inspector would keep a lid on things.'

Mary raised a thin finger. 'They shot each other. *Bang*. *Bang*. We heard the noise. It was very loud.'

'Right,' I said slowly. 'What was behind the flare of hot tempers?'

'Well, they had words at dinner…it was quite silly. They had been bickering since they arrived,' Lady Rose replied. 'We've asked everyone in the house if they know of any deeper reason why they should shoot each other, but no-one does. It is most inconsiderate.'

'Constable Kibble came from the village on his bicycle,' Mary added. 'He said they'll hang.'

'But one is already dead, dear.' Lady Rose turned to her.

'Yes, dead already,' Mary repeated. 'Dreadful.'

I glanced at Persi, who was very determinedly keeping a straight face.

'Fossett.' I turned to him. 'Take notes, would you?'

'Yes, sir. Sorry sir.' He'd been staring at the old ladies in bemusement. He straightened up, then opened his satchel and dug about for his notebook and pencil. 'Ready now, sir.' He stood poised.

'You must take our names,' Lady Rose told him. 'This is how things are done, isn't it? I am the widow of the late Lord George Wilfred Edward Bancroft. He was the sixteenth Lord Bancroft. There is no seventeenth,' she said, her voice catching on the words. She cleared her throat and continued. 'And Mary is my companion, who has been with me for many years now. I simply could not manage without her.'

Mary smiled vaguely.

'Yes, very good,' I said. 'What happened before the duel?'

'Nothing. We were asleep in our beds,' Lady Rose said.

'So was I,' Mary echoed.

'What about the evening before?' Persi asked in a kindly tone.

'Oh, it was a lovely evening.' Lady Rose brightened. 'We had a glorious dinner – one of Flambert's masterpieces. He is a French chef, we have hired his services whilst we have guests. We are most fortunate to have him! Such flair with the pastries. And exquisite sauces.' She beamed.

'The very best,' Mary said. 'But quite costly. Quite an extravagance.'

'Mary keeps the accounts, don't you, dear?' Lady Rose said as Mary nodded.

'You said the two duelists had words during dinner,'

Persi reminded them. The warmth of the fire had brought colour to her cheeks, and bright sunlight from the tall windows caught strands of gold in her blonde hair. She looked quite radiant.

'They did, it was about the pudding,' Lady Rose replied.

'The pudding?' I repeated.

'Bombe surprise,' she replied. 'One of Flambert's specialities. It is exceedingly difficult to bake to perfection, yet he managed it beautifully. And then Bernard Wilmslow was quite rude, saying that ice cream was indefensible in the cold winter months. He declared it a foreign affectation and added he would prefer a proper English pudding.' She paused to sigh loudly. 'Unfortunately one of the staff relayed this back to Chef and he stormed from the kitchen to upbraid Wilmslow. Wilmslow retaliated, of course, and was very rude to Flambert, particularly about France and the French in general. Chef became terribly angry and shouted–'

'He was red in the face,' Mary interrupted. 'He is quite short but very fierce. He threw his hat on the floor.'

Lady Rose nodded. 'The Gallic temperament, you know. He threatened to leave. Naturally I had to placate him, we have paid for him to stay for a whole week to cater for our guests. After Flambert returned to the kitchen, Charles mocked Wilmslow for being parochial and small-minded, they had high words…' She tailed off.

'Redfern diverted them.' Mary took up. 'With the pistols.'

'Erm, sir?' Fossett raised a hand, still clutching the pencil. 'What's a bombed surprise?'

'Bombe surprise,' I corrected in poor French. 'It's meringue baked around ice cream.'

'Oh, right.' He scratched through a note and rewrote it carefully. He was an amiable lad, thick brown hair carefully combed beneath the helmet, a long face, and plenty of good country common sense in his head.

'What pistols?' I switched to the more interesting point.

'The thirteenth Lord Bancroft was…' Lady Rose replied, shifting slightly in her seat, 'well, he was a keen duellist. Quite renowned, actually. It was in the early eighteen hundreds when duelling was fashionable. He had a pair of pistols made to his own design. They are kept in the glass case in his honour. Over there.' She indicated a tall Elizabethan oak dresser near a lofty window.

I stood up to go and have a look.

'They have been removed, Major,' Lady Rose said. 'Redfern has locked them in the gun room now. We couldn't return them to the case under the circumstances.'

'They were used in the duel?' I guessed and sat down again.

'They were, yes.' She nodded, her chins wobbling over her lace frill. 'Such a shock. The thirteenth Lord fought many duels, but he never killed a man. It was always a matter of honour. The meadow next to the house is named the duelling ground because of it.' She reached in a pocket hidden in her voluminous skirts for a handkerchief. 'And now his famous pistols have been involved in a death.' She blew loudly into her handkerchief. 'And the pistols may be taken away from us, and we have lost so much already.' Tears trickled down her plump cheeks. She dabbed at them, which unfortunately also lifted her face powder. She sat clutching the hankie, looking patchy and forlorn.

'Poor Rose,' Mary commiserated. 'The weight of tragedy hangs heavy on the house.'

Redfern entered with a laden tray, providing relief all round. He blinked when he spotted Lady Rose's tears but soldiered on regardless. 'Earl Grey and glazed fruit tarts, m'ladies,' he announced and proceeded to pour tea into dainty Meissen cups.

Lady Rose dried her eyes and accepted a cup and saucer. Redfern then placed a matching plate with a small but perfectly confected glazed tart on the end table at her elbow. Then he served everyone else, leaving me till last, even after Fossett. It's extraordinary what authority a police uniform can confer.

The tart was delicious and the pastry first-class. It seemed the unfortunate incident hadn't deterred the chef from his work.

'Would you care to attend the ball this evening, Major Lennox?' Lady Rose asked after she polished off her pastry. 'Accompanied by your beautiful wife, of course.' She smiled at Persi, who looked enquiringly at me.

'You're going ahead with the ball?' I asked in surprise.

'Of course. It is our Valentine's Day Ball,' Mary said.

'The highlight of our year,' Lady Rose added. 'We have extended invitations to you in the past, Major Lennox, whilst you were still in your bachelor days.'

I frowned. 'Have you?'

'We have,' she carried on. 'And never once did we receive a reply.'

That was probably because I'd have thrown them on the fire. After the war I returned to my home, the manor at Ashton Steeple, and craved nothing but peace and solitude, apart from Greggs of course. And Cook…and Tommy, and Foggy, and Tubbs…

'But now the major is a famous detective!' Mary said to Lady Rose.

'I know, dear, and he is so handsome,' Lady Rose said. 'Such a shame he is wed.'

Persi laughed then put her hand over her mouth and watched me with dancing eyes.

'I am not a detective,' I said firmly. 'Swift is, he's trained with Scotland Yard. I'm just a consultant.'

'We know dear,' Lady Rose assured me. 'We are just being kind.'

Persi laughed again. I frowned at her.

'I'm going to be a detective,' Fossett declared.

'Are you?' Persi turned to him.

'I've been studying it, milady.' He nodded. He'd taken off his helmet while he sat down to eat his tart. 'And I've got a list of questions that are supposed to be asked.' He turned to me. 'I can do it if you like, sir?'

'Yes, why not,' I agreed.

Redfern raised the teapot and his brows to enquire if I'd like a top-up. I nodded and he duly poured.

Fossett finished his tart and turned to the elderly ladies.

'Did anyone hear Mr Bernard Wilmslow and Mr Charles Flyte leave the house this morning?'

'I don't believe so,' Lady Rose replied. 'Redfern, did any of the staff mention it?' She looked at the factotum.

'They did not, milady, but the staff are exceedingly busy preparing for the ball this evening. I suspect the two gentlemen came in here to collect the pistols before dawn and left the house immediately after.'

'Dawn's around seven o'clock,' I mentioned, it being when I take Foggy out.

'Indeed sir, and is the time the staff would be awakening,' Redfern said.

'Rather late for the staff to still be abed,' I said.

'No, it is our rule in the house,' Mary cut in. '*None should stir on a winter's day dark, lest the lady steals away with your heart.*'

We all looked at her.

'It also helps keep the electricity bills down,' Lady Rose added.

'Which lady?' Persi asked.

'The Lost Lady de Lisle,' Mary said, as though it were perfectly obvious.

'Who is the Lost Lady?' Persi continued, her eyes now sharply focused.

'Excuse me, milady,' Fossett interrupted with a determined tone. 'I haven't finished asking questions yet.'

'Sorry.' Persi smiled. 'But it sounds quite interesting.'

'I will relate the story later, dear Lady Persi,' Lady Rose told her.

'Mr Redfern.' Fossett turned to the factotum, pencil in hand. 'Lady Rose said you created a diversion after dinner. Did you demonstrate the pistols?'

'I did, sir,' Redfern admitted. 'The pistols are of exceptional quality and it is a tradition to demonstrate them to the Saint Valentine's guests. We do so every year.'

'Are they kept loaded?' I asked, keen to see them.

'No, sir, they are not. I allow each guest to handle the pistols, then I take each gun and show how the powder is poured into the barrel and pan, and the shot lightly wrapped so I can remove it, and tamped down. Very few gentlemen are familiar with the process and my lecture has always been most popular,' he said, then his face fell and he looked sad.

'And the pistols are acclaimed,' Mary repeated. 'It was so romantic…but…but…now the death.'

'We will not be downhearted, Mary.' Lady Rose rallied her troops. 'The ball is tonight, we have more guests arriving, and it will be splendid. I'm certain Charles Flyte will recover and give a satisfactory account of himself to the police.'

'Huh, he's not going to get away with it just because he's rich.' Fossett didn't agree. 'Now who else heard the shots, other than you two ladies?'

'No-one, I should think,' Lady Rose replied. 'My suite overlooks the east front and Mary has rooms next to mine. We place our guests at the other end of the house. That's the more recent wing. Elizabethan, you know.'

Fossett duly wrote this down. 'And who found the bodies…I mean one body and the one that wasn't dead.'

'I did, sir,' Redfern admitted. 'Lady Rose rang for me, and informed me she had heard two shots from the direction of the duelling ground. I went to the door of the watchtower and looked out. It was very frosty, clear and cold, the morn had barely broken. However, I could see a dark bundle lying upon the ground. I crossed the garden as fast as possible…' He paused and shook his head. 'Well, I was astonished, sir. Two men lying in their own blood. Both with a pistol in their hands – the very duelling pistols designed and owned by the thirteenth Lord. I could scarcely believe it. I went to Mr Wilmslow first, he was patently deceased. Then I went over to Mr Flyte and realised he was still breathing. I ran to the house calling for Meg, the housekeeper, to telephone the doctor and an ambulance.'

'Dr Frazer came.' Mary turned her gaze to the fire. 'Such a blessing.'

Fossett pricked up. 'We'd best talk to him, sir.'

'Later. We should try talking to Flyte,' I decided. I'd had enough of sitting around.

'I very much doubt he will be conscious yet, sir,' Redfern said.

I stood up. 'We'll find out. Come on, Fossett,' I told him. 'And I need to find my dog.'

'He is in the kitchen, sir,' Redfern replied. 'Enjoying some roast lamb provided by Monsieur Flambert. Chef has asked me to present his compliments on your dog, sir. He thinks Mr Fogg to be a noble creature.'

'Does he?' Any number of words have been used to

describe Fogg, but I don't recall noble ever being among them. 'Strange chap…anyway, lead on,' I told him.

'Would dear Lady Persi care to stay here with us?' Lady Rose asked. 'We can tell her all about the Lost Lady de Lisle.'

'Yes, I would,' she said determinedly.

'Fine. Come on, Fossett,' I said.

'Right behind you, sir.'

CHAPTER THREE

'Mr Flyte has been placed in the watchtower, sir,' Redfern said as he led us down to the echoing great hall and then around and through a doorway passing beneath the stairs. 'He is rather a robust gentleman and we were unable to convey him back to his room.'

'What is all this Lost Lady stuff, Redfern?' I asked.

'The Lady de Lisle, sir,' he replied as he pushed open a studded oak door set in a stone-built archway. 'She was the wife of the first Lord Bancroft. A French lady. She disappeared one day and was never seen again. This tower was built on the side of the great hall and used by the Lord and Lady as their private quarters.'

'What's the burnt structure at the top?' I asked.

'That is the old beacon, sir.' He continued into a sparse, and icy-cold corridor. Our boots clattered on the stone floor. 'It was part of a medieval warning system that crossed the country. Once one beacon was lit, the others would spot them and follow suit. Due to the hall being in a valley, the Bancroft beacon was built on top of the tower.'

We'd entered the ground floor of the square-built structure; there was nothing but a plain bench seat to furnish it. Another studded door was set into the opposite wall, opening to the outside world judging by the draught. Two arrow slit windows, both fitted with thickly opaque glass, allowed narrow shafts of sunshine in.

'Warning about what?' Fossett asked.

'Rival militias, sir. Civil wars raged for centuries after the Norman invasion. A king had to be a warrior, or he would fall to a rival, and his men would fall with him. England was rarely a place of peace in those turbulent times,' Redfern explained as he led us across the floor to a set of stone stairs built against the far wall. 'Mr Flyte is abed in the chamber on the next floor. His valet, Gilbert, has remained at his side in case of need.'

The ground floor had exuded the usual smell of mouldering damp, but I caught the whiff of carbolic and ammonia as we trooped up the worn steps.

A narrow passage met us. Redfern halted at the only door midway along it and turned the iron hoop to push it open. 'Mr Gilbert?' he called as he walked in. He stopped, and gasped. 'Oh, good Lord.'

I sidestepped past him, Fossett did the same.

'Oh sir, they've been done in!' Fossett darted to the man lying near a fire smouldering in a simple stone fireplace.

I strode to the bed. 'He's been shot.' I stared at the dead man, there was blood and feathers everywhere. Someone had taken a pillow from under him and shot a bullet through it. And him.

'Actually, this one's not dead, sir.' Fossett was kneeling over the man on the floor. 'I think he's drunk. He stinks of whisky, and there's an empty bottle next to him.'

'Oooooh,' a groan escaped Redfern. 'This is a disaster…' He was leaning against the wall, ashen-faced, his mouth fallen open. 'The end…the end.'

I ignored him. 'Fossett, go and telephone Swift.'

'What? Now, sir? In Scotland?'

'He's in London.' I lifted the pillow to look under it, white goose-down feathers drifted about. Blood covered the man's bare chest, it had pumped out from a bullet hole and soaked into his pyjamas and the sheet beneath him. More feathers were stuck to the blood, a sticky mass of red and white. 'Ask the operator for The Stafford Hotel, St James's Place.'

'I…righto, sir.' He went to Redfern. 'Could you tell me where the telephone is, please?'

This seemed to bring the old man round. He straightened up. 'I…I will show you.'

'And don't tell anyone else,' I ordered as they made for the stairs.

'Won't say a dickie bird, sir,' Fossett called as he exited.

That left me and the corpse, and the drunk, although he hardly counted.

Where to start? Swift usually dealt with the details. I had once investigated a murder on my own at Melrose Court when some blighter had tried to set me up to hang. Although the experience hardly helped as I hadn't a clue what I was doing at the time.

What would Swift do? He'd make sure the victim was actually dead. I didn't need to bother with that because it was patently obvious. Charles Flyte was a big chap, not as tall as me by the looks of him, but well fleshed out. Burly, I suppose would be a good description, and handsome in a dissolute way.

His mouth gaped open, his eyes were closed, as though he'd been peacefully snoring. His head was laid on a single pillow, dark hair slicked with sweat. That was probably a reaction to having the pistol ball removed from his shoulder this morning. He had a fleshy nose, square chin, aged around early thirties... same as me, and his skin was almost as pale as the sheet he lay on. A wool blanket was neatly pulled up to his midriff, and a neat white bandage was wound around his right shoulder. I put the pillow back on his chest, causing another cloud of feathers to float upwards.

I pulled out my pocket watch, it was ticking, which made a change. Twenty to three. I picked up one of Flyte's hands: it was flaccid, and still warm. He must have been killed within the last hour, meaning it could have been done while I'd actually been in the house.

I sighed, then decided to search the room. I bent down to check under the bed; it was old with a carved headboard in mahogany. The floor was stone. There was nothing on it apart from a light layer of dust and more feathers.

A matching cabinet stood next to the bed. A jug of water, glass tumbler, and an opened pack of tissues were neatly arranged on its top. I opened each of the drawers, but they were all empty. Actually, it was a bit unlikely the culprit would have left anything in them.

I went over to where the valet, Gilbert, I think he was called, was lying on his side, his back to the smouldering fire. He'd apparently fallen from a stool which had toppled over next to him. I gave him a prod with my finger. He groaned but didn't wake. A thin man, boney almost. His nose long and sharp, so were his cheeks, and grey hair sparse and lank. His clothes hung on him. The bottle next to him was empty; it was Talisker, a good whisky and a damn waste to drain in a drunken stew.

'Ahhhh,' a screech suddenly sounded behind me, making me bound upright.

'What the devil–'

'You fiend! What have you done?' a young woman shrieked at me. 'Get away. Get away from him.' Her eyes flashed in fury, she didn't show an ounce of fear.

'I'm the police,' I said, 'and he's not dead.'

'Absolute rot, you're wearing tweeds. And that's a bullet hole in the pillow.' She pointed at Flyte on the bed.

'I meant the valet,' I retorted.

Fossett dashed back in. 'Inspector Swift wants to speak to you, sir.'

The woman looked at Fossett in full police rig, then me. 'Oh, so you are…well, I apologise, but…Charles… he's dead, isn't he?' She went over to him, her hand tentatively reaching for his.

'You mustn't touch anything, miss.' Fossett followed her over.

'I won't,' she murmured, retracting fingers to clutch to her chest. A fashionable young woman, she wore eye makeup in shades of charcoal and grey around hazel eyes, lips painted pink in a cupid's bow, with her straight brown hair held by a diamanté-studded headband. Dressed in lilac silk ruched at the knee, she wore a long strand of knotted pearls about her neck. Expensive, and stylish, but more suited to a London salon than an old country house on a cold winter's day. 'This is murder, isn't it?'

'Could I ask who you are?' I said.

'Annabel Cresswell,' she replied, a crack in her voice. 'I can't believe Charles is dead. Who could have done such a thing?' She regarded him, shock growing on her fine-boned face.

'Sir,' Fossett reminded me. 'The telephone is in a little parlour just by the boot room. Mr Redfern is guarding it for you.'

'Fine,' I said. 'And I think you need to clear the room, Fossett.'

'Will do, sir.' He looked at Annabel Cresswell. 'You'd best leave, miss, and please don't mention this to anyone,' he told her. 'It must be handled by the police.'

'He was rather a cad,' I heard her say as I left to trot down the steps.

Redfern was actually in the hall, still pale, but in better command of himself. He didn't speak, simply led me to a door under the shadow of the minstrel gallery. The telephone parlour proved to be a small room with a lattice window, an ancient chair, equally aged desk, and the telephone.

I picked up the receiver lying on the desk.

'Lennox.' Swift sounded terse. 'Fossett said Flyte's been murdered.'

'Yes, I know.'

'How?'

'Shot again. The second time today.'

'What happened?' The line was surprisingly clear. I could hear his every word.

'He was in bed after the doctor removed the ball,' I said. 'Someone went in with a gun and used his pillow to muffle the sound, although he's in a stone tower so I don't know why they bothered.'

'What type of gun?'

'Something with a smaller bore than the duelling pistol.'

He cursed under his breath. 'We'll try to catch the express train.'

'Florence is coming with you?'

'Well, there's no point in leaving her here,' he said, then sighed. 'It was supposed to be a romantic weekend, just the two of us. We were going to the opera.'

'What on earth for?'

'Because we like opera, Lennox,' he sounded exasperated. 'I'll call Billings at Scotland Yard before we leave.'

'Fine,' I said, not having thought of that. 'See you later.' I put the receiver back, its cable curled and twisted into loops. It was an old device, suspended on brass arms above a wooden box which had to be wound with a handle. It had been new before the war, just as the central heating had been.

33

Redfern had gone off somewhere so I made my own way back to the tower and up the stone steps.

'Oh, it's you, sir.' Fossett looked round as I entered. He was holding a magnifying glass aimed at the dead man. 'It took ages to get that lady to leave. She kept asking questions, even when I refused to answer any. Why are they all here, anyway?'

'Lady Bancroft goes in for upper-class matchmaking. A sort of latter-day Saint Valentine.' Flyte's skin was becoming blotchy and sallow, his full cheeks beginning to slump. 'Did you dust for prints?'

'Yes, sir, and drew them that I found. There was loads on the door handles but all of them were smeared. I took the victim's prints and that drunk's too.' He indicated the comatose man. 'I dusted the whisky bottle. There was only his fingers been on it. I've put the bottle in my bag as evidence, sir.'

'Excellent.' I was impressed.

'Now I'm examining the body for foreign objects, like bits of fabric torn from the killer's clothes, or blood or dirt under the fingernails from a fight. Best evidence would be a strand of someone's hair caught in a signet ring.'

'He isn't wearing a ring,' I said. 'And he was sedated when he was shot, so he couldn't have fought his attacker.'

He carried on with the magnifying glass regardless. 'I know, sir, but it's good practice. I'm studying detecting and there are pages and pages about examining the victim.'

'Which page are you on?'

'Eight, but I skipped ahead to see how it ended.' He sounded quite serious.

I shook my head then noticed the dead man's hands lying neatly either side of him. They were very clean, apart from the ink; not even a smear of dirt, which considering he'd been lying outside on the grass after being shot the first time, was rather unexpected. 'Do you think they washed him?'

'What d'you mean, sir?' Fossett frowned.

'After they brought him indoors.'

'Oh, good thinking! Yes, they might have done, because of taking the bullet out. Doctors are always going on about cleanliness and infection, my mum's the same.' He looked about. 'Have you searched the room, sir?'

'Yes…but I'll do it again,' I offered because there wasn't really much else to do. I shoved my hands in my pockets and gazed about while he leaned back over the body. There was a very old embroidery hanging over the bed, it had been placed in a picture frame with glass over it, to preserve it probably. It was threadbare in places, but very colourful. The section at the base had mostly mouldered away.

This room was lit by a large window, probably modified from the original. I went to look out but the glass was covered in a fine layer of moisture. I wiped it with my sleeve. It didn't achieve much, so I gave it up. 'Where did you read about detecting, Fossett?'

'A book called *The Basics of Detecting* from the police library, sir. I rang up Oxford Station and asked if I could borrow any proper training manuals and they sent it over.'

'Well, it's good to hear you're being methodical.' The search done, I turned to lean on the window sill. 'You'd better go and break the news to the old ladies.'

'Can't you tell them, sir,' he objected. 'They'll just make a fuss and cry and all that. And they're toffs, like you, and I'm not.'

I sighed. 'Fine, I'll do it. You can make sure Flyte's bedroom is locked, and Wilmslow's. There's no doubt this is a murder enquiry now.'

He'd taken his helmet off and left it on the bedside cabinet. Without it, he looked more like the fresh-faced farm lad he actually was. 'Yes, sir. I'll hold on to the keys, too.' He put the magnifying glass back in his satchel. 'When's the doctor coming?'

'I…erm. You'd better go and call him,' I said. 'And ask for an ambulance, too.'

'You mean you didn't telephone them? Sir, you're the senior detective!'

'And I'm allowed to delegate, so I'm delegating it to you. Off you go.'

He looked inclined to argue but grabbed his helmet, stuck it on his head and marched out. I waited a moment before going to the cabinet, picking up the jug of water on it and pouring it over the drunken valet's head.

CHAPTER FOUR

I found Lady Rose with Persi and Miss Mary Lovelace standing in the hall, admiring the large tapestry hanging between the huge mullion windows. I hadn't taken much notice before. It appeared to be an earlier version of Bancroft Hall, with the surrounding gardens, and dominated by a couple dressed in medieval style with a little whippet sitting between them. Persi was examining it with interest.

'That is the first Lord Bancroft,' Lady Rose was saying, her plump finger pointing at a man in a rich red tunic. A prosperous looking chap with a gold chain of office over his ermine-trimmed cloak and a green felt cap adorned with a large gold insignia. 'He was a big man and a valiant warrior.'

'He's our hero,' Mary sighed.

'The lady next to him is Lady Madeleine, his lost wife,' Lady Rose continued, pointing to a short slim figure with blonde hair pinned under a pointed hat, and long blue dress in classic medieval fashion. 'There are flowers scattered all around them, it's a style called millefleurs.'

'A thousand flowers,' Mary said. 'So pretty.'

'Persi,' I spoke quietly to her.

'Lennox.' She turned and smiled.

'Would you…erm…' I led her to one side and whispered to her while the two elderly ladies looked on. 'He's dead. Flyte. Shot again, properly this time.'

She stared at me, her smile fading. The ladies realised something was up.

'Major Lennox?' Lady Rose advanced.

'I think we should return to the drawing room,' Persi declared.

'Is there something amiss?' Mary asked, her voice a thin quibble.

Redfern can't have been far away because he now crossed the hall in our direction. 'Milady. Miss Mary.' He spoke almost breathlessly. 'I have served brandy-buttered crumpets in the drawing room.'

'Aaargghh.' Lady Rose held a hand to her heart as she staggered backwards. 'Has war been declared?'

'No, milady.' Redfern stepped forward, arms outstretched as though ready to catch her. 'Mr Flyte is dead.'

'Oh, is that all?' She released a shuddering breath. 'Really Redfern, brandy-buttered crumpets should only be served in the case of national emergency.'

'Indeed, milady, but in the circum–'

I gestured at him to shut up.

'Dead?' Mary said and stopped in her tracks. 'Why is he dead?'

'The wound, Mary, the wound.' Lady Rose made the assumption.

An unknown man strolled into the hall. 'There's a policeman in the telephone room telling someone old Flyte's been shot,' he called out to us. 'We all know he was shot, why's he repeating it?'

'Because he's dead,' Lady Rose told him.

'Is he by Jove!' The chap's brows rose in surprise. 'He wasn't that badly injured. I helped carry him up to the tower. He should sue that bally doctor for incompetence.' He waved an arm in imperious fashion.

'Bit difficult if he's dead,' I stated.

'I mean his family should, of course,' he cavilled.

'Doctor Frazer is not in the least incompetent,' Lady Rose replied tartly, then forced a smile and simpered. 'But, I do understand your concern, dear Rupert. And you may rest assured, we have a professional on hand who is looking into things.'

He turned his focus on me. 'Another quack are you?'

'No, I'm–' I didn't get very far, because he suddenly spotted my wife.

'Oh, I say.' His eyes lit up and he slid a hand over his slicked-back brown hair. 'Are you here for the ball? I'd like to claim a couple of dances, I'm a whizz at the waltz.'

'Actually I'm–' she said as she held her hand out.

He grabbed it to plant a kiss. 'Rupert Featherstone, enchanted to meet you, haha,' he laughed in an ingratiating manner. Expensively dressed in a grey suit expertly tailored to disguise his lightweight frame, he was a typical chinless wonder.

'This is Lady Persephone Lennox,' I said coolly. 'My wife.'

He dropped her hand as if it were electrified. 'Wife? Good lord. My apologies, old boy. Didn't mean to trespass.'

Persi suppressed a laugh as she came to put her hand through my arm.

'*Ahem*,' Redfern cleared his throat loudly. 'The crumpets will be cold, milady.'

'Ah, of course. The drawing room. Come along Mary,' Lady Rose said.

Redfern sighed quietly and herded them towards the stairs.

'Does this mean we are two men short now, Rose?' Mary asked as they began a slow climb upwards.

'It does,' Lady Rose agreed, shaking her head. 'It will affect the ball. Such a tragedy.'

'They should have thought about that before they had the duel,' Mary replied.

'Indeed, yes. Most inconsiderate,' Lady Rose murmured. 'And what was it all for? Not the pudding, that's for sure.'

'Pride,' Mary replied. 'It is always so with men.'

'I do believe you are right, Mary,' Lady Rose replied. 'The crumpets will be a comfort.'

'As will the brandy butter,' Mary added.

'Did someone say crumpets?' Rupert Featherstone looked after the ladies hopefully.

'No,' I said, and glowered at him.

'I am a guest here, you know.' He shoved his hands in pockets. 'An honoured guest, actually.'

I ignored him and led Persi toward the stairs to follow the tottering procession.

'How did anyone manage to shoot Flyte?' Persi spoke quietly. 'I thought his valet was with him?'

'Drunk.' I looked down into her lovely blue eyes. 'I tossed water over the damned sot, he didn't stir an inch.'

The chinless wonder followed us up the stairs at a distance, and then into the drawing room.

'What tea have you brought with the crumpets, Redfern?' Lady Rose asked the factotum.

'A pot of first flush Darjeeling, milady.' He busied himself with cups and whatnots over at the Elizabethan dresser, where he'd placed the tray.

'I'll have one,' the chinless wonder chimed up. 'And a crumpet please.'

'Dear Rupert.' Lady Rose sat in the chair we'd found her in earlier. 'You will be spoiled for choice at the ball tonight. Two men dead, and no-one fresh to stand in.' She finished on a sigh.

I took a breath. 'Lady Rose, I'm afraid Mr Flyte didn't die from—'

'I just heard!' Another young woman strode in, rather plain-faced with long mousy hair and a determined chin. She wore a drab dress in green with thick black stockings. 'Annabel told me Charles has been shot again. Dead this time, with feathers everywhere. That's the second time today.'

'What?' Lady Rose's eyes rounded in shock.

'Shot again?' Miss Mary echoed and dropped the blanket she'd been trying to spread over her knees. 'Another duel?'

'No, it was murder. The detective found him. Apparently

he's a real dreamboat, and he's brought a dog and a constable…' She focused a sharp gaze on me. 'Ah, that must be you. Are you Major Lennox?'

'Yes,' I replied. 'And this is my wife, Lady Persi.' She was sitting next to me, but we both now rose to our feet.

'I'm Edna Kent.' The young woman offered her hand with a friendly grin.

'Delighted,' Persi said.

'Murder?' Lady Rose grabbed the arms of her chair. 'You mean…someone has killed him deliberately?' She sounded aghast.

Edna nodded, then plonked down in a spare armchair. She wasn't particularly attractive, her nose being too large and her matter-of-fact manner rather intimidating, but there was a spark about her that would appeal to an intelligent man. 'Annabel saw him and the constable confirmed it.'

Rupert Featherstone came closer. 'I heard him on the telephone, but he didn't say anything about murder. You aren't ribbing us are you, Edna?'

'No, it's true, I've just been to see him myself,' Edna replied. 'He's definitely dead.'

'Aaahhh,' Mary squealed. 'Murder!'

'Redfern, is Mr Flyte truly murdered?' Lady Rose demanded.

He looked at her apologetically. 'I am afraid so, milady.'

'Oh, drat it, the stupid man,' she said in irritation. 'Mary, we must cancel the champagne.'

'Cancel the champagne?' Mary turned to her.

'The ball. We cannot hold the ball!' Lady Rose was almost shouting. 'Not with murder in the house.'

'But…the musicians, and the invitations… Oh, what a tragedy…' Mary plucked at her blanket.

'I really don't think Charles is worth cancelling the ball for,' Edna said.

'Don't you?' Mary looked hopeful.

'We must,' Lady Rose said decisively. 'Etiquette dictates that one cannot dance after a murder in the house.'

Fossett came in. 'Excuse me ladies, and sir. The ambulance is on the way, and the doctor is downstairs.'

'Excellent,' I said, keen to escape. 'I'll go and deal with them. You can find the other guests and gather them in here.'

'What? Everybody?' Rupert demanded. 'Why?'

'Because you're all suspects,' I replied.

They stared at me, then broke onto objections, including Fossett.

'They won't listen to me, sir, they're a bunch of toffs. It's always the same–'

'Ask Lady Persi to help, they won't argue with her.'

He grinned. 'Now that's a good idea, sir.'

'They can write statements,' I continued, 'and you'd better take their fingerprints and all the usual whatnots. I'll see you later.' I made a rapid exit and headed downstairs to find a man standing in the great hall with a medical bag in hand.

'Hello?' he said. 'I'm Dr Frazer. I was called on the telephone regarding Charles Flyte.' He spoke in a rich Scottish accent. A tall man, dark-haired with pleasant features, broad shoulders, black scarf, grey wool coat, and a frown of concern between thick brows.

'Major Lennox,' I told him. 'Flyte's still in the tower. When did you see him last?'

'Noon. I…may I ask why you are involved in this?' He hadn't moved from his spot near the front door.

'Consultant detective to Scotland Yard,' I said without so much as batting an eyelid.

'Ah.' He seemed quite impressed. 'You got here quickly.'

'Lady Rose rang me, and then we found the man shot dead.'

'Dead…you mean he's been murdered?'

'Well, he hardly shot himself. Come on,' I replied then explained what I knew as we headed towards the tower.

The valet was snoring; someone, presumably Fossett, had propped him up against the wall. His hair was still wet, his chin rested on his chest. He looked thin, pale, and crumpled. I would have felt pity if he weren't drunk.

'What happened to him?' Dr Frazer asked.

'A bottle of good whisky,' I said.

Frazer eyed him with irritation as he walked over to the bed and put his leather bag on the end of it. 'Ach, someone's made a proper job of it.' He removed the pillow to peer at the blood-rimmed bullet hole in Flyte's chest. 'And it wasn't a duelling pistol that made the hole, it was something modern.'

I nodded, having deduced the same myself. 'You have experience of bullet wounds?'

'I was a surgeon with the CCS. Abbeville at first, then wherever the fighting took us.' He glanced over at me. 'I'm sure you'll know how it was – assuming you were there.'

'I was RFC,' I replied. 'Injured near Verdun.' I knew that CCS was the Casualty Clearing Station. They moved with the battle lines, taking their tents and huts with them. It was easy to see where they'd been by the cluster of cemeteries left behind. 'Would Flyte have survived the injury he received from the pistol this morning?' I asked. The corpse was now a rather ghastly grey. Death did not become him.

'There was no reason why he shouldn't have. I was very careful to clean the site.' He pulled back the bandage wound around Flyte's shoulder and bent over for a closer look. 'Damn, that would have been a neat scar,' he muttered and straightened up. 'Not much I can do for him other than write out a death certificate. Do you know who's responsible for killing him?

'No.'

'It's a bad business. I assume the ambulance is on its way.'

'It is,' I said. 'Where are his clothes?'

'I gave them to Redfern to burn. I had to cut them from him, they were badly bloodied.'

'Did you wash his hands?'

He regarded Flyte's strong hands, the fingertips now black. 'No, I had no reason to, they weren't dirty. Is that ink? It wasn't there before.'

'The constable took his prints,' I said. 'You seem to know your way around here?'

'The old ladies have any number of ailments,' he said wryly. 'They call me out frequently.'

'Are you married?' I asked.

His lips twitched a wry smile. 'No.'

'Hum.' He looked likely fodder for the matchmakers. His voice was deep and smooth, the Scottish accent appealing, and he was a medical man. Just the sort who'd be popular with the ladies. 'Didn't happen to be here last night, did you?'

'I was invited to dinner. They're always trying to pair me off. It's a hobby of theirs – they hold a Valentine's Ball every year, to which I've been given a standing invitation,' he added.

'Tonight is cancelled,' I replied. 'What happened at dinner?'

'Not much. The food was good.' He left the body and went to lean back against the wall next to the dying fire. 'There was some sort of quibbling over dessert, but I was conversing with Serafina Deville, or trying to anyway. The chef had a bit of a tantrum before storming off. French. He's hired in. I think he was just adding colour to the drama.'

'Hum… The lady you were talking to, is she a guest here?'

'She is,' he said.

'Wealthy?'

He shrugged. 'I believe that's one of the prerequisites set by Lady Rose.'

I nodded. 'What time did you leave Flyte after operating on him?'

'It was just before noon. I went to speak to Redfern and then I joined the house for lunch. All the guests were there. Astonished, of course, at the news of the duel and the outcome.'

'Did anyone act oddly?'

'Difficult to say. I don't know any of them very well, apart from the old ladies.' He was observing me with a faint smile on his face. 'No-one cried or became emotional, if that's what you're asking.'

Typical British reaction, I thought but didn't say. 'Did you see Flyte again before you left?'

'No, I'm afraid not. I'd left him to rest with orders to leave him be. Gilbert was with him.' He indicated the valet. 'I thought he would attend to whatever was required. Rather disappointing to see him like this. He seemed quite attentive this morning.'

Questions were buzzing in my mind. 'Did you notice any obvious enmity between the guests?'

He thought about it. 'There may be some jealousies, but nothing malicious that I've seen, certainly nothing I'd believe would lead to murder.'

I gave up, he didn't seem to have anything to add. 'Constable Fossett will be taking statements in the drawing room, you can make yours there.'

He took it for the dismissal it was, picked up his medical bag and went off. I mooched about the room for a while longer. Grey fingerprint powder was evident on the head-board where Fossett had forgotten to wipe it off. I tried shaking Gilbert, which caused him to slump onto the floor.

I contemplated sticking a pin in him to see what happened, but I didn't have one.

We should probably move him somewhere and lock him up, just in case. I could get someone to help from the drawing room, but I was in no mood to join the inevitable contretemps. Nervous tension was already rippling through the house. I decided on a walk with my dog instead.

It didn't take long to find him. I stood in the great hall and whistled very loudly. He came racing in, ears flapping, bright eyes full of joy and enthusiasm. I stopped to ruffle his golden fur, then opened the front door wide.

'Swift? What are you doing here?'

CHAPTER FIVE

'What?' Swift said.

'I mean, you're earlier than expected.'

'We managed to catch the express train.' He walked into the hall; Foggy greeted him ecstatically, yipping and leaping about his feet. He bent to calm him with quiet words, then explained to me, 'Florence got off at Ashton Steeple. I carried on to Stratford-0n-Avon then took a taxi down here… Is that a real suit of armour?' He eyed it, then turned to the minstrel gallery. 'How old is this place?'

'Predates Agincourt. Persi says it's an old hall house.'

'Hum…where's the body?'

'The watchtower.' I looked down at Foggy, who had sat down with his tongue hanging out. 'Stay,' I told him. He followed us as far as the tower then turned around and scooted off. He'd never liked anything dead, the body would have upset him.

I wasn't too happy I'd missed out on our walk, or about revisiting the corpse for the umpteenth time today, but at least Swift could take on some of the questioning.

Actually he spent the next fifteen minutes questioning

me while examining the body, the room, and anything else he could think of.

'I thought you said the drunken valet was in here?'

'He was,' I replied. 'He must have slunk off, thoroughly ashamed of himself.'

'He's a witness, Lennox. What's his name?'

'Gilbert. We'll find him, he can't have gone very far.'

'Someone should have kept an eye on him, or locked him up.'

He was right, but I didn't say so.

Swift was leaning over the body. 'His hands look clean for someone who was lying on the ground,' he remarked.

'He could have been wearing gloves,' I replied.

'No, look, there's a tiny residue of gunpowder.' He'd taken out a white handkerchief and rubbed it across the man's palm.

'Right. Jolly good.' I should have thought to do that myself.

Swift was pleased. 'It's fortunate they didn't wash his hands or this evidence would have been lost.'

'Yes,' I agreed.

'We should search his bedroom,' he declared once he'd exhausted the tower.

'Fine. Is that a new coat, Swift?'

He suddenly looked sheepish. He was wearing a brand new trench coat over his dark grey city suit. 'I thought I might replace the old one, now that I'm back with Scotland Yard.'

'We're only consultants,' I said.

'Yes, but it's still the Yard, Lennox.'

We walked from the tower back through to the hall. Fossett was there with two ambulance men.

'Broke down again, it did,' one of them was saying. 'Had to bash the carburettor with a hammer.'

'Did the trick, though, didn't it, Bert?' the other said.

'You men.' Swift advanced on them.

'Sir.' Fossett instantly jumped to attention and saluted. 'I didn't know you'd arrived.'

'Caught the express. Where's the valet?' Swift demanded.

'I…um, isn't he with the body, sir?'

'No, he must have come round. Show these men the body then go and find him,' Swift rapped out orders. 'Where's the victim's bedroom?'

'I've locked it already, sir, and the other bloke that was shot,' Fossett spoke smartly. 'But I haven't had time to make a proper search yet.'

'Keys?' Swift held his hand out.

'There's only one, sir.' Fossett handed him a large brass key. 'It works on both the doors. Might even work on all the doors for all I know.'

'Right.' Swift frowned and dropped the key into his pocket.

'Is Lady Persi still in the drawing room?' I asked Fossett.

'Yes sir, she's trying to make them write statements,' he replied. 'But we were having a right job getting them gathered together. Half of them are still wandering about the house somewhere. I came out to find them, but then the ambulance arrived, so I'm here now.'

The ambulance men had a stretcher with them and were standing either end of it, ready to move into action. They were ruddy-faced from the cold and wore the usual brown jackets with flat caps and heavy winter boots.

'We already took one body away from here this morning,' one of them said.

'Shot dead he was,' the other said.

'Where?' I asked.

'Bull's-eye right in his forehead. Must have been a good shot, whoever did it,' the first man replied.

'Not just chance then?' I said.

'Might be,' he replied. 'Ye never know, do you?'

'Did the bullet lodge in the skull or exit through the back?' Swift asked.

'T'wasn't a bullet, it were a ball. The butler said they'd fought a duel with old-fashion pistols. Like Dick Turpin had when he was holding up old carriages in days yon gone,' he said.

'That's right, Bert. Him as had Black Bess.' The other one nodded.

'So where's the ball now?' I asked, realising they couldn't have known it was a ball unless they'd seen it.

They looked at each other, then one shoved his hand in his pocket and dug about.

'I was goin' to give it if some'n asked fer it.' He looked sheepish as he handed it over. 'It went through 'is head and was lyin' on the ground not far from where we plucked him up.'

'We washed the blood off,' the other man said. 'Not often we get intrestin' deaths. Usually they're just lyin' around in bed, or on the floor. Found one in 'is attic once. Been there a bit 'cos they thought he'd gone to the races.'

I assume the chap was keen on horses.

Swift and Fossett came to stand next to me as I turned the lead ball in my palm. It was flattened on one side, presumably where it had encountered Wilmslow's skull.

'Where did you pick him up?' Swift asked.

'Off the field out yonder.' The other chap pointed vaguely outside. 'The other bloke was still alive, they'd taken 'im inside and called the doctor. Dunno how they both could shoot each other like that. Dun't make sense,' he said. 'So who are we takin' away, then? We was told there was another'un snuffed it.' He looked from me, to Swift, to Fossett.

'It's the one who survived the duel,' I told him. 'He was shot again.'

'Again?' Bert repeated, looking shocked. 'Ye mean twice?'

'In one day?' the other said.

'Yes, dead this time,' I said. 'Fossett will take you.'

Fossett took charge. 'Right, you follow me and keep it respectful. There's gentry around and they'll be complainin' if you're chunnerin'.'

'And find that valet,' Swift repeated the order as they trooped off.

'Aye, sir,' Fossett replied.

'Lennox, there's more to this than just a duel. We'll start by searching the victims' rooms,' Swift decided and went to ring a brass bell on the oval table with the vase of flowers.

A lady arrived dressed in a long, navy-coloured frock,

drying her hands on her white apron. 'Good evening, gentlemen.' She spoke with a local accent. 'We're all at sixes and sevens. Oh, and now look, more people traipsing on the floor with dirty boots.' She pointed at the grubby footprints left behind by the ambulance drivers. 'Why can't they just wipe their feet like civilised folk?'

'Chief Inspector Swift, Scotland Yard,' Swift announced.

'Ah!' She bobbed a curtsy. 'Sorry, sir, I never knew we had a proper police inspector here…I'm Meg, the housekeeper.'

'Where is Mr Charles Flyte's bedroom?'

'Oh, you don't want to go there yet, sir.' A strand of grey-streaked hair had escaped her starched white cap and curled over her forehead. 'I haven't had time to tidy up. Nor the other man's room. We've been making ready for the ball, but now it's called off. Chef is having a tantrum, banging and bashing at pans, but I told him there's no point in getting in a lather. All the food'll go to the hospital, they'll appreciate it there, poor souls.' She seemed a chatterbox, but it may have just been nerves.

'Could you just show us to Mr Flyte's room, please,' I asked politely.

She looked at Swift for confirmation.

'Now,' he said in an authoritative tone.

Her pale cheeks flushed, she bobbed another curtsy, then turned to take the stairs. 'If you'll come along with me then.'

We passed the closed doors of the drawing room, humming with voices. A large and stately library was a little way beyond it and, at the end, a magnificent ballroom, its doors wide open to show a glittering chandelier and numerous chairs and tables fringing an empty dance floor.

Another flight of stairs led to a long passageway that took us to a quieter wing. All the doors were firmly closed. The grey carpet was relatively new, so was the blue paintwork.

Swift paused at a radiator, placed his hands on it, then carried on.

'Now, these are the guest quarters for the gentlemen, sirs,' Meg told us. 'It was all refurbished just before the war, and the heating was put in too. Best money they ever spent, to my mind. Didn't do much use though because there weren't any guests then, they were all away getting themselves shot at.' She sighed. 'And we lost the young man then. Christian, he was called. He was the last of the Bancroft line. Poor Lady Rose was beside herself. We all were,' she said sadly, and placed her hand on the third door down. 'This is Mr Flyte's room, and Mr Wilmslow's is next door. I don't know what's going to happen now,' she told us. 'Scandal won't do anyone no good, and Valentine's is all the ladies have got left to look forward to.' She sniffed suddenly, then walked quickly away, wiping a tear from the corner of her eye.

Swift had the key. We entered Flyte's room first. Clothes were strewn all over the floor, an open trunk with underwear and shoes jumbled in the bottom. The curtains were still drawn and an electric lamp was lit beside the unmade bed.

'Consistent with his going out before dawn,' Swift said as his eyes swept the room.

I went to the wardrobe. The door was partly open to show nothing had been hung up in it. 'That damned valet should have put his clothes away.'

Swift pulled open drawers in the tallboy. 'There's nothing in here either.'

We both stopped. Flyte's clothes had never been properly unpacked.

'Gilbert's not a valet,' I stated the obvious.

'Then what the hell is he?'

'I'll go and find out. It's time we found this blighter and questioned him,' I said in irritation, and made an exit before Swift could object.

The ambulance men were struggling down the stairs with the stretcher carrying the blanket-wrapped body of Flyte.

'Where's Fossett?' I asked them.

'Gone outside. He's been lookin' all over for some drunk bloke, or so he said,' the first answered.

'Right,' I said and made for the tower. The outside door was slightly ajar. It was dusk, with a heavy mist obscuring everything a yard from my face. 'Fossett?'

'I've searched high and low, sir. He's not in the house, he's run off,' Fossett called back, invisible in the mist. 'Oh, damn and drat it!' He suddenly swore. 'Sorry, sir, nearly lost my footing. The puddles are all covered in ice.'

'Any footprints?' I strode in the direction of his voice. I had my own torch in my jacket pocket and lit it.

'No, ground's frozen. I don't know where he went to, there's nothing out here as I can see.'

I caught him up, and we walked around, the light from

our torches skimming the ground, seeking signs of broken blades in the hoar-rimmed grass.

'Gilbert hadn't hung any of Flyte's clothes up or put things away,' I said, my breath a cloud of white. 'He isn't a valet.'

Fossett stopped swinging the torch. 'What is he then?'

'No idea. Swift's still searching the bedrooms. I suppose we should go and tell him.'

He looked at me; I could barely make his face out in the misty dark, and the shadows thrown by his helmet didn't help. 'He isn't goin' to be very happy, and I wanted to do a good job an' all. This in't goin' to impress him is it, sir?'

'Don't worry about Swift,' I said in a reassuring tone.

He sighed. 'Watch your feet going back in, sir. Everythin' iced up.'

We found Swift in Wilmslow's room, he'd been sifting through the cold ashes in the fireplace. He stood up as we entered, brushing his hands clean.

'Gilbert's done a runner, sir,' Fossett told him in a leaden voice.

'Damn it.' His reaction was predictable. 'He must have been feigning drunkenness,' Swift lectured. 'And he was in the room with the victim around the time he was shot, that makes him the primary suspect.'

'Yes, sir.' Fossett wilted. 'Sorry, sir. I should have locked him up somewhere.'

'It didn't occur to me either,' I said in support of the lad.

'You should have considered it, Lennox,' Swift lectured. 'Is he likely to get far?'

'Wouldn't think so, sir,' Fossett replied glumly. 'It's pretty dicey out there. Thick fog and pitch black beyond the house. It'll be dangerous in the dark. There could be a ditch or pond or canal, or what have you. If he falls in, he'll not last long in this cold.'

'What about the railway?' I asked Swift.

'There's only Stratford, and it's twelve miles away,' Swift replied. 'The local village is just a scattering of cottages and farms, according to the taxi driver who brought me here.'

Typical of him to have learned that already. 'He'll hole up, Swift, we can send an alert out,' I told him. 'Did you find anything in here?' I looked around Wilmslow's bedroom. It was tidier than Flyte's. Expensively tailored clothes were hung in the wardrobe, a set of brushes, shaving gear, hair oil and the like on the dressing table. It was decorated in the same unadorned style as Flyte's with blue-painted walls, ancient furniture and a plain wool rug on a lino floor.

'No,' he said. 'And there was nothing in Flyte's room to indicate what the duel was about.'

'We should check the valet's room–' I began.

'I've been,' Swift cut in. 'It's cleared out. Nothing in there at all; he must have collected his belongings before he ran.'

Fossett shook his head, still upset. 'I can't believe he was pretending to be drunk, listening to what we was saying and just waiting to escape… That's really devious, sir.'

'And indicates premeditation,' Swift said.

'Should I dust the rooms for fingerprints, sir?' Fossett offered, keen to do something to redeem himself.

'We can do it tomorrow,' I said.

'No, Lennox–' Swift instantly countered.

'There's nothing more to learn and the primary suspect has fled,' I said. 'We can take the statements home. Florence will be waiting for us,' I added, knowing he wouldn't leave his wife alone for long.

He bit his lip, then sighed. 'Fine, but I have to call Scotland Yard first and tell them to put out an all ports alert for Gilbert.' His face fell. 'Damn it, we don't know a single thing about the man. We're going to look like fools, Lennox.'

'Nonsense, Swift. There's more to this than some murderous valet.'

'Such as what?'

'I have no idea, but we'll find out,' I said with far more conviction than I felt. 'I'll find Persi and see you both outside,' I told them and walked out before they could think of any other objections.

CHAPTER SIX

It was far too cold to discuss anything on the way home. Despite the gloves, my hands were practically frozen to the steering wheel by the time I drew up outside my house, the manor at Ashton Steeple.

Greggs was waiting for us, the front door wide open, bright light pouring into the misty darkness. The smell of woodsmoke, car exhaust fumes, and rich country earth filled our nostrils as we piled out of the car and into the house.

We'd left the inhabitants of Bancroft Hall astonished but relieved when we'd told them Gilbert was probably responsible for the murder of Flyte. Every police force in the country was even now being put on alert to find the escaped valet, they'd even sent out a team from Stratford to scout the area. I was pleased we weren't with them and was looking forward to a quiet evening.

It wasn't quiet at all, but actually really rather entertaining. After we'd told Florence about the murder, the missing valet, and the assorted guests at Bancroft Hall, Persi insisted on explaining all she'd learned of the Lost Lady Madeleine de Lisle.

'The tapestry in the great hall is a much larger copy of an original made by Lady Madeleine herself,' Persi explained as we ate roast beef, creamy mashed potatoes and Yorkshire puddings with a thick onion gravy. It was utterly delicious and just what I needed to thaw out – along with a couple or three glasses of rich red wine.

'There was an old embroidery in the tower where the dead bloke was,' Fossett told her. We'd asked him to stay and he'd removed helmet and jacket to sit down at the dining table with us.

'I'd like to see that.' Persi switched her gaze to him.

'I'd like to see the house,' Florence said. 'Do you think we could go with you tomorrow, Jonathan?' She turned to Swift.

'We're investigating a murder–' Swift tried to object.

'But you said the valet was probably the murderer,' Florence countered in her soft Scottish accent.

'Exactly,' Persi said in support. 'And we won't be in your way. We will create a nice diversion for Lady Rose and Mary. They were terribly upset at having to cancel the ball.'

'Not to mention two dead guests,' I added dryly.

'How come this Lady Madeleine de Lisle got lost then?' Fossett asked. He was surreptitiously sharing bits of beef with Tubbs, my fat little cat, who had jumped onto his knee under the table and kept pushing a sooty black paw up towards Fossett's plate.

'She mysteriously vanished in the dead of night and was never seen or heard of again,' Persi said in a mock scary voice.

'So the first Lord Bancroft killed her and buried her in a ditch,' Fossett replied with a grin.

'He'd bury her in the graveyard,' I said. 'That's the best place to hide dead bodies.'

'Actually, I would quite like to know what really happened,' Florence said.

'I would too,' Persi replied more seriously. 'Lady Rose told me that there's a diary from the 1790s written by Violet Bancroft. She was the twelfth Lord Bancroft's daughter, and frail from birth. She spent as much time as she was able researching the family archives for information on the lost Lady Madeleine.'

'It would be fascinating to read her findings,' Florence said, smiling with enthusiasm. She was dressed in a pale pink wool dress with a light blue cardigan which enhanced her delicate colouring. 'Were there truly papers in the house from the early fourteen hundreds?'

'There was a copy of her dowry.' Persi had finished eating and placed her knife and fork neatly on her plate. 'It was written in Latin, and a letter in old French from Lady Madeleine's sister to tell her that her previous affianced had been released from prison.'

That raised all our brows.

'Prison?'

'That is what it is reported to say,' Persi replied. 'I'd like to read it myself as it would be a matter of translation. The ex-fiancé was Chevalier Pierre de Mortier and it's unlikely a high-ranking nobleman would be imprisoned in those days.'

'They bought their way out of trouble,' Swift surmised, his socialist tendencies never far below the surface.

'They wouldn't have ever been in trouble,' Persi replied.

'They were effectively above the law unless they'd upset royalty.'

That sounded perfectly reasonable to me.

'So it's hardly worth an investigation if Bancroft was above the law,' I stated. 'He killed her, disposed of the body and married another heiress.'

'Her family would have demanded reparation if that were the case,' Persi replied.

'That's true,' I agreed. 'There would have been a price to pay, and they would have demanded the dowry back.'

'Lady Rose said there was evidence that they remained on good terms,' Persi said. 'So whatever happened, her family knew about it.'

'How intriguing,' Florence said. Lady Florence was a pretty woman, gentle and kind with pale blonde hair, blue-grey eyes, and the only child of the Laird of Braeburn. She and Swift lived in Braeburn Castle in the Scottish Highlands with their little boy, Angus, and despite Swift's austere temperament, I'd never seen him happier.

'Why do they all say she's lost, then, if her family didn't kick up a fuss?' Fossett said.

'She probably ran away,' I concluded. 'Like the valet.'

That shifted the conversation to why Flyte had taken Gilbert to Bancroft Hall with him, who Gilbert really was, and why he'd murdered Flyte.

'Doesn't anyone know what caused the duel in the first place?' Florence asked with a shake of her head.

As none of us had discovered the real reason why the two men had fought the duel, this led to us rendering increasingly unlikely scenarios throughout a pudding of jam roly-poly and custard.

'Greggs,' I called out as he topped up our wine glasses. 'You're a man of the world, what do you think?'

'A woman, sir,' he replied gravely. 'Manly pride pricked by a rival over a lady's hand.'

'It's the most obvious,' Persi agreed with him.

'But what of Gilbert?' I said.

'Was he a handsome man, sir?' Greggs asked.

'No, he was old and very thin,' I replied.

'Therefore he was not involved in any romantic entanglements.' Greggs pondered, red wine decanter in hand. 'Perhaps there was a financial aspect to the situation, sir. Blackmail, or the erm…*ahem*, the purchase of a lady's affections.'

None of us had considered that and we all turned to look at him.

'Very impressive, Greggs,' Swift congratulated him.

'The benefit of age, sir, is extensive experience of the human condition,' he said with a puff of the chest.

'So you have experience of purchasing a lady's affections,' I said.

That set him all aflutter. 'I certainly have not, sir. I was merely postulating a hypothesis.'

I narrowed my eyes, he huffed, and we'd probably have carried on if Persi hadn't announced we'd been invited to join the Valentine's dance at Ashton Hall.

'We'll give you a lift, Greggs,' I told him, 'once you've finished pouring that decanter.'

He duly did and, after finishing our drinks, we changed into more suitable evening wear and piled into my Bentley to motor into Ashton Steeple. The party proved to be an entirely informal affair, with villagers and local gentry invited to drink, dance and make merry to a local band of music makers. It was a jolly good fun and we all thoroughly enjoyed ourselves.

***

Shafts of sunlight sent long fractured rays through glazed ice on the inside of our bedroom window early next morn. Dust motes drifted in the air above me, caught in the glimmering light of dawn. I lay under the warmth of wool blankets and eider-down quilt, listening to the rise and fall of quiet breath as Persi, Foggy, and Tubbs slept peacefully beside me. I'd have stayed longer but Foggy snuffled awake, black nose twitching, long ears trailing and tail wagging, to remind me it was time to take him out.

Wrapped in a thick winter dressing gown over my pyjamas, slippers on freezing feet, I crept quietly downstairs to wander the garden. Tubbs had decided to come, but only on provision I carried him in my arms. He purred while Foggy pottered about in unhurried spaniel fashion. I paused to admire the sparkling beauty of a spider's web, white with tiny crystals of ice glinting in the glassy sunshine. The house stood framed by a pale blue sky, wood smoke already drifting from sooty chimney pots, the red brick walls pink under a layer of frost, sparkling spikes of sharp icicles hanging from gutters and the stone portico sheltering the front door. I breathed a contented sigh, called Foggy to come and headed back indoors.

The sound and scent of breakfast being prepared emanated from the kitchen as we entered the warmth of the house. I had one foot on the bottom stair, thinking to head back to bed for half an hour in my wife's arms, when the damned telephone rang. Foggy started barking. I cursed and went to pick the receiver up. I had the devil of a job to hear whoever was on the line.

'What?'

'It's Billings, are you deaf?'

'No, Foggy shut up.'

'Are you telling me—'

'No, my dog…'

Swift came rushing downstairs. 'Is it the Yard?'

'Yes, it's Billings,' I told him.

'Lennox, are you listening?' Billings rapped in my ear.

'Roger. Fire away,' I rapped back. Foggy stopped yapping to bound around Swift in greeting.

'Gilbert was an ex-copper, a detective sergeant with the Met. He was hired by Flyte.'

That gave me pause. 'Wait.' I relayed the information to Swift, who, typically, had his notebook and pencil in his dressing gown pocket and proceeded to write everything down.

'How do you know?' I asked Billings.

There were a few expletives, then, 'Flyte was already growing paranoid. We haven't found out why, but then he started receiving death threats. We searched his London house last night and found them. Five. Written in block capitals on cheap notepaper. No envelopes and no clue who sent them.'

I told Swift, then thought about it. 'Could Gilbert have written the threats himself to get close to Flyte?'

'We don't need guesswork, Lennox. We need facts,' Billings' voice rasped through the crackling line. 'Just listen. Gilbert was said to be a good man, he left the force with an exemplary record.'

'Why did he run away then?' I replied.

'That's what you're there to find out,' he snapped back.

I refrained from making a sharp retort, but my mind was sifting the news. The man can't have been found or we wouldn't be having this conversation. 'Constable Fossett has the bottle Gilbert was drinking from. The dregs should be analysed. He may have been drugged.'

'You should have thought about that yesterday. We'll send a courier to your local station, they can bring it to our lab here. And Flyte was an important man, one of the OceanFlyte family. I've got the chief breathing down my neck, so you'd better not mess this up, Lennox.'

I didn't deign a reply, merely handed the receiver over to Swift and went upstairs to explain the latest turn of events to Persi while donning my warm winter tweeds.

Half an hour later we entered the breakfast room together. Greggs wasn't on duty, he'd declared himself hors de combat, having executed an over-exuberant foxtrot the evening before. Cook had ordered him to rest until a hot water bottle could relieve the problem.

That meant we had to make do with a 'help yourself' breakfast. It was rather disorganised until Persi took control and we sat down to eat bacon, sausages, fried bread, mushrooms, and eggs whilst debating the latest news.

'If Gilbert is innocent, then the murderer is still at Bancroft. It might be dangerous,' I said.

'Nonsense.' Persi was dismissive. 'Why would anyone want to murder us?'

'To scare us off, or some such,' I replied. 'Greggs could come and keep an eye on you.'

'Heathcliff,' Persi replied sternly. 'You are not to drag Greggs out of bed to play nursemaid to us.'

'I'll come, sir,' Tommy offered. He'd arrived with a stack of toast in a silver rack. 'I can watch out for miladies. No-one would sneak up on them while I'm around. I'm dead good at watching out. I could be a spy, like Bulldog Drummond. I've read the book by Sapper and seen the film at the picture house. I'm going to be just like him and lead a life of thrills and adventure!'

'I thought you wanted to be Ivanhoe,' Persi said.

'I do,' he was quick to reply. 'But we haven't got any armour and Constable Fossett said they had a really old suit at that Hall you're going to. If I came with you, I could try it out.'

'Tommy,' I said as I speared a slice of bacon. 'Go and fetch the eggs from the orchard.'

'Oh sir,' he complained.

'And check the fencing is secured. The foxes will be out hunting in this weather.'

'I think I should go with him,' Persi said as she put her napkin on the table. 'The chickens' water will be frozen and we'll need to carry a hot kettle with us.'

'I can do that milady,' Tommy instantly offered.

'I'll carry the kettle, you can bring the corn,' she said. 'And don't forget the egg basket.'

'I'll come too.' Florence made to go with them. 'We will see you later.' She bent to kiss Swift on the cheek, which brought a smile to his lean face.

I pushed my plate aside and reached for my teacup, as they made their way out with Tommy chattering ten to the dozen.

'Billings dictated the threatening letters found in Flyte's house.' Swift pulled his notebook from his pocket and opened it on the breakfast table. '*You cheating rat, this is the last time you play this game,*' Swift read. 'Billings thought that was the first letter, then… *Keep looking over your shoulder, I'll be there, right behind you.*'

'I wouldn't really describe those as death threats, Swift.'

'There are more,' he said testily. '*You deserve what's coming. You've broken my heart, you louse. There's a bullet waiting for you.*'

'That sounds more serious,' I said. 'Particularly as he was actually shot.'

'*You lied, everything you said was a lie. It's all just a game and you don't give a damn who gets hurt.*'

'So, it was an affair of the heart,' I said.

Swift turned a page. '*You lying cheat. Everyone's going to know what you did.*'

'The lady sounds rather upset, sirs.' Greggs came in with a fresh pot of tea.

I raised my brows in his direction. 'I thought you'd hurt your back?'

'Indeed so, sir, ever since the crash in France…'

'Greggs, you fell out because you didn't strap yourself in,' I reminded him rather tersely. I'd crashed my aeroplane after being dogged by the Boche on a ferry flight to a new base; Greggs had been my batman during the war and had insisted on coming along. He'd played the martyr ever since the incident and it was hardly my fault he hadn't been able to fit the seat belt around his paunch.

'Nevertheless, sir, I would not neglect my duty.' He turned stuffy. 'I have taken aspirin and a shot of brandy as a temporary respite.'

'Brandy?' Swift raised a brow.

'An old remedy, sir, and most efficacious.' He poured tea for both of us and eyed Swift's closely written script. 'Should such letters really be taken seriously, sir? Those who are apt to act, do so. They do not waste time with mere threats.'

I pondered that. My old butler was an unlikely Romeo, and yet he had a great deal of experience in the petticoat line. Far more than I ever had, or Swift, probably.

'You could be right,' I agreed.

'Has Fossett arrived?' Swift was focused on the investigation.

'He telephoned, sir. He asked me to inform you that he must give a lecture at the school this morning. He had promised Mrs Summerour, and she was very particular that he honour his commitment.'

'Mrs Summerour is Tommy's school teacher,' I reminded Swift.

'We can't waste time–' Swift began in irritation.

'Fossett can come later with Persi and Florence,' I said. 'Persi told me they were going to the library in the village this morning and will join us later.'

'How are they going to get to Bancroft Hall?' Swift asked.

'*Ahem*, if you will excuse me, sir. I will be downstairs,' Greggs said and promptly skedaddled.

I took a breath. 'Persi has her own car.' This was still a rather sticky subject.

He frowned. 'What sort of car?'

'An Aston Cloverleaf.'

He whistled. 'That was generous…I thought you'd exhausted your funds on house repairs?'

'I did, but Persi thought we could make a few savings in the household accounts, so I said she was welcome to try. She's cut back on all sorts of expenses and saved us a small fortune. Then she found some share certificates in my library. I didn't realise I had them and she sold them at a rather good price, so I offered to let her buy something for herself as a reward. She bought the car…it's red.'

He grinned as though it were somehow amusing. 'Good, so your financial worries are over.' He stood up. 'And we can get going.'

'Hmm,' I muttered darkly.

71

'Come on, Lennox.' He headed downstairs to where Greggs would be waiting with our coats.

I followed at my own pace. I was pleased Persi had solved our financial misfortunes but wasn't sure about her deep-rooted independence. Our home was at the very heart of my life, but for Persi it seemed more like a hub from which she came and went. That might be part of her peripatetic past, I suppose, always away on digs in appalling locations, but I had a niggling fear that she wasn't as deeply rooted in Ashton Steeple as I was.

Swift had donned his trench coat. I didn't say a word, merely shrugged into my great coat and strode out of the front door, fastening my flying helmet firmly over my ears.

The sun had risen further in the expanse of blue sky to set the frost glittering on leafless twigs and glossy evergreens. The day was too beautiful for petty fears and my spirits lifted as I started the Bentley up. Swift jumped in, Foggy came haring around the side of the house to leap in beside him, and I opened up the throttle, put my foot down and roared out of the drive.

CHAPTER SEVEN

'Ah, sirs.' Redfern had opened the front door. 'The household are still abed. It was rather a late night. After the news of Gilbert's dreadful deeds there was a surge of exuberance last evening, followed by an impromptu dance.'

'No weeping and wailing then?' I remarked.

'If there was, sir, it was done in private,' Redfern replied solemnly.

'Hmm,' I muttered as we walked into the great hall. 'Could you bring us the duelling pistols, please?'

A flicker of anxiety crossed his face, but he nodded. 'I shall do so, sir. If you will excuse me.' He turned and went off toward the door below the minstrel gallery.

I was of half a mind to follow, thinking to see the gun room, but the housekeeper came bustling in from behind us.

'One moment.' Swift held up a hand.

She stopped, raising her greying brows. 'Yes, sir?'

'Meg, isn't it?' he asked.

'It is, sir.' She was dressed as yesterday in housekeeper's navy blue with a white apron. 'Now I think you're going to want to know about that Gilbert, aren't you? We were just fair flummoxed when we heard he went and killed Mr Flyte and then ran off. There's nothing ever happened like that in the house.'

Given the age and history of the place, I thought that unlikely.

'Had Gilbert been here before?' Swift took out his notebook and pencil.

'He hasn't and he had nothing to do with us downstairs even while he was here,' she replied. 'He was polite enough but kept his distance. Most guests don't bring servants, they don't want their romantic lives gossiped about back home. And Gilbert was really familiar with Mr Flyte, which we all thought a bit odd. Not that it's for me to say anything.'

'How was he familiar?' I asked as Swift pulled out his notebook.

'Well, the way he talked to him. He did call him sir most of the time, and sometimes it was Mr Flyte, but it's like he wasn't used to being in service.'

That fitted with what we'd learned from Billings.

'And,' she continued, 'he followed Mr Flyte all over the place. We all remarked on it. Even when Mr Flyte had an assignation with Miss Deville.'

Swift looked up from his writing. 'Who?'

'Miss Serafina Deville, she's a guest here, sir,' she answered. Meg was a chatterer, and very probably enjoyed a gossip. Her plain face was animated, brown eyes alight. 'Miss Serafina and Mr Flyte took walks around the grounds on their own. Although they all do that. It's what it's about isn't it?' She smiled, her voice warming. 'Getting them together so they can fall in love. They were close though, he even tried to hold her hand, but she wouldn't let him. I saw it myself.' She nodded, her arms crossed under her bosom. 'She's far too good for him, doesn't matter how much money he's got. Miss Serafina could have anyone she wanted, even royalty, I reckon.'

I recalled Dr Frazer saying he'd been trying to talk to Serafina Deville over dinner the night before the duel. Miss Deville must be quite the beauty.

'There aren't any royals here, are there?' I asked.

She laughed. 'No, but we live in hopes of a minor. I reckon they'd come if they was asked. It'd be a real notch up for Lady Rose. Although we do have Lord Hector Sommerton, he's the heir to an earldom.'

Swift was looking less than impressed. 'How long have the guests been here?'

'Four days now,' she replied, seemingly impervious to Swift's demeanour. She looked over her shoulder before lowering her voice. 'Usually the ball is the highlight. It's when they pair off and dance the night away. It's nice when they find someone, because it's no fun being on your own, is it? We've had quite a few weddings, you know. And we all love a wedding, don't we?' she ended with a beaming smile. Perhaps she was a busybody, but she seemed kindly with it.

'Was anyone else close to Flyte, or the other victim, Wilmslow?' Swift remained focused.

'Hard to tell really. Most like to keep their feelings to themselves.' Her brow creased as she thought about it.

'You'd think some of them would be in tears, wouldn't you, but none of them was that I could see…'

'*Ahem*.' Redfern had returned and cleared his throat. 'The breakfast room, if you please, Meg.'

'I'm on my way now, Mr Redfern,' she said to him, still smiling. 'I've just been helping these gentlemen.'

He watched her go up the main stairs, then turned to us. 'Meg is a most efficient housekeeper, sirs, although apt to be talkative,' he explained. 'Here are the pistols.' He raised the polished cherrywood case held in his hands.

'Thank you, Redfern.' I gave him a grin as I took it; there was something tantalising about a pair of duelling pistols. The catch was unlocked and I went to a side table to put the case down and lift the lid.

Swift was right beside me. We both picked a pistol up and balanced them in our hands.

'They're not loaded?' Swift asked Redfern.

'No, sir, I have not touched them since I recovered them from the duelling ground.'

'But you left them loaded the evening after demonstrating them?' I asked him.

His face drooped further. 'As has ever been my custom, sir. It would never occur to me that someone would use the pistols to kill. I always remove powder and ball the following morning, clean them thoroughly and place the pistols back in their glass case.'

There was nothing we could say to that. I peered at a streak of grey powder on the frizzen. 'They have dust on them.'

'Constable Kibble dusted them for fingerprints, sir. He was the first policeman on the scene, he lives in the village…'

'Telephone him and have him come here,' Swift ordered.

'I will do so, sir,' Redfern replied. The look of anxiety had returned to his eyes.

'And then meet us outside on the duelling ground,' I told him.

He glanced at me. 'Very well, sir.' He bowed and left for the little parlour housing the telephone.

'Come on, Swift, we can test these out.' I put the pistol back in the case, picked it up to put under my arm and headed for the front door.

Foggy came bounding over as we exited the house. He'd cleared off into the garden when we'd arrived, and now his fur was ragged and wet with little balls of ice stuck between his paws. He *woofed* in delight that we were joining him, then hared off across the white frosted lawn for no good reason.

'The duelling ground is next to the tower,' I said.

Swift didn't reply; he seemed very taken with the pistol in his hand. 'There's more powder and shot in the case, isn't there?'

'Yes,' I replied. Foggy came back, ran circles round us then followed with his tail aloft and a dusting of ice on his soft muzzle.

'We'll check the accuracy,' Swift continued. His face was keen, lean cheeks accentuating his hawk-like features.

I glanced at him as we walked down stone steps from the garden and onto a wide, flat meadow edged with shrubs and winter-bare trees. 'Fine. Have you ever fired flintlocks before?'

'No, but I'm sure you'll know how.'

He was right about that.

Two pools of dark blood marked the spots where both men fell.

We stopped at the first. The frozen ground stained reddish black, the bruised and flattened grass telling its own tale of the fallen man, and those who had come and carried him away.

We paced out the distance to the other bloodied patch. Swift counted: '…30, 31, 32, 33, 34.'

'They're supposed to take twenty paces each,' I said.

'Yes…why didn't they?' He looked back to where we'd started. 'Right, let's load the pistols.'

'We're going to shoot each other?'

'Tempting, but we're just recreating the scene.' He strode back to the case and pistols we'd left on an old tree stump bordering the meadow. Foggy had remained with the guns, not being keen on the smell of spilled blood.

'I'll load, you can watch,' I said as I took the cap off the powder flask.

'Fine.' He grinned. 'I've always wanted to fire one of these.'

'They can have a kick, but these have heavy barrels which should reduce the recoil,' I told him. I'd learned how to handle flintlocks at an exclusive Oxford club run by an old military man who'd taught us how to fight with sword, knife, and fists. And guns, of course.

I demonstrated how to load powder and ball and prime

the pan, then did the same with the other pistol. 'Right, and do not shoot me, Swift.'

'I'm not an idiot, Lennox, and you can see the gun isn't cocked. Are you ready?'

'Obviously.' We were standing back to back, white breath streaming in the cold air.

'One, two…' He strode off.

I walked to the bloodied patch and turned to face him. Foggy hadn't moved but now gazed from one to the other of us.

'Bang!' Swift shouted.

I didn't say a word, merely raised the gun to a point above his head, then lowered it again. It wouldn't be easy to hit someone with any degree of accuracy from this distance. 'These pistols never killed anyone when they were used by the thirteenth Lord Bancroft, until now,' I remarked as I walked back to join him at the stump.

'The distance could be the reason, or they've been modified in some way,' Swift said, the grin still on his face. He appeared to be enjoying himself. 'Let's use that tree as target practice.' He indicated a huge old oak on the periphery, then headed for it. 'The scar from that sawn-off branch is the target.'

I followed with gun in hand.

Swift marked out thirty-four paces from the tree, cocked the pistol and fired. The ball missed the target by a narrow margin. The sound of the shot reverberated around the shallow valley, frightening a dozen or more crows out of nearby trees.

'This gun fires slightly high and to the right,' Swift said, then stood back.

'Understood.' I aimed with arm outstretched, took the shot and missed the damn target too. I frowned. I was a fairly good shot with these types of weapons. 'They've been modified, both of them fire high and to the right.'

'Yes,' he agreed. 'A couple of degrees out of true.'

'Which is why the thirteenth Lord Bancroft never killed anyone,' I said.

'Or was killed,' he concluded. 'Flyte couldn't have shot Wilmslow unless he knew about the modification.'

'So what really happened?' I was trying to visualise it.

'Wilmslow must have taken the first shot…' Swift was thinking as he spoke. 'He hit Flyte in the right shoulder, injuring him, but Flyte managed to return fire and kill Wilmslow.' He looked at me, dark eyes narrowed. 'That doesn't add up, Lennox, nor does the ball lodging in Flyte's shoulder.'

'No.' I'd been thinking the same. 'The ball from Flyte's pistol had enough force to go right through Wilmslow's skull, and yet it never could have done so from thirty-four yards.'

'Flyte's pistol could have been filled with more powder than Wilmslow's,' Swift suggested.

'And yet the guns had been primed by Redfern the night before…unless Flyte tampered with them.'

'In which case he deliberately set out to murder Wilmslow.'

'Had either of them practiced with these pistols, Redfern?' I called out to him.

He'd been making his way slowly over the grass towards us.

'Sir,' he said when he arrived; the poor chap was out of breath. 'They had not done so to my knowledge.'

I didn't believe him. 'You knew about the modifications to the barrels.'

He had lifted the cherrywood case and now held it up as we put the pistols back in their places. 'I did, sir. But that information has not been widely broadcast.'

'You should have told us.' Swift was terse.

He caught his breath. 'You are quite correct, sir…it has been…' his hands were trembling as he closed the clasps, 'really quite dreadful. But when the valet was declared to be the culprit we thought to retain the secret.'

'The secret of the modifications?' Swift asked in his pedantic way.

'Yes, sir. Lady Rose considered it to be a chivalrous story. Duels without bloodshed, each man's honour upheld, as it were.'

'How many did she share the secret with?' I asked.

Colour seeped into his pale cheeks. 'I could not say for certain, sir. A select few over the years.'

'Had Wilmslow and Flyte stayed at Bancroft before?' I asked.

'They did, sir.' Redfern sounded miserable.

I thought about the ramifications, and the likelihood of the duel playing out in the way it was presented. 'There was someone else out here, wasn't there?'

'Was it you?' Swift instantly demanded of Redfern.

'It was not, sir...' His shoulders sagged. 'But I had noticed what appeared to be another set of footsteps in the frost, leading from the tower to the edge of the field.' He hesitated, then raised his eyes to us. 'I was barely thinking, sir. The shock. Two men lying in their own blood. The pistols I had loaded the evening before...it didn't seem possible.'

Despite our attempts to act the hardened detectives, the poor chap's distress caused us to soften our tone.

'Redfern we need to find out what happened, please just tell us what you know,' I told him.

'I am doing my best, sir,' he replied, and attempted to straighten his thin shoulders.

'Where was each man lying?' I continued.

'Where the blood stains are.' He pointed. 'Mr Wilmslow was to the left, sir, and Mr Flyte was to the right.'

Swift took out his notebook and made a quick pencil drawing of the field and position of each protagonist in relation to the tower. 'Good, now show us where you saw the third set of footsteps.'

'If you would like to come this way, sirs,' Redfern said. He set off back towards the tower, gun case still in hand. We went behind, and Foggy, who had not liked the sound of the shots at all, decided to be brave and come too.

'Over there, sirs.' Redfern returned to the tower door and pointed towards some distant shrubs. 'I noticed them as I came out of this door, they went in that direction. The heavier sets were going to the duelling ground, and it was those that I followed. I wasn't thinking of anything other than the fallen men, but I have since reflected on the matter and concluded there must have been someone else present.'

'Stay there,' I told him.

Swift and I strode over to a scrub of brambles and hawthorn under a few trees. There was nothing to see on the ground, the frost of yesterday had left the earth too hard to register footprints.

'Someone could have hidden here,' Swift said.

'Gilbert?' I offered.

His buoyant mood slid away. 'If he did murder Flyte then it makes sense…but he'd been with the force. Billings said he was a good man.' He glanced across to the duelling ground again. 'It goes against everything he would have stood for.'

'Then why would he have run away?' I repeated, because the apparent contradiction was troubling me.

'I don't know, but we shouldn't jump to too many conclusions.'

'On the assumption that he's the killer?' I questioned.

'On the assumption that there's a killer here and we don't know who it is.'

'Fine, but without Gilbert, we'll have the devil of a job untangling this,' I replied as we strode back to where Redfern was holding the door to the tower open.

CHAPTER EIGHT

'Ah, you must be the detectives.' A chap was crossing the echoing great hall as we entered behind Redfern. 'Hot on the trail of the valet, I assume. Or would varlet be a better term?'

'There's a nationwide alert for him.' Swift had stopped to remove his trench coat, still in pristine condition.

'Well, let's hope they catch him and we can all sleep safely in our beds.' He smiled. 'Sir George Lovell, at your service.' Debonair, handsome, and courteous, he held a hand out to Swift.

'Inspector Swift, Scotland Yard,' he said, which was a new one on me. He usually declared himself retired, but since he was now an official consultant to the force, I suppose it was correct.

'Lennox,' I said and shook the man's hand.

'Ah, spouse of the exquisite Lady Persephone,' Sir George said with a disarming grin. His thick dark hair was touched with grey at the temples, he wore a superbly tailored light grey suit with a blue tie embroidered with the insignia of the Royal Naval Officers' Club. 'I had the honour to be introduced yesterday. She was intrigued by the story of the lost Lady Madeleine – as am I. I do hope she is returning to continue her quest.'

'What quest?' I frowned.

'To uncover the mystery, of course.' His grin broadened. 'I have offered my humble services. I thought we'd make rather a good team.'

Extraordinary how a man might seem perfectly affable one minute and an oily snake the next.

'My wife will be aiding Lady Persi,' Swift said, handing his trench coat to Redfern. 'And we are investigating the murder of Flyte.'

The smile had frozen on George's lips, but he didn't miss a beat. 'Naturally I will be delighted to cooperate in any way I can.' He made an elaborate bow then turned to the factotum, standing quietly to one side. 'Redfern, I am in search of coffee.'

'A fresh pot will be served in the breakfast room very shortly, sir.'

'Very well, *à la prochaine*, gentlemen,' Sir George spoke lightly then turned to climb the stairs.

'We need an incident room, Redfern.' Swift turned to him.

'I…erm…a what…sir?' he stammered.

'We could use the tower?' I suggested. 'Top floor, not the one where Flyte was murdered. The bed would be in the way.'

'Good idea,' Swift agreed. 'And it should be easy to secure.'

Redfern looked askance but recovered himself. 'Very well, sir. I will inform Lady Rose of your decision.'

'Right, at least that's settled.' I gave him a grin, and my great coat, which he folded over his arm.

He sighed. 'Indeed sir.'

Rather than go straight to the tower, Swift insisted on going to search Gilbert's room again.

'You've already done it,' I objected.

'Yes, and now we're doing it again,' he replied, then added, 'I didn't make as thorough a search as I should have, Lennox.'

We trooped up to the top floor where all the servants' quarters were. It was freezing cold.

He insisted on dusting for fingerprints.

'Fossett took everyone's prints yesterday,' I said as he stalked around the dreary room, badger brush in hand.

'I know, he gave the sheet to me.' Swift paused to remove a folded paper from his jacket pocket. 'Here, hold onto it and check them carefully with your magnifying glass.'

'I haven't brought a magnifying glass.'

'Why not?' he stopped dabbing the brush to demand.

Actually it was in my coat pocket down in the hall but I wasn't going to trail all the way down there to get it.

'Really Lennox, you should come prepared. You must have learned something about procedure by now,' he lectured, then pulled his own magnifying glass from another pocket. I knew he'd have one.

I used it to peer at the iced-over window panes. 'Fossett's doing a good job, he even took Gilbert's prints while the man was pretending to be in a drunken stupor. And he's reading a detecting manual.'

'You could take a few lessons yourself.'

I ignored that. 'If Gilbert were the culprit, he wouldn't have left anything to find,' I said. I scanned the few fingerprints Swift had turned up. There weren't many. Given the cold in the room, Gilbert had probably worn gloves most of the time. 'They're all Gilbert's,' I said once I finished following Swift around. 'Here.' I handed back the magnifying glass.

'Gilbert was an ex-copper, he might have hidden his notes. Those habits die hard.' Swift went to the bed and knelt down to check under it with his torch, which he also kept in a pocket.

'He'd have taken them with him, along with the rest of his belongings.' I went back to the window. The room was painted dull grey. An ancient wardrobe, an iron bed, cheap dressing table and chair, and a ragged rug made up the furnishings.

'Possibly, but it's no excuse for shortcuts.'

'Fine,' I said and walked over to the wardrobe to move it away from the wall. There was nothing other than dust and thick cobwebs clinging to the rough plaster. I reached up to run my hand over the top of it and found more dust and cobwebs. 'Come on, Swift, we're wasting our time.' I wiped my hands on my jacket.

He sighed as he straightened up. 'Wait. What's that?'

'What?'

'On your sleeve, it must have been stuck to the cobwebs.'

I raised my arm and plucked off a neatly cut lock of hair. 'Dark red hair…'

The strands were bound by the cobwebs, which I gently brushed away with my fingers.

'It looks quite old,' Swift said and whipped his magnifying glass back out.

'How can you tell?'

'Hair can become brittle after it's cut unless it's well cared for.' He stopped examining it and dug in his jacket for an envelope. 'Drop it in here.'

I did so.

He folded the envelope over, then made a note of where and when it was found. 'Well done, Lennox,' he said, then moved the chair to step up and make a more thorough search of the wardrobe. Nothing else came to light.

'Satisfied?' I said.

He nodded. 'Let's go and set up the incident room.' He strode off, quite obviously enjoying himself.

We trod the stone steps up to the chamber at the top of the watchtower to find it occupied.

''Ello…are you them detectives from Scotland Yard then?' A round-faced young constable had been loading logs onto a freshly built fire in a large stone fireplace, but stopped and straightened up as we entered.

'Are you Kibble?' Swift said.

'I am, sir.' He saluted, standing firmly upright, podgy tummy to the fore, buttons on his straining uniform polished and gleaming. 'Constable Kibble. Ready to serve, sir.'

'I'm Inspector Swift, this is Major Lennox.'

'A major?' Kibble's eyes lit up. 'I never knew we 'ad majors in the police. Ee, you must be ever so clever.'

Swift frowned. 'How long have you been in the force, Kibble?'

'Twenty-eight days, sir. But I've been learnin' since I were a little lad on account of my dad bein' a policeman before me.' He beamed, his cheeks pink in a round face, blue eyes full of enthusiasm. 'Even give me 'is helmet he did.' He pointed to it on his head. It was at least two sizes too small.

Swift closed his eyes for a brief moment. 'Have you had any training?'

'Aye, lots.' Kibble nodded. The helmet wobbled precariously. 'I know how to put handcuffs on, and what's what with a truncheon. I've put fingerprint powder on stuff and I'm right good at cleanin' out the station. I've me own mop an' bucket an' everything.'

'Jolly good,' I told him. 'We need a table, four chairs, a thick floor rug, a cabinet of some sort, and tea and muffins.'

'And a blackboard,' Swift added.

'Swift we don't–' I began.

'Oh, yes, sir! Blackboards are great for puttin' up ideas on,' Kibble said, excitement in his voice. 'I'll ask at the school. They'll have one. I can have it brought over on the milk cart.'

'Bring the table and chairs first,' I told him. 'And the tea.'

'Aye, sir. Right away, sir.' Kibble saluted again then went off, his boots stomping on the bare wooden floorboards.

Swift went to finish piling logs on the fire, which was now blazing, but making very little difference to the icy temperature in the stone-built room. 'He'll be no use whatsoever.'

'He might be.'

He glanced at me, then tossed another log into the fire. 'Doing what?'

'Spying,' I said. 'He could be the new boot boy, or footman.'

'What?'

'The people here are supposed to be tied up in romance,' I said. 'They won't be willing to talk about their love lives, Swift.'

'And how exactly do you expect Kibble to spy on them?' He was incredulous.

'He can listen to conversations.' I was wavering a bit. It may not have been my best idea.

'The guests will all have seen him.'

'I doubt it, and even if they did, they wouldn't have taken much notice. People rarely look beyond the uniform.'

'Then have Fossett do it.'

'He and Persi made them write statements yesterday, and he took their fingerprints, they'd recognise him after that.'

He shook his head then went to look at a set of stone steps rising from the far corner of the room. They led to a hatch in the ceiling. 'I'm going up, Lennox.'

'Right…' There wasn't much else to do, so I went with him.

The hatch was heavy but worked on oiled hinges; we pushed it open and climbed out into the very top of the tower. A slate roof was suspended high above us on metal poles, it held a raised platform at waist height, and took up most of the space.

'The old warning beacon,' I said, tapping the huge sheet of blackened metal. 'But it can't be medieval. The iron would have long since rusted out.'

'They'd have replaced it numerous times.' Swift put out a hand above a heap of grey ashes in the centre of the platform. 'It's warm.'

I'd felt the warmth too. Then spotted something on the walkway and bent to retrieve it. 'Burned-out firework.' I showed it to him.

'There are more amongst the ashes,' he said.

'They had a party last night, perhaps they set them off.'

'And lit the beacon,' he added, nodding. 'They'd probably prepared it for the ball before it was called off.'

'Hmm,' I muttered agreement and turned my attention to the surrounds. I'd never been keen on heights but the perimeter wall seemed sound enough. I leaned on it and gazed out. The grounds extended right to the hills, still glazed white with sparkling frost. Grassy meadows, fields lined with hedgerows, magnificent ancient trees in the distance and a few rickety byres to shelter horses or deer. All the usual elements of an old country estate. A small lake lay beyond the duelling ground; we hadn't spotted it earlier because it was screened by trees and bushes. The drive lay in the other direction. I watched as a red speck trailing grey and white exhaust fumes raced towards the house. 'Persi.'

Swift turned to look. 'And Florence.'

'Come on,' I said and we trotted back down the steps,

out of the upper chamber and kept on going all the way to the ground floor.

Lady Rose and Mary Lovelace had beaten us to the front door. I assumed Redfern had alerted them. He was taking their coats.

'Hello, my love.' Persi kissed my cheek as she walked to meet me. She was in archaeologist's colours, a cream sweater and dark green skirt. Florence was in the blue and pale pink outfit of last evening.

'Florence.' Swift turned soft in the presence of his lovely wife.

Fossett was with them, but he merely nodded stiffly.

'Have you had breakfast?' Lady Rose twittered. 'Come and take muffins with us, and Darjeeling.'

'We have plenty,' Mary added. 'We thought there would be stayers-on after the ball, but we had to cancel. We have champagne too. I do like champagne for breakfast.'

'Tea and muffins sounds very nice,' Persi said, smiling.

She introduced Lady Florence of Braeburn Castle while Fossett stood at the rear as though he'd been stuffed.

'Braeburn?' Lady Rose mused. 'Now I recall a very handsome laird of the name back in the day. Oh, how many years must it be?' She shook her head. 'Before I was wed, I'm sure of that!'

Florence's eyes widened. 'My father has been laird for the whole of my life, but before that it would be my grandfather.'

'Craig, I believe his name was.' Lady Rose crinkled her brow as she tried to remember.

'Yes.' Florence smiled in delight. 'The old laird was Craig-Dunbar of Braeburn. My grandfather.'

'Now isn't that marvellous. I simply adore family connections. Do come and take tea and we will talk of him. Mary, to the drawing room!' Lady Rose gave a rallying cry and led the way to the stairs with Mary tottering along beside her.

'And we're very much looking forward to reading the diary about the lost lady Madeleine,' Persi said as she and Florence went with them.

'I wouldn't mind tea and muffins,' Fossett said as we all watched them go.

'Kibble should be arranging that,' I said.

'Kibble?' he asked. 'Isn't that the local bobby?'

'Did the courier from Scotland Yard pick up the bottle, Fossett?' Swift demanded of the lad.

'He did, sir,' Fossett confirmed. 'And said we might have the results by tomorrow. And he knew Gilbert from right back when they were in London together on the beat. He said Detective Sergeant Gilbert was a good bloke, although he liked a bit of a tipple now and then. And he brought down the threatening letters that was found in Mr Flyte's London house. Inspector Billings said you should have them, sir, so you can compare the paper, or writing, or whatever.' He made to open his satchel.

'We'll go to the incident room, we can examine them there,' Swift said and marched off toward the tower.

'We got an incident room?' Fossett asked as he followed. I strolled behind them, wondering if Sir George Lovell was likely to encounter the ladies and attach himself to them.

'Ee, there you are.' Kibble was back in the incident room, his sleeves rolled up and his helmet put aside. 'There's a tray on the table with a warm pot of tea an' a pile of hot muffins. I 'ad one myself and they was the best thing I ever tasted.'

The young constable had excelled himself. A large table with four upholstered dining chairs had been placed in the room. The fire was now blazing. A low bookcase with a couple of drawers was under the window, along with an oil lamp and a rug in front of the fire. My dog had made himself comfortable in front of it but came over for a fuss, tail wagging as he leapt about me.

'Constable Fossett,' Fossett introduced himself with a smart salute.

'Sir!' Kibble instantly straightened up and returned the salute.

'At ease,' Fossett told him.

'Shall I pour the tea, sir?' Kibble seemed to regard Fossett as senior, although Fossett was probably younger than him, and they were both the same rank.

'Go ahead,' Fossett replied.

I noticed Swift was suppressing a grin as we went to sit down. Fossett unbuckled his satchel and pulled out an official-looking brown envelope. 'Here's the threatening letters, sir. And there's a report in there about Mr Wilmslow and Mr Flyte.' He carried on shuffling through the satchel. 'And here's the statements the folks wrote yesterday before Gilbert disappeared.' Fossett added another pile of papers to the stack.

'And the sheet of fingerprints,' Swift added as he unfolded the paper he'd taken from his jacket.

'Help yourselves to milk an' sugar,' Kibble said as he pushed teacups towards us. 'I brought extra of everything 'cos you never know who might turn up.'

I reached for a muffin and bit into it. It was utterly delicious with added cherries and a sprinkling of sugar on top.

'I don't think Inspector Billings thinks Gilbert did it, sir,' Fossett said as he sat down opposite Swift.

'We have to keep an open mind,' Swift replied. 'Spread the statements out along the table, and don't spill tea on them.' He eyed me as he said that. 'Then place the threatening letters alongside the papers for comparison.'

He did so and we quietly observed the writing as we ate the muffins.

'I think they wrote the letters in their wrong hand,' Fossett declared after he finished eating.

'Like their left, instead of their right,' Kibble said.

'Yes, that's why the writing's all wobbly,' Fossett agreed.

I took the page covered in inky black prints, then the fingerprints Fossett had found in the room downstairs where Flyte was shot, and compared the whorls. 'Annabel Cresswell,' I said. 'She came in when we were examining the body.'

'Yes, and there's another lady's there too,' Fossett said. 'Edna Kent.'

I remembered her from the drawing room yesterday, a plain young woman, and plain spoken with it. 'She said she'd heard about Flyte being shot dead, but didn't say she'd been in the room.'

'Ooh, that might be significant,' Fossett said.

'They shouldn't just go in and out like that. He wasn't even properly dressed,' Kibble quibbled as he finished his tea.

Swift had been reading Billings' report sent along with the threatening letters. 'According to this, Flyte was a playboy. One of the footmen employed in his house said he had any number of lady friends coming and going.' He read out the report. '*OceanFlyte International was started in London 86 years ago by Michael Patrick Flyte. It now operates out of Singapore and is a trading and shipping company. Charles Flyte is one of eight direct descendants of Michael Patrick Flyte. Each descendant holds a proportion of non-voting shares in OceanFlyte International. None of the Flyte descendants are involved in running the company, they merely receive dividends…*' He turned a page and his eyes widened. 'Very large dividends, according to these figures. *The trustee company manages all their assets, including houses, estates, vineyards and yachts. When any of the Flyte descendants die, their shares are divided between the surviving family members.*'

'So he probably wasn't killed for his fortune,' I cut in.

'Unless the other seven paid for an assassin to finish him off–' Swift began, before being interrupted again.

'You think Gilbert was a hired assassin!' Kibble's eyes were almost bulging. 'I've read about them in books.'

'Don't be ridiculous, Constable,' Swift said then carried on. 'Three ladies who are also guests here have frequented Flyte's Mayfair home in recent weeks. Annabel Cresswell, Felicity Carr, and Serafina Deville.'

I refrained from raising my eyebrows.

'I took Felicity Carr's statement, and she seemed really quiet,' Fossett said. He'd been making notes in his own notebook. 'I had to drag every word out of her. I thought she was shy, but it might be anything really.'

'Yeah, like guilt 'cos she shot 'im,' Kibble said.

'You have to keep an open mind, Kibble, not just guess all the time,' Fossett told him. 'You find evidence and question witnesses and then write everything down. I've got a proper book on detecting.' He nodded in emphasis. 'Not some penny dreadful from the market.'

'Those books are twopence halfpenny,' Kibble replied, then added, 'sir.'

'Well if you want to learn, you have to listen and watch the detectives,' Fossett lectured. 'And write everything down.'

'Righty-o,' Kibble said. 'I'd best sharpen me pencil then.'

Swift had been sorting through the pile of papers. 'The report on Wilmslow...' He scanned the typed sheet. 'Family estate in Devon...mother elderly but still alive. *Wilmslow is the youngest son of four siblings, an elder brother and two sisters. He has no job, but received rental income from various properties which he dissipated as fast as it arrived in his bank. He lived in a flat off Belgravia, he employed a valet who also cooked and a charlady who came in to clean. There was mention of ladies but no names...*' He scanned the page. 'Typical toff, living in clover.'

Kibble was leaning on the table trying to write in the smallest notebook I'd ever seen; he could barely get a complete sentence on a page.

'Motive wasn't money by the sounds of it, sir,' Fossett said.

'No,' Swift agreed.

'Kibble,' I said. 'We need a spy in the house, and you're it.'

'What?' Kibble and Fossett said at once.

'Oh, sir, I don't know how to be a spy,' Kibble said. 'An' they'll soon spot me 'cos of my uniform.'

'You won't wear that uniform,' I said. 'You can be a footman.'

He sat looking at me as though I'd just declared he had to fly to the moon. 'But…but…'

'Won't they already have seen him, sir?' Fossett said.

'Have they seen you, Kibble?' I asked him.

'I…um, no I don't think so, sir. Lady Rose might 'ave done but she was all in a lather. I was mostly helping Mr Redfern. We locked the guns away. They'd already called the doctor afore I arrived but I didn't see him neither 'cos he was cutting the ball out from Mr Flyte's shoulder.'

'What about Wilmslow? Did you see him?' Swift asked.

'Yes, when he was lyin' dead outside, and then when he was bein' carted out to the ambulance, sir.'

'Right.' Swift seemed to have made a decision. 'Fossett, go and find Redfern, tell him to arrange with Lady Rose to take on a new footman or whatever they need. Have them find a uniform to fit Kibble. They'll have something in store, these places always do.'

'But sir–' Kibble attempted to object.

'Go with Fossett and don't be seen,' Swift cut him off. 'Dismissed.'

They both looked nonplussed then trooped out.

'It isn't illegal or anything, is it, Swift?' I asked.

'Impersonating a footman?' he replied, reaching for another piece of paper off the pile. 'Not as far as I know.

A knock sounded on the door. It opened.

'Hello?' A woman put her head round it. 'May I come in?'

'Yes,' Swift replied, putting the brown envelope over the top of the stack of papers.

'I'm Felicity Carr,' she said. 'And I have a confession to make.'

CHAPTER NINE

'I didn't kill him,' she said as she sat down. 'But I'm glad he's dead.'

Swift was quick to wield his fountain pen.

'Muffin?' I offered. It was the last one.

'No, thank you, I've only just finished breakfast.' Her voice held a tremor; she pulled agitatedly at a long curl of soft brown hair.

'I assume this is regarding Charles Flyte?' Swift intoned in a professional manner.

'Yes, of course,' she replied. A young woman, around Persi's age, average height, slim, dark eyes, shoulders slightly hunched, she was practically twitching with nervousness.

'Would you like to write your confession down?' Swift continued.

'No, I…' She let the curl drop and tugged her red cardigan together over the white cotton blouse she wore. 'We… Oh dear lord, this really is excruciating. I am furious at Charles, he could be such a heartless brute. I absolutely refuse to mourn for him.' She pulled a damp handkerchief from the sleeve of the cardigan and balled it between her hands.

'Did you write threatening letters to him?' I asked.

Her eyes darted to mine. 'I…yes, I did.' She hung her head. 'I'm ashamed. It was stupid, but I was angry. Anyway, that's what I wanted to tell you.'

A frown creased between Swift's dark brows. 'Thank you. Perhaps we should introduce ourselves–'

'Oh, I know who you are,' she said. 'Everyone does. Lady Rose told us all about it. You're Inspector Swift from Scotland Yard,' she said, then turned to me. 'And you're Major Lennox, the dashing war hero with the terribly clever wife.' She tried a smile, it was tremulous.

Swift's frown deepened. 'You made a statement to Constable Fossett yesterday afternoon…' He picked up the papers and shuffled through them until he found hers. 'Is this your handwriting?' He showed it to her.

'It is.' She nodded.

He read through it before continuing. 'You said you knew Flyte but *only as another guest and had very little to do with him*. You also stated that you did not know the cause of the duel.' He eyed her narrowly. 'Was any of that true?'

She raised her chin, then lowered it to gaze at the tightly balled handkerchief in her hands. 'No. I knew him in London…we…he was my…*ahem*…' She raised a hand in front of her lips. 'My lover,' she whispered. 'I think they may have been fighting over me.'

Swift looked sceptical. 'Why?'

Her cheeks flushed pink. She gazed over at the sunshine falling through the window. 'Bernard Wilmslow had been growing quite keen on me. We met here last year at the ball, and saw each other at different events and parties in London–'

I interrupted her. 'What was Wilmslow like?'

She blinked at that. 'Oh, I suppose you haven't met him. Well, he was good looking, slim, fashionably dressed, not terribly tall, but all in proportion…' She paused, as though switching her focus from Flyte to him. 'He could be wasp-ish for no good reason. Sometimes it was like walking on eggshells around him. I've no idea why he was so touchy, he had everything you could imagine.'

'Charles Flyte was at last year's ball, wasn't he?' Swift asked.

'Yes, but he hadn't taken any notice of me; he was chas-ing Clarissa Weston at the time. Charles is awfully popular, and incredibly rich. He's invited everywhere…I suppose I should say he *was*. I haven't adjusted to him being dead yet.' She began to pluck at the long brown curl again. 'Three months ago Charles suddenly took a shine to me…I was quite flattered. He asked me out, and then, well, he took me everywhere, even to the Riviera. It was sensational. He has a yacht, and estates, and houses in all the best places. Paris, Seville, Rhodes, London of course, and Antibes. There were so many servants, he said he didn't know how many, or who they even were.' Her lips briefly lifted again. 'I suppose all that sounds as though I was dazzled by his lifestyle, and I think I was. Bernard was annoyed, but he'd been seeing someone else before me anyway, and I don't think he'd actually stopped seeing her, even though he swore he had. Anyway, we parted with a few harsh words and I spent more and more time with Charles. Then one day he said he had a proposition for me and he'd tell me about it soon. Naturally I assumed it would be marriage. I mean what other type of proposition is there? I told my girlfriends, they were thrilled, we laughed about what colour bridesmaid dresses they would wear…' She crushed the handkerchief into an even tighter ball. 'I even told my parents…' She hung her head again, long brown curls fell to obscure her face. 'He asked me to dinner at the Goring, saying it would be memorable. We were about to order dessert when he smiled and reached for my hand across the table. Then he…he asked me if I would be his *special girl*.'

She sniffed, and put the handkerchief to her nose, trying to stop the sobs escaping. We waited. The ink dried on Swift's pen. He shook it. I eyed the muffin.

'When was this?' Swift asked the typical policeman's question.

'In the new year. He'd gone to Paris to stay with friends for Christmas, or so he told me, then came back and asked me for dinner. He said he'd missed me…' She sobbed briefly, then banged her fist on the table. 'Damn him,' she hissed.

'And what did being Flyte's "special girl" entail?' Swift continued in the same formal tone.

'It was what we'd already been doing, but he said he wanted to formalise it.' She heaved a breath. 'It meant going away with him, and attending parties, evenings out, and weekends away on his yacht.' Her voice had fallen to a barely controlled monotone. 'He would pay for it all, including my clothes. He was very keen to choose clothes for me. He said my taste was too modest, and I needed to wear something more stylish. And then he stated I would have to be his *exclusively,* but would have to understand that he had *other* special girls. I would have to accept this, and not make a fuss.' She suddenly raised her voice again. 'The beast. He didn't want to marry me, he wanted…he wanted to buy me,' she yelled, and suddenly threw the balled handkerchief across the room. Foggy watched, perplexed, as it bounced off a wall and onto the rug. 'I was incensed. How dare he assume I am some sort of…' her mouth worked as she searched for the word, 'strumpet! The louse! I should have thrown my drink at him. Or the whole bottle, but I just sat in the middle of the restaurant and wept.' She put her elbows on the table and her head in her hands. 'I was wearing makeup. It ran down my cheeks. Everyone around us was so embarrassed.' She spoke through clenched teeth. 'One of the waitresses came and asked if she could help, and led me out to the powder room. Then she found a taxi for me. And Charles did nothing. Not a thing. He just waved for the head waiter, told him to forward the bill and walked out. I hate him, *hate* him.' She banged a fist on the plain oak tabletop, making it reverberate.

'*Ahem,*' Swift cleared his throat. 'And you sent threatening letters to him after that?'

'Yes,' she muttered, then dashed the tears from her eyes.

'Could you show us how you wrote those letters, please?' Swift passed her a sheet of paper and another pen he'd taken from his inside pocket.

'I feel such a fool,' she said quietly as she leaned over the table to write awkwardly with her left hand. 'I told my friends about his proposition, they were livid. And I told Bernard. He'd finally split up once and for all from his girlfriend and came to see me. We were both at a loose end, and we sort of…took up where we'd left off.'

That raised my brows. 'So you and Wilmslow were, erm…'

'Lovers? No, Major Lennox, what do you take me for?' Her eyes flashed. 'Good Lord you men are as bad as each other.'

'I meant…it was just…' I babbled.

Swift cut in. 'We're merely trying to ascertain facts, Miss Carr.'

'Yes, precisely,' I said, then shut up when she glared at me.

'Did you enter the room Charles Flyte was in on the day of his death?' Swift threw in a question designed to throw her off kilter. He often did that, it was one of his tactics. 'We have fingerprinted the room,' he added.

'In that case you will realise I did not,' she said firmly.

Swift made a point of writing that down. 'Did you witness the duel?'

'No. I had no idea they were going to shoot each other,' she replied.

'But you said you thought it may have been fought over you,' I put in.

She glared at me again, then sighed. 'Well, it's possible, and if I didn't know the valet had murdered Charles, I never would have told you all this. Why haven't you caught him?' she suddenly demanded. 'He can't have gone very far in this weather.'

'An alert has been raised. Police forces across the country will be looking for him, including the force at Stratford-up-on-Avon,' Swift replied in a monotone.

She sniffled again, her shoulders more hunched than before.

Swift lightly tapped the end of his pen on his notebook to prompt her to resume talking.

She stopped sniffing. 'The duel might have been about Bernard's old flame.'

'Who was?' Swift asked, pen now poised.

'Annabel Cresswell,' she replied bitterly.

He wrote this down.

'Why would they fight over her?' I asked.

'Bernard found out that Annabel had been seeing Charles,' she replied.

'As well as you?' I said, and received a glare in response.

'Was she one of his "special girls"?' Swift asked.

'I believe she was, actually,' she replied stiffly.

'Who told Bernard Wilmslow this?' Swift asked.

I expected her to say she did, but she didn't.

'Probably Charles' other *special girl*, Serafina Deville,' she said. 'And neither of them seem to give a fig for them being dead. Even though they have behaved like trollops,' she declared.

'Why did you come here if you knew Flyte would be present, along with his other *special girls*?' I asked, because it seemed to be provocative at the least.

'To show them that Bernard and I were together, and that we weren't going to be intimidated by them,' she said haughtily. 'Nor were we going to descend to their level of degeneracy.'

I flicked a hand towards the death threats. 'Really?' I said.

'I have already said that I regret them,' she retorted, then hung her head. 'And I do. Honestly, I am utterly ashamed of myself for being drawn into Charles' debauched world. I was dazzled, and stupid, and I regret it. But at least I said no to his disgusting proposition.' She raised her chin, then sighed loudly. 'And now poor Bernard is dead and he's done nothing to deserve it.' She looked over at her handkerchief lying by the fire. Tears began streaming down her face; she ran to pick it up and dabbed at her eyes. 'I'm sorry, I really must go,' she stuttered and dashed from the room.

Swift put his pen down. 'Well, I suppose that provides a motive.'

'Embarrassment?'

'No, revenge.' He turned a page in his notebook. 'Felicity Carr – lover of Bernard Wilmslow and Charles Flyte.'

'She said she wasn't Wilmslow's lover,' I corrected.

He raised a cynical eye. 'She didn't admit to it, but it doesn't mean she wasn't.' He put a question mark at the end of the note anyway. 'Annabel Cresswell was Wilmslow's long-term 'flame' but double-crossed him with Flyte. So did Felicity Carr, but she threw him over when he didn't offer marriage. She was not one of Flyte's mistresses, but Annabel Carr and Serafina Deville were, according to Felicity.'

107

'The term was "special girl".'

'Semantics, Lennox.'

I reached for the muffin. 'Looks like a pattern,' I said, between bites.

'Hum,' Swift agreed. 'Flyte stealing Wilmslow's girlfriends.'

'Which could be the cause of the duel.'

'Possibly.' Swift wrote it down.

'Sir.' Kibble walked in with Fossett behind. 'I can't go round dressed like this. I look like Humpty Dumpty.'

He was right. Dark green trousers too short at the ankle and a black jacket too short at the cuffs. The mustard-coloured waistcoat fit very snugly across his tummy though.

I laughed. 'Either that or Tweedledee.'

'Tweedledum more like.' Fossett grinned. 'And it's not the clothes that make you look like that.'

Kibble frowned at him. 'It's not fair, sirs–'

A tap on the door shut him up. A young maid came in, shy and diffident. She stopped to bob a curtsy. 'Hello, sirs. Miss Meg said I was to come and tell you I'm to help the new footman settle in.' She glanced shyly at Kibble.

Kibble and Fossett didn't say a word, just stared at her. She was quite short and slim, pretty in a milkmaid way, with soft eyes, thick lashes, and honey-brown hair tied neatly behind her white cap.

'And you are?' Swift asked.

'I'm Mouse, sirs,' she spoke softly. 'I've always been called that. My real name is Maud.'

'Which do you prefer?' I asked her.

She darted a quick look at me. 'Mouse, sir. They call me that kindly, sir.'

'Kibble, are you prepared to act as footman?' I asked him.

'Erm…if this lady is going to help me out, sir. I think I might be just fine at it.' He suddenly beamed at Mouse. She gave another shy smile.

'Actually, I don't think it's a good idea,' Fossett said. 'I bet this lady has more important things to do.'

'If she's willing…' Swift said.

'I am, sir,' Mouse agreed.

'Right. Well, I'll be going then,' Kibble said. 'After you, Mouse.' He gave a nod of the head and wafted his hand in courtly manner.

They went out, closing the door behind them. I eyed Fossett. He'd fallen for a maid at Belvedere House when we'd been investigating a murder there. He was too quick to lose his heart.

'I don't think he should be working with the staff like that,' Fossett huffed. 'That's fraternising, that is, and coppers are supposed to keep suspects at a proper distance.'

'Is she a suspect?' I asked.

'Well, we don't know, do we, sir,' Fossett muttered as he picked his pencil back up.

'I'm sure Kibble will find out,' Swift said lightly.

Fossett huffed again and sat down to write in his notebook with shoulders hunched.

Foggy had opened his eyes from his position curled up on the mat in front of the fire, but was just blinking back to sleep when Redfern came in with a quiet tread.

'Sir, Mr Doggett has requested you meet him in the drawing room.'

'Who?' I asked.

'Mr Frederick Doggett is a guest, sir. He prefers to be known as Freddie.'

'Why does he want to talk to us?'

'He would not say, sir.'

'Right.' Swift stood up. 'Come on, Lennox.'

CHAPTER TEN

I'd half expected to find Lady Rose and Mary Lovelace but there was just a tall, slim chap, sitting in Lady Rose's chair by the fire. He stood up and gave us a friendly grin.

'They've all gone to the library,' he said in response to my inquiry. 'With a couple of very attractive visitors, and George, of course.'

'Sir George Lovell?' I asked.

'Yes, all the ladies think he's wonderful,' the chap said. An amiable enough type, carefully combed hair the colour of straw, pleasant features radiating with goodwill, an exquisitely tailored jacket, a club tie, pristine shirt and fashionable slacks. 'I don't even know why he came here. He's a naval captain, you know. Girls adore that kind of thing, they just fall all over him. Lucky devil.' he grinned.

'You're Freddie Doggett?' Swift asked.

'Spot on, yes!' He chortled. 'But then you're detectives, so you'd deduce that, wouldn't you? Anyway, delighted to meet you and all that.' He shook our hands warmly as we made the usual introductions.

'Why do you want to talk to us?' Swift sat on the nearest sofa.

A frown formed between Doggett's sandy brows. 'Well, to ask why you're still in the house. I mean, if the valet killed Charles...'

'There's no proof the valet killed anyone.' Swift cut him off. 'Unless you can provide some?'

'I...I...no, of course not,' he spluttered. 'I was simply... well, you know, rather confounded. And you said he had done it.'

'We said *probably* done it,' Swift instantly replied.

'Right, yes,' Doggett was even more confused. 'Well, um...Is there any danger? Should we be on the alert? We have the fairer sex to think of. And the old ladies,' he added.

'What was the cause of the duel?' I asked him.

'Haven't the foggiest,' he replied, then added, 'there was only the nonsense about the bombe surprise.'

'Which upset the chef,' Swift said.

'It upset everybody!' Doggett's voice rose an octave. 'It was quite unnecessary. Charles was arrogant, as usual, trying to belittle Wilmslow, and Serafina was withering. Then Wilmslow tried to join forces with her, and Charles became really angry. There was something going on there, you know.' He fidgeted in his seat. 'Not that Serafina would fain to notice, she's too far above that sort of thing, or anything really. Her name means fiery angel, but she's more of an ice maiden. The sort that would be worshipped, if anyone were the worshipping sort, of course. Haha.' He gave an unconvincing laugh.

'Oh, Freddie, you here?' A young lady came in, elegant and poised, slim, with pale blonde hair, blue eyes and a classic "peaches and cream" complexion. 'And you will be the detectives.' She came across towards us.

Doggett sprang to his feet as we both rose to ours.

'Clarissa,' Doggett said. 'Would you like to take this seat, it's perfectly warm by the fire.' He was suddenly overly animated, trying hard to please the lady.

'I'd rather not,' she replied with a polite smile. 'I always think of that as Lady Rose's chair.' She turned to us. 'I'm Lady Clarissa Weston.' She held her hand out and we formally introduced ourselves. 'I imagine you must be wondering what on earth has been happening in this house.' She sat on the other end of the sofa to Swift, ankles crossed, hands in her lap. Doggett shifted to a different chair and perched on the edge, leaning towards Clarissa, a nervous smile fixed on his face.

'You made a statement to the constable,' Swift began in friendlier fashion. 'Is there anything you'd like to add?' he asked her.

'I wish I could,' she replied. She wore a simple dress in lavender blue under a matching cardigan and a string of perfect pearls. Classic and understated. 'There are inevitably a few rivalries here, but I'd never have thought them intense enough to lead to a duel.'

'I thought the same,' Doggett chimed in. 'It's just what I said, apart from the argument over pudding.'

Clarissa cast him a glance of mild indifference, then turned back to us. 'When Lady Rose organises the Valentine's Balls, she hopes we will meet someone special, but

I really don't think there are any serious matches at all this year,' Clarissa replied. She seemed very straightforward in a direct, country way.

'Presumably Lady Rose had specific partners in mind when she made the invitations,' I said.

Clarissa cast another glance at Doggett. 'Freddie, Annabel was hoping to find someone to go for a walk in the garden with her, why don't you–'

He was on his feet in an instant. 'Was she really? I could go with her,' he spoke with enthusiasm. 'Where is she? I'll find her and offer my arm.' He grinned at Clarissa. 'Tally-ho,' he said cheerfully and dashed off.

'I take it he is keen on the lady,' I said dryly.

She laughed. 'He's keen on all the ladies, he's like an over eager puppy. It's sweet but a bit wearing after a while. He's been badgering Lady Rose to be invited to the ball.'

'Who was matched with whom?' Swift was poised with pencil and notepad.

'Oh, let me see…' She raised her head in thought, her thick blonde hair falling back from her face. 'George Lovell with Barbara Boden–'

'Wait…' Swift stopped her. He was writing a heading on a fresh page. 'Thank you. Please carry on.'

'Barbara Boden's the tall one with black hair?' I asked. I was about to add cherry-red lips but decided against.

'And regally imperious with it,' Clarissa laughed. 'She's closest to George's age, but I believe he's keen on having a family and I doubt that features in her ambitions at all.'

Swift made a note. 'Who was Charles Flyte supposed to be partnered with?'

'Serafina Deville,' Clarissa said. 'Although Charles was running after Anabel Cresswell, which infuriated Felicity Carr.'

That chimed with Felicity Carr's confession to us in the tower, although I was already becoming confused with who was who.

'What about Bernard Wilmslow?' Swift was focused on his notebook.

'He had been matched with Annabel, and Lady Rose had understood it was just a question of time before he popped the question to her,' Clarissa said. 'But it seems they had some sort of falling out and Annabel was quite cool with him. So Bernard was matched with Felicity.'

Thinking of what Felicity Carr had told us about Annabel being one of Flyte's "special girls", that would hardly be a surprise.

'Do the guests know who Lady Rose has matched together?' Swift asked without looking up.

'No, not at all, and nor should they know or it would feel too forced,' she said and neatly recrossed her slim ankles.

'But you do?' I asked.

'Yes, Lady Rose is my godmother, she confides these things in me.'

Swift glanced up from his note-taking but then continued writing.

'How well does Lady Rose actually know these people?' I asked.

'She knows them by reputation, mostly,' Clarissa said.

'And by that I mean chit-chat among society's grand dames. They all correspond. Lady Rose and Miss Mary no longer travel, but they have old friends in London.'

I very much doubted high society matriarchs would really know who's doing what with whomever, because amorous exploits are kept very carefully hidden from the grand dames.

'Do you tell Lady Rose the true relationships between her guests?' Swift asked with a frown.

'Heavens, no,' Clarissa laughed. 'It would spoil her rosy-eyed view of us all.'

'If Lady Rose had known about the rivalry between Flyte and Wilmslow, they may not now be dead,' Swift said dourly.

I reacted instantly to that. 'That's out of order, Swift, you can't equate the two.'

Clarissa looked shaken. 'I can't imagine it was anything to do with what I said, or didn't say. The rivalry could have erupted anywhere with a similar result. And they chose to come here, no-one forced them.'

Touché, I thought.

Swift looked suitably abashed. 'I apologise,' he said. 'Nevertheless both men are dead and these romantic entanglements are probably the cause of it.'

Clarissa took the apology to heart and gripped her hands together. 'You're quite right. I'm sorry. What can I do to help?'

'If you could tell us the complete list of who were expected to form couples, and the reality of the relationships, we would have a clearer picture,' Swift said politely. I gazed over at him, wondering if this was a new tactic.

'Of course,' Clarissa said eagerly. 'Well, I'll repeat Lady Rose's list: George Lovell with Barbara Boden, Serafina Deville with Charles Flyte, Bernard Wilmslow with Felicity Carr, Annabel Cresswell with Rupert Featherstone, Freddie Doggett with Edna Kent, and,' she took a breath, 'I am paired with Lord Hector Sommerton.'

'We haven't met Sommerton yet,' I said.

'He isn't being very sociable at the moment. He's terribly annoyed about everything,' Clarissa said, her face troubled.

I wanted to ask more but there was a flush to her cheeks – she was obviously embarrassed by the subject.

Swift had finished writing and turned a page. 'Who is actually romantically involved with whom?'

'Oh, that is much more difficult to answer. I think I've covered most of them…really it was Charles who created the ructions. He was utterly selfish and thought nothing of leading women on, only to drop them if they wouldn't dance to his tune.'

'You mean if they wouldn't agree to become his mistress,' Swift spoke plainly.

She blushed again. 'It wasn't being a mistress in the concubine sense; he was offering them a slice of the high life, and he would pick up the bill. His dalliances usually only lasted a short while, but he ensured the ladies were exceptionally well treated.'

So she knew about this too. 'That's a remarkably tolerant interpretation,' I remarked, wondering where her morals were and had I misinterpreted her.

'Perhaps.' She shrugged. 'But Charles had an entirely

different attitude to most of us – much more modern. Laissez-faire, one could say. I don't subscribe to it, but I do think young people need to be allowed more leeway to learn about life, and the opposite sex. We're all so cloistered, and I've seen the most terrible mistakes made. Couples shackled together for life, becoming more and more unhappy, and making their whole family miserable. Marriage is such a momentous decision, it should only be made for the right reasons.'

She had a point there, and since the war the deeply ingrained attitudes of Victorian times have been slowly eroding away. Although youthful frolics, particularly in public, could still sully a reputation and that wasn't anything a decent young woman would want.

'It didn't sound as if Flyte was "learning about life", it sounded as though he was setting up a harem.' Swift was direct.

Her eyes fixed on his. 'I suspect you've been talking to Felicity.'

'We don't disclose confidential information,' Swift replied.

'Felicity is from a very good family, but doesn't have a bean,' Clarissa said. 'She has decided that she must marry a husband with enough money to keep her, or she'll end up in the typing pool. She's already had one job in a chemist shop and found it utterly demeaning.'

'Why?' Swift asked with a slight frown.

'She was at the beck and call of all sorts of people. I imagine she thought it was beneath her to deal with the public. We've all told her that money is the worst reason to marry, but she seems quite determined.'

'Or desperate,' Swift added.

'Yes, quite,' she agreed.

'Did Flyte make a point of stealing women from Bernard Wilmslow?' I asked, thinking back to the discussion earlier.

Her eyes flew to me, then she tilted her head slightly to one side. 'Possibly, though Charles would chase any girl if she gave the slightest hint his attentions would be welcome.'

Swift's brows drew together at that. It gave a different slant to the tale Felicity Carr had told earlier.

A tap on the door interrupted us. Kibble walked in, stopped, puffed out his chest and announced, 'Hello everybody. I'm sent to tell you that lunch is served. Ye'd best come quick cos it'll be gettin' cold. Thank you.'

Swift glanced at me and rolled his eyes. I grinned.

Lady Clarissa bit her bottom lip, trying to suppress a smile as she regarded him. 'Are you the new footman?'

'I am, miss.' Kibble waited as we all rose to our feet and followed him out.

'You look awfully like the constable from the village I met yesterday,' she said. 'He was looking for Redfern and I directed him.'

'Oh, right.' He stopped walking for a moment. 'Erm… That'll be Kibble, he's my cousin…twice removed,' he added. 'I'm Kipp from, erm…Binton, near Stratford.'

'Oh, really?' Clarissa broke into a smile. 'I know it well, there's a very nice bookshop there.'

'Is there?' Kibble, or rather, Kipp said. 'I don't read much. Now, here's the dining room.' He threw open the door; it was the billiards room, and deserted.

Clarissa laughed. 'Come along, I'll show you.' She led on.

The hubbub of voices gave it away before we arrived.

'Here we go,' Kibble said and swung the door open.

CHAPTER ELEVEN

'I saved a seat for you.' Persi smiled at me and patted the chair next to her.

I sighed as I sat down. The chatter subdued as Swift took the vacant spot next to Florence.

'Hello there, the detectives,' Freddie Doggett called out amiably. 'I've been introduced to your dog.' Foggy was sitting next to him, probably because Doggett seemed the sort to hand out goodies.

Lady Rose stood up, a thick paisley shawl around her shoulders over a formal black frock with a high lace neckline, presumably in deference to the dead. 'I don't think Inspector Swift and Major Lennox have met everyone just yet?' She turned to us, a smile on her face; she seemed to enjoy being in company, it gave her eyes a sparkle. The half full glass of red wine in front of her may have added to her radiance.

'Correct.' Swift stood and made a brief bow, then introduced himself. 'Inspector Swift, Scotland Yard.'

I was more interested in lunch, and the wine bottles lined up on the long refectory table standing between the tall windows flooded with winter sunshine.

'Major Lennox,' I said and sat down again.

'You know who I am,' Barbara Boden said, a curl to her cherry-red lips. 'We've already met.' She had dressed in black again, although this time with a glittering diamond necklace to add dazzle to the silky outfit.

'And me,' Freddie Doggett said gaily.

'We have also met.' Edna Kent raised a hand to wave.

'And I,' Felicity Carr added, her face composed, shoulders hunched. She seemed withdrawn and rather sad.

'I spoke with the major yesterday.' Rupert Featherstone, the chinless wonder, was less than friendly. 'I think it commendable Scotland Yard have sent Inspector Swift, at least he is a professional, but I can't think why they're still in the house rather than out hunting for that valet of Flyte's.'

'The entire British police force is on the alert for Gilbert,' Swift answered coldly. 'Major Lennox and I are investigating the cause of the deaths of Bernard Wilmslow and Charles Flyte.'

I suppose that was as good an explanation as any.

'I do hope that answers your question, Rupert.' Lady Rose waved a hand. 'Now, Serafina will be down shortly, and I will introduce Lord Hector Sommerton, who had very graciously agreed to attend our ball again this year.'

Lord Hector Sommerton rose to his feet and bowed stiffly in our direction, then sat down again. Thick brown hair combed above a square face. An aquiline nose and heavily lidded eyes that observed us with sharp intelligence. He wore a tweed jacket at least as old as mine, a plain green waistcoat and a dull red bow tie. He looked more like a high court judge than the heir to an earldom. 'Good afternoon gentlemen.' He spoke with a refined accent. 'Inspector Swift, you spent some of the war in intelligence?'

'I did, yes,' Swift spoke warily.

'I'm an acquaintance of Thomas Patterson,' Sommerton said. 'I telephoned him earlier. He is keeping a close eye on your progress.'

The sinews in Swift's hawkish face tightened. We had only dealt with DCI Billings. Patterson was the chief constable, and the last thing Swift would want is him breathing down our necks.

'I'm sure he'll be very impressed.' Lady Rose broke the moment of uncomfortable silence. 'Now if only Serafina would arrive we can begin.'

The door opened almost as she spoke. Kibble entered in solemn dignity. 'Miss Surfina Devil,' he announced loudly and then wobbled an extravagant bow.

'It's Serafina Deville, you idiot,' Rupert Featherstone said and stood up to pull out the chair next to him.

'I'm not an idiot,' Kibble instantly retorted, and went to hold the chair out himself. 'And that's my job.'

'Who are you?' the chinless wonder demanded.

'Kibb...Kipp. I'm the new footman.'

'Well go away and do some serving or something,' Featherstone retorted.

The woman herself remained entirely impassive, her serene features untouched by the faintest hint of emotion. She seemed to glide across the floor in a sapphire silk dress; lithe and long-limbed, pale blonde hair flowing in waves down her back. She could have been a goddess from ancient myth. Freddie Doggett described her as an ice maiden and it was clear to see why: her skin was perfect and pale, cool blue eyes the colour of a winter sky, and long slender neck holding her head high.

'Don't be a bore, Rupert,' she said as she slid into the chair.

Featherstone let go as though he'd been electrocuted, and Kibble pushed her chair forward with a look of triumph.

'Your napkin, miss.' Kibble picked it off the table and laid it over his arm, then presented it to her.

A look of faint puzzlement crossed her beautiful face, and I heard stifled laughter as Serafina lifted the white linen with one graceful movement and placed it across her lap. 'Thank you, Kipp,' she said and glanced up at him with an unblinking gaze.

He beamed. 'That's alright, miss. Happy to be of service. Anythin' else I can get for you?'

'I think we are all waiting for the soup,' Lady Rose said loudly.

'And a white wine for me,' Mary said next to her.

'Right you are, then,' Kibble said, and casting a withering glance at Rupert Featherstone, he went off, presumably to join Redfern.

'I was hoping to hear more of your quest to uncover the mystery of the Lost Lady de Lisle,' Lady Clarissa said to my wife. She'd taken the seat next to Lord Hector Sommerton, who had opened a leatherbound journal on the tablecloth and was methodically making notes in it.

'We've had a marvellous morning in the library with Lady Rose and Miss Lovelace.' Persi smiled back at her. 'We went through the diary of Violet Bancroft from 1798 and read her findings.'

'Lady Persi made some fascinating discoveries.' Lady Rose broke in and finished what was left of the red wine in her glass.

'She reads Latin, and medieval French,' Mary Lovelace added. 'So clever.'

'Persi is an archaeologist,' I said and grinned at my lovely wife.

'We know,' almost everyone replied. I decided to shut up after that.

'There were two documents kept with Violet's diary,' Persi explained. 'She had tried to translate them, but her Latin was quite basic and although her French was excellent, she wasn't familiar with Occitan, which would have been used in the Lisle region at the time.'

'I was able to offer some help with the Latin,' Sir George added. 'Although Persi's language skills are far superior to mine.'

I frowned and reached to put my hand over Persi's.

Redfern arrived to pour drinks, followed by Kibble, who presumably was in training. He doggedly followed Redfern, watching everything he did. The ladies all opted for white wine, apart from Clarissa, who had water, and Lady Rose, who stuck firmly with red. I had red, too. It was actually very good; I'd half expected a cut-price vintage, but she'd invested in a very respectable Bordeaux.

'The letter from Lady Madeleine's sister was apparently informing her that her previous affianced, Chevalier Pierre de Mortier, had been imprisoned,' Florence was telling everyone, 'but it may be that Violet misinterpreted it. The writing was terribly faded and the words arrayed so tightly it was very difficult to decipher them. We think…' she turned to Persi, 'you should tell them, you unravelled it.'

'Well it's more of a theory–' Persi began.

'But a very good one,' Sir George Lovell added.

Persi smiled. 'It's possible Pierre de Mortier had been taken hostage, not prisoner. The letter goes on to mention "Lo Rei" which in Occitan is "the king." There's also mention of "rescatar" which could be rescue, but it's more likely to be ransom.'

'Which comes from the Latin "rescaptare",' George Lovell said, with a self-satisfied grin.

'You're assuming, therefore,' Lord Hector Sommerton said in measured tones, 'that Lady Madeleine's ex-fiancé had been captured, held hostage, and been freed upon payment of a ransom.'

'And of course, he would have fought at Agincourt,' Lady Rose broke in. 'This is what we've been discussing all morning in the library. Isn't it fascinating?' she enthused, then took another long drink from her replenished glass.

'Agincourt,' Mary echoed. 'Where the first Lord Bancroft fought and was ennobled.' Then she drained her glass of white wine. Redfern immediately filled it again; he'd been standing in readiness behind her.

'Interesting.' Hector Sommerton nodded as he wrote

notes. 'So while Lady Madeleine was wooed and wed by the victorious English knight, her captured French lover lay in a dungeon waiting for his ransom to be paid.'

'Well, it's certainly a good story,' Barbara Boden said, then took a sip of her wine.

'Evidence would be required to make it compelling,' Hector stated.

'Lady Persephone and Lady Florence have already begun researching this,' George Lovell replied from across the table. 'I sat in with them this morning. I'm convinced by the evidence they supplied.'

Felicity Carr spoke up. 'Oh, of course, George. I'm sure they will have hit upon the right track if you were guiding them.' She forced a smile.

He looked slightly bemused at that.

Kibble arrived with a tray holding a large Meissen soup tureen. Mouse, the maid, came behind him. 'Don't say anything,' she whispered too loudly at the new "footman". 'Let Mr Redfern do it.'

'I was only going to say hello, nice and polite like,' Kibble hissed back.

Redfern frowned at them and they both shut up.

Animated talk broke out about Persi's revelations around the lost lady as cream of mushroom soup was served. I watched the guests, particularly the ladies said to be Flyte's mistresses.

Serafina was the most enigmatic. Why would anyone gifted with such beauty and grace sell herself to someone like Flyte? Assuming she actually did. I glanced at Felicity

Carr sitting to one side of Rupert Featherstone. She was quietly stirring her soup, her red cardigan buttoned up over the white blouse. I wondered if she regretted her confession to us. Her information could have been interpreted in different ways; I wondered what the truth had been.

According to Clarissa, Felicity was looking for a wealthy husband to avoid work she considered demeaning. Dr Frazer said they were all wealthy, but they couldn't be if Felicity had to find work.

What of the lock we'd found in Gilbert's room? It was the colour of autumn leaves. No-one here had dark red hair…unless they dyed it. How could one tell?

Freddie Doggett spent most of the time gazing in moon-struck awe across the table at Serafina. Perhaps she truly was an ice maiden, and had made the cold calculation to capture Flyte for his fortune. It would hardly help her cause if he were dead. The housekeeper had said she'd seen Flyte try to take her hand in the garden and Serafina had not allowed him to do so. That didn't chime with Felicity Carr's account. Although perhaps they had fallen out?

Annabel Cresswell sat to my right, darkly made-up eyes focused on her soup. She took no part in the lively discussion. She'd changed into a black frock though, and caught her hair in simple grips rather than the glitzy headband of yesterday. Her cupid's bow painted lips were downturned and she seemed quite tragic.

'Major Lennox.' She turned to speak quietly to me. 'I hope you discover what is behind all this because I knew both men well, and none of it makes sense.'

'I'd heard you were going to marry Bernard Wilmslow, but it didn't work out,' I said, hoping it was a suitably tactful approach.

'That is not true, we were never going to marry,' she replied.

'Really?' I broke a crusty bun into the mushroom soup.

'Bernard and I were friends,' she carried on, her voice low, talking in an undertone so as not to be overheard. 'We've known each other for years. Everyone thought we were together, but it wasn't ever anything romantic.' She let her spoon rest in the soup and gripped her hands together under the table. 'But when Charles suddenly swept me off my feet, Bernard's whole attitude changed—'

'You swine!' Barbara Boden leapt to her feet and slapped Rupert Featherstone across the face. 'Keep your damned hands to yourself,' she yelled.

'I…what? Why did you hit me?' Rupert held a hand over his cheek, aghast and trying to push his chair away from her.

'You touched my knee,' she shouted, glaring at him with dark eyes narrowed in fury.

'I did not.' He leapt to his feet and faced her. 'I would never touch a lady, not like that.'

Barbara Boden turned her gaze to George Lovell. 'George did you hear what he did?' she demanded.

'I doubt it was deliberate,' George replied. 'Featherstone doesn't have it in him.'

That simply added fuel to the fire and they began a tirade against each other. George simply carried on eating his soup.

Foggy came to sit at my feet, liquid brown eyes fixed on me, or rather my food. He'd woven through people's legs under the table to reach me.

I looked at Persi, who had guessed immediately. She took charge.

'Miss Boden, I think it was our dog. I apologise, he must have brushed against you.' She had to raise her voice to make them listen.

'What?' Barbara Boden snapped.

'I–' Persi tried again.

'A dog?' Barbara retorted, the frown deepening between her black brows.

'It was a dog?' Rupert turned toward Persi.

'He's my dog,' I said.

'I demand an apology,' Rupert postured.

'Fine.' I looked down at my dog. 'Foggy, you should apologise.'

Lady Rose burst into peals of laughter. She'd just finished her third glass of wine. I saw Clarissa cover her mouth; Lord Hector's shoulders shook, and he leaned in to Clarissa as they exchanged amused glances.

'Did you mean *I* should apologise?' Barbara directed her fury back at Rupert.

'I…no.' Rupert deflated and sank back down in his chair. 'Barbara, I have a great deal of respect for you. I'd never dream of touching you in such a dishonourable manner.'

That made a number of people stare, including me. My opinion of the chinless wonder suddenly rose a notch.

'Well said, Rupert! Spoken like a gentleman.' Freddie Doggett raised his glass to him.

There were other murmurings of approval around the table, including George Lovell.

'Well, I appreciate your consideration, Rupert,' Barbara said, and tilted her head as she regarded him. 'I think I have misjudged you. And I'm sorry I shouted, it was bad manners.'

'I'm sorry too. I've always thought you admirable, Barbara.' Rupert turned towards her, his soup going cold in front of him. 'Any woman who can make a fortune from scratch deserves acclaim.'

'I agree,' Felicity Carr suddenly spoke up. 'I wish I were so clever.'

The hard sheen in Barbara's eyes softened. 'Thank you… I'm very touched.' She suddenly smiled and even looked quite tender.

'What was that about?' I whispered to Persi. 'Boden & Locke; *Luxury you can afford*,' Persi whispered back.

'What?'

'She owns factories that make soap.' Persi finished her soup. 'It's quite renowned, haven't you seen the adverts in the papers?'

'Why would I look at adverts?'

'Heathcliff…' she warned, so I shut up and finished my soup.

CHAPTER TWELVE

The conversation resumed in a lighter mode and everyone joined in this time, including Serafina. She talked in the way a member of royalty would address a commoner – lofty but diffidently polite.

'And you consider your theory of Lady Madeleine's amour to be likely?' she asked.

'We think it quite feasible,' Florence answered.

'But,' Serafina said, then paused for a second, 'would not Pierre du Mortier be obliged to challenge Lord Bancroft to mortal combat?'

'If he were the same status, he might,' Persi replied. 'But it would be very risky for a foreigner to approach a high-ranking English noble in medieval times; the law would offer him no protection. Bancroft could kill Du Mortier out of hand.'

'Would there be no repercussions?' Serafina continued. 'Surely a nobleman's family would demand blood money?'

'They would, but I doubt the English courts would support a pursuit,' Persi replied. 'Although Du Mortier could have started a feud in France against Bancroft's wife's family, if the dispute was caused by Lady Madeleine breaking her promise to Du Mortier.'

'Which she had apparently done,' Serafina replied.

'This would hardly regain his lost bride though,' Florence said.

'Ah, then perhaps he came to England in disguise, found his lost maiden and spirited her away,' Serafina stated and then smiled as though the mystery were solved.

'You mean he kidnapped her,' Edna said.

'Possibly,' Serafina replied, unperturbed. 'Or she chose to go with him. You can't know which man her preference lay with. She may have simply been sold to the English conqueror while her own fiancé was held ransom in a dungeon.'

'I think it unlikely her preference lay with Du Mortier,' Florence rejoined. 'Her family fell into difficulty some time after the lady was said to have vanished. Her mother sent a letter asking for financial support, and Lord Bancroft gave it.'

'That's correct,' George added. 'We translated the document this morning. Lord Bancroft wouldn't have sent money to his mother-in-law if his wife had abandoned him to run away with a lover.'

'Then I was right about the kidnap,' Edna said.

'Tell them about the tapestry, Lady Persi,' Lady Rose called; she was on another glass of red. Mary was sitting next to her with glazed eyes staring straight ahead. They both seemed rather fond of a drink.

'The tapestry in the hall?' Lord Hector asked. 'It's a copy, the dyes are chemically enhanced, it cannot be medieval.'

'We are aware it's a copy,' Persi said. 'The original is in the tower. Lady Rose has agreed to let us take it down and examine it this afternoon. We will make a detailed drawing of it to help in our interpretation.'

'I could help,' Edna Kent volunteered. She'd finished her soup and then had seconds. 'I've done tons of embroidery and I'm quite a proficient artist.'

'You're more than proficient, Edna,' Freddie suddenly said, having torn his gaze from Serafina. 'I've seen the pen and ink portraits you did, they were jolly good.'

'I didn't know you did portraits, Edna,' Clarissa said. 'Whom have you drawn?'

Colour rose in Edna's cheeks. 'Well, I did one of Bernard actually, and one of Charles…it was pure chance,' she said, her eyes flitting to Swift, who had been listening in silence throughout the first course.

'Why them?' Swift asked.

'Bernard asked me,' Edna replied. 'And I couldn't resist doing Charles, he was as handsome as he was duplicitous. He pretended to be annoyed, but that was just part of the act. Everything was just a game to him.'

Annabel's eyes flew to Edna's when she said this, a sharp look on her face, which she then let drop, as though accepting the truth of Edna's words.

'Now, I hope you're all hungry,' Kibble called out as he came into the room followed by Mouse. Both were carrying laden trays of tureens and covered dishes. 'Chef's roasted lamb with a baked crust what's made of apricots, crushed nuts, an' mint an' stuff. Never smelled nothin'' as good.' He beamed and placed the tray on the long refectory table.

'Thank you, Kibb–, Kipp.' Redfern stopped topping up glasses and went over to him. 'I shall serve with the help of Mouse. You can return to the kitchens.'

'But I–' Kibble tried.

'Now, if you please,' Redfern said sharply, suddenly becoming quite forceful.

Kibble sighed loudly, causing his waistcoat buttons to strain dangerously, but he went off as told and Redfern began dishing out the delicious-smelling meal.

I glanced at Edna Kent, wanting to question her further, but she appeared to be in close conversation with Mary Lovelace, who was nodding vaguely, her eyes quite glazed. 'Persi, do you have a notebook?' I asked her.

'Yes, I've got yours,' she replied with an air of innocence.

I looked at her.

'I thought you might need it.' She slipped it out of her pocket to put in my hands, then gave me a big smile.

She had a habit of teasing, and was always at least one step ahead of me. For which I was eternally grateful.

I flicked through the pages. It was bound in blue leather; I'd used it on a previous case, so it was full of ink-spotted scrawl, lots of crossings out, various musings and lists of suspects. I found a clean page and dug about in my inside pocket until Persi passed me a fountain pen.

Redfern was serving the ladies, so I made a quick list of names to remind me of the supposed pairs.

Lady Clarissa Weston - Lord Hector Sommerton.

Barbara Boden - George Lovell
Felicity Carr - Bernard Wilmslow (dead)
Serafina Deville - Charles Flyte (also dead)
Edna Kent - Freddie Doggett
Annabel Cresswell - Rupert Featherstone

Apart from Clarissa and Hector, I hadn't seen any of these 'pairs' acting remotely romantic. And those who were matched with both victims weren't exactly in the throes of heartbreak either. Actually that wasn't correct, Annabel Cresswell did seem upset, and she and Barbara Boden were both in black today. The dresses were actually cocktail dresses, but that shouldn't be a surprise as they'd have hardly brought mourning gear to a Valentine's bash.

Annabel seemed to be at the centre of it all. She had straightened up and was eating her food rather than picking at it. Perhaps Edna's words about Charles Flyte's duplicitousness had resonated in a dose of reality.

She must have realised I was observing her, as she glanced up, her eyes shadowed by the dark makeup she wore.

I gave her a grin, she smiled back, then returned to her food, her painted lips slightly smudged, as was her eye shadow.

Why do people adopt these fashionable trends? It's hardly an expression of individuality. I'd always assumed that such a person is trying to hide themselves within a crowd of lookalikes. Was she presenting a compliant persona to the world in order to hide her true character? Or was she simply weak, and easily influenced?

'May I offer roast potatoes, sir?' Redfern broke into my musings as Mouse slid a plate piled with slices of pink lamb in front of me. The rim of the meat was encased in a thick layer of crispy glazed confection, the apricot, nuts, and mint I assumed.

'Yes, please,' I said and he added perfectly roasted potatoes, then some greens and lots of gravy. It smelled absolutely delicious.

'Redfern,' I said as I picked up my fork. 'Was there a fire lit on the watchtower last night?'

'I…um, yes, there was, sir. There were fireworks too. It is a tradition held at midnight on St Valentine's,' he admitted, then turned to serve Swift.

'He had the luck of the Irish.' Mary suddenly put down her empty glass.

'Whom do you mean, dear?' Lady Rose was cutting into a sprout.

'Oh, what's his name?' Mary was sitting upright, she hadn't seemed to notice the food on the plate in front of her.

'You mean Kipp, the new footman?' Lady Rose replied.

'No,' Mary carried on. 'The family are from Ireland. A bad business.' She turned. 'Hector, you know who I mean.' She tried to focus on him, but failed.

'I'm afraid I do not, Miss Mary,' he replied genially.

'There are many families with landholdings in Ireland. Including the Duke of Wellington,' Lady Rose assured her. 'It is perfectly acceptable. Now do eat your food, Mary, or it will become cold.'

'Charming, but hot-headed,' Mary said. 'It is a trait,' she added, then picked up her knife and fork and sawed at the lamb.

'Felicity told me you were going to join me for a walk this morning, Freddie,' Annabel addressed him.

His eyes flew open, obviously startled. 'I…well I did hope to find you, but failed, I'm afraid. Story of my life really.' He laughed nervously. 'But I'd be very happy to escort you for a ramble this afternoon, if you like.'

'Actually, I thought it would be a nice diversion to skate on the lake, the ice seems more than thick enough,' Annabel said.

'We have plenty of ice skates of all sizes,' Lady Rose called gaily. 'The water is mostly shallow and ices over quite solidly. Skating in this sunshine would be such a pleasant outing.'

'I think it's a lovely idea,' Clarissa said and turned to Hector.

He smiled, dispelling his air of austerity. 'I shall be most pleased to attend, Clarissa. I haven't skated since I was at Cambridge.'

'I'll have to change into slacks,' Edna Kent said.

'You wear slacks?' Barbara Boden sounded horrified.

'Yes, they're practical,' Edna countered. 'I love being outdoors, riding and walking. Frocks are dreadfully inconvenient. I'm forever risking my modesty in the woods.' I could hear the tease of humour in her voice; she may be plain-looking but she was fun, and engaging, and talented too by the sounds of it.

'What are you doing in the woods to risk your modesty?' George asked with a gleam of devilment in his eye.

She laughed. 'Just climbing over fallen trees. I love hiking and the routes can be pretty rugged.'

'That shows spirit,' George said. He'd finished his meal and leaned in her direction. 'Perhaps you'd like to go for a trek with me sometime?'

Her cheeks showed a touch of pink, she seemed almost shy. 'Yes, I think I'd like that.'

Eyes darted back and forth for an instant, the air catching a frisson of tension.

'I walk around my estate a lot,' Rupert broke in. 'I was thinking of buying an Alvis, they're said to be robust enough to drive on cart tracks. I've got ten thousand acres and it's far too big to ride a horse around. I never get to half of my outlying villages.'

'You have ten thousand acres of land?' Felicity asked in awestruck tone.

'Yes, it's been in the family for generations,' Rupert replied. 'I've had to oversee it all myself since Mummy died last year, and it's a dashed responsibility. Mummy did it all before…' He trailed off.

Barbara Boden feigned sympathy. 'I totally understand. I own three factories and have hundreds of employees. There's no end to the problems.'

'What an appalling weight of responsibility,' Serafina uttered as she put her knife and fork neatly on her plate, having eaten very little food.

'You may put all your worries behind and enjoy your

skating this afternoon,' Lady Rose said merrily. 'Redfern will show you where the skates are kept after lunch! Annabel, how clever of you to suggest it.'

The chatter slowly rose again. I realised there was a degree of jousting going on, each of them showing whatever they thought were their best attributes, be it wealth, sense of humour, charm, or sophistication. It was nothing new, most dinner parties were the same, but there was an underlying element of competitiveness here. Potential partnerships forming, or falling away as rivals interjected politely polished barbs. All part of the mating dance I suppose; then I took my dear wife's hand and squeezed it, silently thanking the man upstairs that my solitary life had ended.

'Flaming tart for pudding!' Kibble came in, red-cheeked and beaming. He held a silver tray at arm's length; it bore a large roundel of apple tart that was burning with a blue flame.

'It is tarte flambé,' Redfern corrected him. 'And a particular favourite of her Ladyship.'

'With brandy and cream,' Lady Rose said gaily, obviously thoroughly enjoying herself.

'Put it on the refectory table, Kipp,' Redfern told him.

'Righty-o,' Kibble called out. 'I've had a taste of the one Chef made for the kitchen staff, and it's better than anything my mam's ever done.'

'Yes, thank you–' Redfern tried to quell his enthusiasm.

'Just a mo, sir, I've been given a message,' Kibble cut in. 'Constable Fossett said he'd like to talk to Inspector Swift and Major Lennox.'

Swift was instantly on his feet. 'Where?'

'In the incident room, sir,' Kibble said. 'The tower,' he added in reminder.

'I know where it is.' Swift was already shoving his chair back.

'Swift, can we finish pudding first–' I objected.

'Come on, Lennox.' He was marching towards the door.

'Damn it,' I cursed under my breath. 'Kibble, bring some of the tart upstairs with tea,' I ordered.

'It's Kipp, sir,' he hissed.

'What?'

'It's K–'

'Right, yes. Just do it, man,' I told him and followed Swift out.

CHAPTER THIRTEEN

'I went down to the kitchen for lunch and the housekeeper said Mr Flyte's clothes were still in the cellar, sir, waiting to be burned.' Fossett was in the incident room leaning over the table, his helmet at his elbow, the fire blazing behind him. 'There was only his jacket there, next to the boiler. It was all cut up and covered in blood. There was a piece of paper in the pocket. It's got blood on it, too, and the writing's almost disappeared.' Fossett was trying to unravel a tightly balled paper, crumpled and red-stained.

'Why didn't any of the Stratford policemen find it yesterday morning?' Swift went straight to join him.

'Dunno, sir, but they should have done. It was just shoved in the pocket.' He tried prising the ball apart without much success.

'Someone must have put it there after his clothes were taken to be burned,' I guessed.

'I agree,' Swift said. 'The police wouldn't have missed this, neither would anyone else. Where is the jacket now, Fossett?'

'I've put it in a sack and tossed it into Major Lennox's car,' he replied.

'What!' I exclaimed.

'To take back to the station, sir,' he replied as if that were some sort of excuse. 'Oh drat it!' he swore as he tried to pull the page flat, which caused it to start tearing along the middle.

'Let me, Constable,' Swift said.

'You're welcome to it, sir.' Fossett stepped smartly aside.

Swift picked up a sheet of thick blotting paper and placed it over the still crumpled page and smoothed it down.

'I reckon,' Fossett said, 'that whoever stuffed it in the pocket did it 'cos the boiler was blazing and they couldn't open the door because the handle was too hot.'

'They could have used the jacket to protect their hand,' I said, having prised open a burning aeroplane cockpit once in the same manner.

'Maybe they didn't think of it,' Fossett replied, then added, 'or they didn't want to get blood on their hands.'

Swift flipped the blotting paper over. The crumpled page was stuck to it. 'I can just make out the writing…' He peered at the paper, the ink was almost washed away. 'Fossett, write this down. *A simple note, a heartfelt line—will you be my Valentine? No promises grand, but hopes to share, a little love with an Irish flair.*' His dry tone rather ruined the rhythm of the rhyme.

Fossett gazed at him for a full second, then pulled out his notebook and pencil, licked the tip and wrote the doggrel down. 'That's really rubbish, that is.'

'I've heard worse,' I said, thinking of the card I'd bought for Persi yesterday. I'd told her to stay in bed, then given the card to Fogg to carry to her. He'd refused, of course, so I put a bit of bacon inside it and he'd promptly chewed it to pieces. I had to tie a red ribbon round our fat little cat's neck instead and offer him as a token of my affections. She'd laughed and cuddled Mr Tubbs, then Foggy, then me.

Valentine's day wasn't all just murder and mayhem.

I picked up the magnifying glass lying on the table and aimed it at the stained page. 'Look, on the top right corner.'

'What?' Swift and Fossett said, leaning either side of me.

'Could be initials…shine a torch on it, Fossett,' I told him.

He did so. 'It says C.F.'

'Charles Flyte,' Swift said. 'It looks like it was pencilled in.'

'Considering what we've learned of the man,' I said, 'This doesn't sound like him.'

'No, someone else wrote this,' Swift said. 'Fossett where are the statements you took yesterday?'

'I tidied them away sir.' Fossett went to the drawer of the low bookcase and brought the sheets to Swift.

'We can compare the handwriting.' He shuffled through them.

'It's Miss Mary Lovelace's!' Fossett exclaimed.

Swift nodded. 'That's interesting.'

'And there's an Irish reference,' I said. 'She was talking about–'

A knock at the door interrupted us.

'Brought some tea an' flamin' tart.' Kibble entered with a tray; Foggy trotted in at his heels. 'Gentry have all gone out to skate on the ice,' he said as he put the tray on a corner of the table. 'I'd have been up sooner, but Mr Redfern said there was coal needed shovelling and could I do it. So I said I would. It's a proper big furnace and ever so warm. I had to be careful not to get coal dust on my uniform, but I'll tell ye somethin' strange.' He rattled the cups and saucers as he laid them out, then picked up the tea pot. 'Your Mr Fogg came along with me, right as rain he was, but then when we got down to the bottom step, he turned about and ran back up with his tail between his legs. It was like he was really scared or summat. I reckon they got ghosts down there.' Kibble put the pot down. 'Now you help yerselfs—'

'Damn it.' I leapt up.

'What?' Kibble's brows shot up.

'Fogg hates anything dead,' I told him.

'It might just have been the smell of blood from Flyte's clothes,' Swift said.

'No,' I replied. 'He might not have liked it, but he wouldn't run off like that. Come on.'

We all strode towards the door, leaving Kibble with his mouth hanging open.

'Where's the cellar, Fossett?' Swift already had his torch at the ready.

'Below the minstrel gallery.' He was slightly out of breath. He'd grabbed his helmet for some reason and was pulling on the strap under his chin.

We entered the great hall and he led the way through an arch under the minstrel gallery that I recalled seeing the housekeeper emerging from. It led to an unadorned area, grey and cold. I could hear the sound of rattling crockery and voices in the distance.

'Here we are,' Fossett said and pulled open a plain wooden door set in the roughly plastered wall. A set of worn stone steps took us down about twenty feet under the house, and arrived at a tunnel-like corridor. An arched ceiling rose above us, built of old brick which had been whitewashed long ago. A string of bare light bulbs hung along the centre; another passageway ran off it.

'I reckon this was the dungeons once,' Fossett said as we walked quickly along the echoing passage to another short set of steps going down.

The smell of smoke and coal dust filled the large vaulted room. This seemed older than anywhere else I'd been in the house. I wondered if Persi had seen it.

'His jacket was there, left bundled up by the furnace.' Fossett went over to the huge cast iron boiler, which gave off a glorious blast of heat. The door, however, was only a spade's width, and might explain why Flyte's jacket had been left unburned. It would have been difficult to shove in, especially given the heat.

'It must run the radiators upstairs.' Swift stated the obvious.

'There will be a coal chute somewhere,' I said.

The place was dimly lit by the glass door in the furnace and a single overhead bulb, but Swift shone his torch over the huge piles of coal going right back under the vaulted ceilings to the furthest wall. 'Look, a hatch to the outside,' Swift said, using his torch beam to point up to it.

'You realise we're under the tower,' I said.

'Sir!' Fossett shouted. 'Just there, look, there's something at the top.'

Swift lowered the beam. Fossett was right, something vaguely pale, barely visible on top of the most distant mound. We'd have never seen it if we hadn't been searching for it.

'I'll go outside and open the hatch,' I decided.

'Right,' Swift said and turned to Fossett. 'You'll have to climb over there.'

'What? But sir, my uniform will be ruined.' He was horrified.

'Take it off then.' Swift wasn't sympathetic. 'You can clean up afterwards.'

'But, sir…'

I left them to it and raced back up the steps, through the great hall and onwards to the base of the tower. I wrenched open the door and headed out towards where the hatch might be. It didn't take long; it was at the rear of the tower, almost butting up against the wall and flush with the surrounding ground. North facing, the area lay in shade and covered by heavy frost. There were signs of recent activity, broken blades of grass and stiff shards of black soil lying on the green painted hatch. I reached down to tug at the handle. It came up quite easily to fold back on iron hinges.

I looked down. Gilbert stared up, eyes wide and unseeing, his mouth gaping like a silent scream. It seemed he hadn't gone very far after all.

CHAPTER FOURTEEN

Fossett had scrambled up the pile dressed in white vest and undershorts, now smeared with black coal dust. As were his face, hands, and legs. He'd kept his socks and boots on.

'Sir.' He had reached the body, and stopped to look up at me through the hatch. 'Are you coming down?'

'No.'

He couldn't stand on the coals, which were already shifting under his weight. He knelt as best he could on the hard lumps, a lighted torch in one hand. 'He's dead.'

'What?' Swift was still by the furnace and shouted over.

'Dead,' Fossett turned to call back. 'Major Lennox is up top.'

'Tell him I'll join him,' Swift ordered.

'I can hear you,' I called down.

'The Inspector's left, sir,' Fossett said. He shone the torch into Gilbert's lifeless eyes. 'I reckon he was dead before he was chucked down here. He's stiff as a board and all purple on the back of his head, and probably everywhere else on his back. Lividity, it's called. I read about it.'

'Pooling blood,' I said. I'd learned this from Swift, and

Persi, who took a keen interest in all things expired. 'Any sign of cause of death?' I asked him. He was only about eight feet below me.

'Not that I can see…' He felt along the man's arms, then chest, and shone the torch along his trousers. 'Nothing obvious.' He aimed the beam back at the man's gaping mouth, then leaned in closer, disturbing more lumps of coal to clatter off down the pile. 'I think there's something…' He bent this way and that with the torch. 'Yeah… more bruising on the back of his head, and there's something funny with his neck…'

'Lennox.' Swift came up behind me, making me jump. 'Damn it, Swift. I almost fell in.'

He grinned, there was nothing like murder to cheer up a detective. 'I found a rope.' He held up a coil of thick hemp line. 'There's a set of steps leading from the cellar into the back garden.' He knelt next to me and leaned over the edge. 'Fossett, are you ready?'

'Just trying to see if there's anything in his back, like a knife or summat.' He was barely audible. I watched him struggling with the corpse. 'He's so stiff, I can't turn him.'

'You said there was something with his neck,' I reminded him.

'Aye, but perhaps he was hit over the head, then stabbed.' Fossett managed to lever up the dead man. He let him fall again. 'Nope, he wasn't.'

It wasn't terribly dignified.

'Tie the rope under his arms,' Swift ordered and tossed the end down to him.

'Right-o, sir.' Fossett, his face and hands now black as a chimney sweep, grabbed it. 'It's cold down here without me togs on.' He quickly attached and tightened the rope. I suspected he'd tied up plenty of livestock at the family farm in the past. 'Ready. You can haul him up now.'

'Right, Lennox?' Swift moved into full pedantic mode. 'When I say heave—'

'Swift just get on with it,' I cut in, then pulled at the rope.

It took a few minutes, the man was heavier than his thin body suggested, and his stiff arms and legs were awkward to manoeuvre through the hatch. I finally managed to grab hold of the back of his jacket and pull him through the frame. Swift twisted him round so he lay on the grass face up.

'I'll come and join you now, shall I, sir?' Fossett called.

'Yes,' Swift replied. 'Go down that other passage, there's a small rear door leading to steps, they'll bring you out into the rear kitchen garden. Hurry up.'

I heard the lad muttering to himself as he clambered down the coals.

'He's wearing the same clothes as yesterday,' I said, gazing at Gilbert.

Swift was already examining his eyes and mouth. 'The state of the body suggests he's been dead for at least twelve hours, probably more. There's damage to the back of the head…and the neck's broken.'

'Fossett said the same.' I looked up at the blank wall of the tower, then strode a few yards to the corner to gaze at the side overlooking the duelling grounds. 'He could have been pushed out of the window then carried or dragged to the hatch and dropped down it,' I said as I walked back to join him.

'It would explain the broken neck.' Swift was rummaging through Gilbert's pockets. 'Nothing there…' He stood up. 'Help me turn him, would you, Lennox?'

We manoeuvred him, the angles of his extended stiff arms and legs making hard work of it. Black dust coated the back of his clothes and hair. Swift knelt next to him. 'No sign of blood anywhere…' He was almost talking to himself. He examined Gilbert's skull under the thin grey hair. 'Only the bruising, and increased lividity…'

I stood back with hands in pockets as he seemed to be doing pretty well without my help.

'You could take notes, Lennox.'

'I could,' I agreed without moving.

He harrumphed then grabbed a fistful of frozen grass to wipe his hands clean. 'Why don't you stay here while I go and call the doctor, and an ambulance.'

'Fine,' I said, ignoring the heavy sarcasm in his voice.

'Right.' He tramped off towards the tower door as I turned toward the pleasant vista surrounding the fine old house. I knew the lake wasn't far off as we'd seen it from the top of the tower. I could hear delighted shouts and laughter coming from that direction. I had half a mind to wander over, but thought I should keep some sort of vigil over the body.

I turned back to Gilbert's mortal remains. We'd left him lying face down, arms outstretched, head unnaturally bent.

He seemed shrunken somehow, his hands thin and claw-like. He'd been a London detective, as Swift had once been.

I sighed, and said a silent prayer, hoping the man upstairs had a place for his soul – assuming he'd earned his place, that is.

A crow wheeled a circle around the top of the tower, a black silhouette against the bright blue sky. Another one came to join it, their heads angled for a better view of the body. Winged shadows of death, they haunted the battle-fields and trenches, ever on the lookout for a fresh corpse.

I suddenly wished Greggs were here. He'd always been a steady presence, comforting and stalwart during the dark days of the war, despite the bombs, mire, and misery. Admittedly he was overfond of Jamesons and tipsy quite a lot of the time, but he'd always be ready with tea and whatever rations he'd been able to garner.

'Rather grubby-looking scarecrow you have there,' a merry voice called out behind me. I spun round: it was Freddie Doggett. He was swinging a pair of wood and steel ice skates by their leather straps. 'Snapped a buckle, I'm just going to find another pair.'

'Right-o,' I said and shuffled in front of Gilbert, not wanting a fuss raised yet.

'Jolly good fun. Old Hector's a bit of a whizz,' he laughed. 'But poor Barbara Boden has spent half the time on her derriere. Rupert's been the gallant though and lent her his arm.' He glanced again at the coal-smeared corpse. 'Broken, is he? Are you going to toss him down the coal hole?'

'What?'

'The scarecrow.'

'Something like that,' I replied.

A frown creased between his sandy-coloured brows. 'Well, cheerio then.'

'Yes,' I replied and he went off, looking briefly back over his shoulder before heading for the front of the house.

A robin sang from a distant tree; the two crows were joined by another. I listened to the sounds of the quiet country day. Birdsong, the harsh cawing of crows, shouts and laughter of the skaters on the ice.

'Where's Fossett?' Swift came round the tower.

'No idea.'

'Hm. Dr Frazer is on his way, and an ambulance…I called Billings, too.'

'Doubt he was happy.'

Swift gave me a wry look. 'He's never happy,' he said dryly, then sighed. 'But he was shaken by the news of Gilbert's death. The man was dying. A brain tumour.'

'He'd lost weight,' I said.

'Yes, I'd thought the same.' Swift had gone to the body to gaze down at it. 'He'd retired to Ireland, his wife is still there. Flyte had employed him recently to act as a bodyguard or investigator or something. Billings didn't know why. He hadn't ever worked with him, Gilbert was much older.' He glanced over at me. 'He thought he may have been short of money.'

I nodded in sympathy. 'Did they have the lab results from the bottle?'

'Yes.' His voice lowered. 'Whisky and traces of phenobarbital. It had been prescribed to Gilbert for epilepsy. The tumour was causing fits.'

'Really?' That raised my brows. 'Phenobarbital was used in the war as a sedative.'

'It can control seizures, too,' Swift said.

'Would he have taken the phenobarbital with whisky?'

'A tot perhaps, but not the whole bottle,' Swift said, his eyes downcast. 'Billings is trying to contact his wife. He said Gilbert was diligent and honest. I can't think how he'd have allowed Flyte to enter into a duel if he was protecting him.'

'And his belongings are missing,' I reminded him. 'Those might have shed some light on it.'

'If it hadn't been assumed he was drunk, he might not be dead now.'

'I know.' I spoke heavily. That was going to haunt me. The fact Gilbert was dying didn't make it easier. Why the hell didn't it occur to me that the man could have been drugged?

'It's obviously someone in the house and Billings is on the warpath. He gave me a hell of a dressing down.'

I bit back a sigh. 'Did he say anything about the chief constable?'

'Patterson? Yes, he's spoken to Billings. Lord Hector really is an acquaintance of his. It's put us under the spotlight.' He shoved his hands in his pockets and looked at me, his face sharpened by the cold air, his shoulders slumped. 'Gilbert died because of our lack of diligence. We can't make another wrong step, Lennox, or we'll be out.'

I was surprised they hadn't given us our marching orders already, though I didn't say so.

Fossett approached, grievance written on his long face. 'Well, that's the most embarrassin' thing that's ever happened.' He sounded distinctly upset.

We both eyed him.

'I couldn't put me uniform back on over my undies, cos they were thick with dust. So I thought I'd leave them off, get dressed then go an' find a bathroom to have a wash. So just as I was taking off me undercrackers, Mouse came into the cellar with a coal bucket.' His cheeks were bright red beneath his helmet. 'An' I fell over, 'cos I was standing on one leg. An' then–' He stopped because we both started laughing. 'It's not funny! Once she got over the fright, and stopped gigglin', she went an' ran me a bath, but I haven't stopped feelin' like an idiot since. I can hardly look her in the face, and Kibble didn't help, he called me Moonbeam.'

'Why?' I asked.

'Because my bum was all white an' the rest was all black.' Fossett frowned in irritation while we laughed even more. We needed that moment of levity to lighten the gloom. 'I'll never be able to ask her to walk out now,' he said through gritted teeth.

'Hello?' a voice called out.

We all instantly shut up.

'Inspector Swift? Major Lennox?' the voice called again, its tone held a distinctive Scottish brogue.

'Doctor Frazer,' I called back. 'We're at the rear of the tower.'

He was dressed as yesterday in the same black scarf and grey wool coat, with his leather case firmly gripped in hand. He gave a grim smile as he approached. 'Another death, I presume?'

'We've found Gilbert, we'd like you to examine his body.' Swift didn't waste time on the niceties.

Frazer spotted the corpse, his pleasant face suddenly wary. 'He's dead?'

'Yes, murdered, and pushed down the coal chute,' I said.

'Right.' Shock tightened Frazer's jaw. He strode quickly to where Gilbert lay. We stepped back as he knelt down. He was quick and deft; he removed his leather gloves and ran hands up and down the limbs. 'Contusions consistent with blunt force trauma, likely sustained in a fall. Cervical vertebrae fractures indicate a broken neck. There is pronounced rigor mortis, with lividity fixed to the dorsal surfaces, suggesting the body remained supine post-mortem. Let's turn him,' he said. 'Constable?' he called Fossett.

'Sir.' Fossett went to help him; they manoeuvred Gilbert over onto his back.

'Was he drugged?' Dr Frazer said as he shone a bright beam of light into Gilbert's clouded eyes.

'The whisky bottle held traces of phenobarbital,' Swift replied.

'Looking back, it seemed strange he didn't stir when I saw him last, but it just didn't occur to me then that he might have been drugged. I was thinking about it again this morning and almost rang you to ask about him.' He shook his head. 'If it hadn't been for the shock of Flyte's murder, I might have given it more consideration at the time. Where did the phenobarbital come from? It's hardly a common drug.'

'He was taking it to control epilepsy caused by a brain tumour,' I explained.

'Ach, that's a crying shame.' Frazer put a thumb on Gilbert's chin to tip the head a little. It wouldn't move so he leaned over the body to stare into the mouth. 'Particles of …feathers, by the looks of it.' He leaned even closer, then pulled out a magnifying glass from his coat pocket. 'He'd have breathed the particles in while he was lying on the floor of Flyte's room – it should have triggered a reflex action, but it doesn't appear that it has. Poor fellow, he must have been already near death.' He turned his gaze to us. 'But his neck's broken, was he pushed out of the window?'

'We think so, sir,' Fossett replied. He'd been standing aside but had moved to watch the doctor's examination.

'Your killer should have been more patient, I reckon he would have died of the overdose soon enough, anyway.'

That didn't make me feel any less guilty.

Swift let out a sigh. 'Did you attend Wilmslow and Flyte's post mortems?'

'Aye, this morning,' Frazer said.

'What did you find?' Swift asked.

'They've sent samples for testing, so there's no blood results yet,' Frazer replied. 'Both men were fit and well before they were shot. Neither had eaten breakfast. Wilmslow was killed by the pistol ball shattering his skull.'

'And Flyte?' Swift asked.

'The bullet through his heart was a .442 Webley,' Frazer replied gravely. 'We found it lodged in his spine.'

'Common enough,' I said. Actually, the country was awash with guns since the war, most of the survivors had brought souvenirs home.

'Was there any gunpowder residue on Wilmslow's hands?' Swift asked.

'There was not,' Frazer replied. 'There were traces on Flyte's though.'

We nodded. We'd already found powder on Flyte's palm.

'Where are you from in Scotland?' Swift shifted the conversation. Probably because he didn't want to discuss the implications surrounding the lack of gunpowder on Wilmslow.

'Invergordon,' Frazer replied.

'East coast.'

Frazer nodded.

'Swift's Braeburn malt,' I said.

Frazer's brows rose and his manner instantly warmed. 'Well, well. My favourite whisky. How the devil did a Sassenach get into Braeburn malt?' He grinned.

'I married the laird's daughter,' Swift admitted, a smile lifting his sharp features.

'Now there's a brave man,' Frazer replied. 'The highlanders are cleaved close, I doubt they'd have thrown the welcome mat down for you.'

'True,' Swift admitted.

Frazer let out a breath, his smile fading. He indicated Gilbert. 'I'm sorry for his death. I should have thought more on it.'

'We thought he was drunk too, sir,' Fossett said. 'It's a bit upsettin' really. Poor man.'

Swift turned to Fossett. 'Constable, stay here and liaise with the ambulance men.'

'I'll stay too,' Frazer said.

'Fine,' Swift replied. 'Come on, Lennox. We have work to do.'

CHAPTER FIFTEEN

Swift and I stopped to examine the window in the chamber where Flyte had been shot, and poor Gilbert pushed to his death. There was nothing to see, not even a scrap of fabric caught on the stone embrasure, or metal-framed window.

'Fingerprints?' I asked Swift.

'It's wiped clean,' he replied and pointed to the thin layer of moisture forming on the cold handle. 'The condensation would show anything up.'

We had another scout round, checking the now cold hearth – which had been cleaned out. I noticed the embroidery had gone. We paused at the window again, imagining someone opening the window and bundling Gilbert out of it.

'Could a woman have done it?' I asked Swift.

'He would have been unconscious, and easy to manoeuvre.' He considered it. 'Yes, a fit young woman could have moved him.'

We gave up and carried on up the next flight of steps to the incident room. Foggy was there, as was Kibble. The dog came cavorting around our feet in greeting before returning to the warmth of the blazing fire. Kibble carried on cleaning a blackboard leaning on an easel against the back wall.

'Ello, sirs.' Kibble grinned. 'I was going to get one of these from the village school, but then I found out they had an old nursery. I said to Mouse, 'I'll bet there's one in there'. We went to have a look and there it was. So we brought it up!'

That cheered Swift's day and he cracked a smile. 'Good work, Constable.'

Kibble saluted in amateur fashion. 'And I got the drawings that the lady did of both the dead blokes. She'd given them to Mr Redfern, and he gave 'em me.' He reached into his trouser pocket and withdrew a folded wad of paper. 'Here you are, sir.'

He held them out; I took them.

'Edna Kent drew them,' I recalled as I unfolded them and scanned the skilful execution. 'They're good.'

Edna had talent, the black pen and ink drawing had caught Flyte's likeness. His eyes held a mix of calculation and amusement. A man full of confidence and vigour, a full face, eminently masculine with a hint of the predator about him. Little of that had been obvious from his corpse, apart from the fact he was marginally overweight, but the portrait gave another aspect to the man altogether.

'Here's a peg, sir.' Kibble held it out. 'Mouse said you'd need 'um.'

I took it and clipped the drawing to the top left of the blackboard.

Swift had discovered a box of chalk left on the easel rim

and was prising it open but stopped to focus on the image. 'That's interesting.'

'Aye, and it looks just like Mr Flyte,' Kibble said. 'He wasn't making much sense when I got here. I'd cycled straight over from the village. I could see he were in a lot of pain. Mr Redfern was with him, trying to stop the bleeding with a towel. Mr Gilbert came in a moment later. He wasn't drunk nor nothing then.'

'What was Gilbert like?' I asked.

'Seemed alright,' he replied. 'Shocked more an' anything. The doctor came then, and so did the police from Stratford. I followed them round. They thought it were stupid, two toffs shootin' each other. Then they went to look outside and I came back into the tower. The doctor had finished diggin' the ball out of Mr Flyte, and Mr Gilbert said he would stop with him. He didn't want any lunch, but I did so I went home. It was stew and dumplings.'

'What time was that?' Swift asked.

'Just after twelve, and after lunch I had to go and help my dad take our old pony to the blacksmith, so I didn't come back cos it took ages.'

I pegged the drawing of Wilmslow next to that of Flyte, then we all stood back to study it.

'Did you get a look at Wilmslow, Kibble?'

'I did, sir, and he looks better in that picture than he did when he were dead,' he said. 'Like that Rudy Valentine,' Kibble considered, his hand on his chin. 'The movie star. My mam's mad keen on him. No wonder he had the ladies runnin' after him.'

'It's Rudolph Valentino,' Swift corrected.

'Aye, maybe it was,' Kibble agreed.

'Kibble,' I said.

'Yes, sir?'

'Pour the tea would you? It'll be stone cold at this rate.'

He sighed and went to the table to rattle cups about.

'I think there was a real rivalry between them,' I said. 'Annabel Cresswell said Flyte swept her off her feet, Felicity Carr said much the same. They were both involved with Wilmslow at the time.' We'd already discussed this, and events seemed to be supporting the theory.

'Hum,' Swift muttered as he proceeded to chalk their names under their pictures, more interested in the blackboard. 'This is excellent,' he continued. 'We can add Gilbert's name as a victim.' He wrote Gilbert's name next to Wilmslow, then yesterday's date, February the fourteenth, underneath.

'Wilmslow shot by Flyte, Flyte shot twice by persons unknown, Gilbert drugged and killed, also by persons unknown,' I remarked.

'Do ye think Mr Wilmslow was drugged as well, makin' him easier to shoot?' Kibble said from the table. He was arranging slices of the flambéed tart onto plates. The tart had gone cold.

'Unlikely, as there was nothing in the stomach,' Swift replied.

I went to sit down and picked up my cup of tea. Foggy came to sit next to my feet, having smelled the tart, not that I'd be giving him any, cake is not proper food for a small spaniel.

'Did the killer come prepared for murder?' I mused between sips of lukewarm tea.

Swift thought about it. 'Gilbert had been prescribed phenobarbital and would have brought it with him…'

'The bullet used to shoot Flyte was a .442,' I said. 'So the killer was armed…although they couldn't possibly have known the duel would take place.'

'The Metropolitan used the Webley .380.' Swift was thinking about it. 'But they were automatic and tended to jam. Most of the officers carried the British Bulldog pocket pistol, which was .442.'

'You think it was Gilbert's gun?' I said.

'Gilbert had the phenobarbital, and he could have been carrying a .442,' Swift stated. 'It's a more likely scenario that it's an opportunist murder rather than planned. Particularly given the duel.'

'In that case, it's a crime of passion,' I said, having learnt the phrase from previous investigations.

'Elementary, Lennox,' Swift replied wryly.

I took my notebook out and leafed through to the page where I'd written the list of names. 'Annabel Cresswell had been close to Wilmslow for some time, but according to Felicity Carr, they'd stopped seeing each other. Flyte had seduced Annabel. I wonder if it was at the same time as Felicity?'

'You mean, he 'ad more than one lady friend?' Kibble was shocked.

'Kibble, go and find Miss Cresswell and ask her to come here,' Swift ordered.

'But she's gone out ice skating, sir. They all have,' he objected.

'Then go and search her room,' Swift continued.

'What? Search a lady's room without the lady bein' there, sir?'

'Kibble.' I raised my voice. 'You're supposed to be spying. Go and spy!'

His plump cheeks turned pink. 'I…oh, alright then, sir,' he huffed, then trudged off.

I reached for a slice of flambéed tart and bit into it. The filling was lemon, lime, and cognac, and despite it being cold, it was utterly delicious. I wrote Annabel's name in the middle of a fresh page, drew a circle around it, then put Wilmslow's initials above and Flyte's below. Then I finished my tart.

'Felicity said Serafina was also involved with Flyte,' Swift said.

'Assuming we can believe her.' I put a dash on each side of Flyte's initials with SD and FC respectively. Then I drew a picture at the bottom of the page with two stick men holding guns facing each other. Wilmslow to the left and Flyte to the right. Then I added another stick figure further back with a question mark over its head, to represent the secret watcher. 'Flyte murdered Wilmslow,' I said, and turned to a fresh page to write that down. 'Flyte had gunpowder on his hand, but Wilmslow didn't. And we know Flyte was closer to Wilmslow than he should have been when he shot him,' I said and wrote this down in proper notes. 'The watcher must have shot

Flyte…He was lying 34 paces from Wilmslow. I think the watcher ran to Wilmslow, realised he was dead, then picked up the pistol from Wilmslow's hand and confronted Flyte.'

'Flyte's pistol would now be useless, having fired the single shot,' Swift added. 'And so he backed off.'

'But the watcher shot him anyway. Then put the pistols into each of their hands,' I finished.

'Which was a mistake,' Swift said. 'Because they'd have dropped them when they fell. So it was staged.'

'Why did Flyte employ Gilbert as a bodyguard…the man was dying…but then Flyte may not have known that.'

'Gilbert was a detective, and was probably there to investigate something,' Swift reminded me.

'Yes, the threatening letters.' I wrote and underlined.

Swift was grinning.

'What?'

'No, no, don't let me interrupt you.' He came to sit down. 'Nice to see you're applying some method.'

I had no idea why he should find it amusing. 'Wilmslow and Flyte had girlfriends in common and a rivalry had built up between them.'

'How would Flyte know about the modifications to the duelling pistols?' Swift stuck a fork into his slice of tart.

I thought about that. 'Someone told him…or he'd found out on a previous visit.'

'Same thing,' Swift said between mouthfuls.

'Yes. Lady Clarissa Weston is Lady Rose's goddaughter and knows the place well. It's possible she could have told him…he must have known about it or he couldn't have hit Wilmslow… Was it a lucky shot?' I mused.

'Possibly, but he must have been close to him. The shot would have hit him somewhere and the size of the ball would almost certainly kill him at close range if it hit somewhere vital.'

'It didn't kill Flyte when he was shot,' I said.

'Proving he was probably further away,' Swift said.

'Yes…' I agreed. 'I think Lady Clarissa is more involved than she's letting on.

'She may even be the heir to Bancroft Hall,' Swift put in, which hadn't occurred to me.

'So you think it's about money rather than rivalry?'

'No, I'm simply throwing in ideas,' he said. 'Just as you're always doing.'

I frowned at that. 'There's no indication Clarissa was involved with any of the murder victims.'

'Felicity Carr said Flyte had been running after Clarissa at the Valentine get-together last year,' he reminded me.

'Ah yes…not that it seems relevant,' I said, but wrote it down anyway. 'But it confirms they have been here before. Clarissa and Hector Sommerton now seem set to get together, and he's probably the pick of the bunch.'

'Rupert Featherstone has ten thousand acres.'

'He's not titled though,' I said.

'You are, and look where it's got you.'

'That's not the point, Swift. Featherstone is an idiot. Anyway, why would Lady Clarissa want to murder Flyte and Gilbert?'

'Exactly, Lennox. This is why procedure is so important. Means, motive, opportunity. I've told you this umpteen times. Find the answers to the right questions,' he proceeded with another lecture. 'Where were all the suspects when the duel took place? What time was Flyte murdered in the tower? When was Gilbert pushed from the window? Where have the means of murder come from? Who knows about the modified pistols? Who knows where the coal hatch is?' he lectured. 'Focus on the facts.'

He was back in full pedantic police mode.

'Swift,' I said.

'What?'

'You write the questions, and then we'll find the answers.'

He opened his mouth to object, then closed it again and picked up his pen.

'Edna Kent doesn't appear to be close to either victim,' I spoke as I wrote. He didn't reply so I carried on. 'We don't know anything about Barbara Boden, and none of the men have any reason to be involved. Which brings us back to Annabel, Serafina, and Felicity.'

'Why did someone put the Valentine letter in Flyte's discarded jacket?' Swift mused. I don't think he'd been listening to me at all.

My reply was lost to Foggy barking at a knock on the door, which was quickly followed by Fossett.

'Ambulance are carrying the body out now, sirs.' He stopped to stare at the blackboard. 'Ooooh, that's good. That's what it says to do in the detecting manual.'

'Did anyone see them?' Swift didn't look up from his writing.

'Don't think so sir. Staff are indoors and the guests are still skating. Doctor Frazer made them go round the outside with the stretcher. He says he's going to go with Gilbert's body to Stratford and attend the post mortem. He's studying to be a pathologist. Can I have a bit of tart now, sir?'

'Yes,' I agreed.

'Gilbert's suitcase…' Swift was still deep in thought. 'He was struggling for money, he probably had a cheap cardboard suitcase. They can't have buried it,' Swift said. 'The ground's frozen.'

'So's the lake, it'll not be thrown in there,' Fossett said between mouthfuls of tart.

I glanced at him. 'Someone must have burnt it, along with his clothes. The furnace door is too small to fit a suitcase in,' I said. 'They lit a fire on the top of the tower last night, that might be worth searching.'

'Good thought, Lennox.' Swift turned to look at Fossett.

The lad scooped up the last of his tart. 'I s'pose you want me to go up and root around in all that dirty ash an' stuff.' He didn't sound thrilled.

'Take a bucket, it'll be easier,' Swift advised. 'There's one next to the fireplace.'

Fossett pushed his plate aside then stood to fix the strap of his helmet under his chin. He grumbled under his breath as he picked up the coal bucket, added the brass shovel to it, and tramped off.

'What do you make of it, Swift?' I asked him.

He moved his pen to the top of his long list of questions. 'What time was Flyte shot in the tower?'

169

'I found him at twenty to three, and I'd say he'd been dead an hour at the most. So, between one forty and two forty.'

'What time did Dr Frazer leave Bancroft yesterday morning?' He was firing the questions.

'He operated on Flyte, then had lunch here, but had left before I arrived around two.'

He wrote it down. 'Did anyone see Flyte alive after he was operated on?'

'Yes: Kibble, Gilbert, and the killer. Kibble left just after midday.'

'You say Gilbert was already comatose when you found Flyte dead at twenty to three... So someone went into Flyte's room, gave Gilbert a drink of whisky laced with phenobarbital, waited for it to take effect, then shot Flyte between one forty and two forty.' He reached for the statements still stacked on the table and put them in front of him to read. It didn't take long; he scanned each in turn. 'They state they were all shocked about the duel, discussed it over breakfast. Gathered for coffee around eleven, talked about it some more, went to their rooms. They read books, drew, wrote, or walked, then had lunch where they were all together,' he summarised. 'After that they did much the same. None of them had alibis for the entire period in question.'

'Some presumably had partial alibis?'

'Yes, either they saw each other in corridors, or spoke briefly together.' He put his pen down. 'We're going to be systematic, Lennox. Interview each of them again–'

'Ello!' Kibble said as he put his head around the door. 'Mr Redfern said the ambulance has just gone and the doctor with it. Anyway, we thought you might still be in 'ere.' He grinned, then shuffled sideways to let Mouse enter beside him.

'Hello, sirs.' She spoke quietly and bobbed a curtsy.

'I found something,' Kibble said and nodded for emphasis.

'I did too,' Mouse said.

'What?' Swift replied.

'Papers, sir.' Kibble came to the table with his hand outstretched.

'Mouse?' I said.

She had held her hand low behind her apron, but now lifted it up. She held a gun by the grip. I leapt up to take it from her. She gazed at me with doe eyes, not realising the damn thing was loaded.

'British Bulldog,' I said as I opened the sidegate and rotated the cylinder. 'One bullet fired.'

Swift had barely glanced up. 'Where did you find these, Kibble?' He indicated the papers in his hand.

'In Miss Annabel's room, sir,' Kibble said. 'It's a will, in't it?'

'Yes,' Swift said. 'It's Wilmslow's will. He leaves everything he owns to his fiancé, Miss Serafina Deville.'

CHAPTER SIXTEEN

'Serafina!' I was astounded. 'What's the date on the will?'

'May the second, nineteen fifteen,' Swift replied.

'It's probably been superseded by now,' I said, trying to take in the strange twist. 'Mouse, where did you find the gun?'

'I was tidying the boot room, they'd left it a mess, coats and shoes all over the place,' she said. 'I picked up one of the jackets and it was really heavy, so I felt in the pocket. It was a gun.'

'Whose pocket?' I asked.

'Miss Barbara's,' she replied. 'But I don't think it was hers, it was just shoved in. The handle was sticking out.'

'Mouse came up to tell me, sirs,' Kibble said. 'I'd just found the will hidden in Miss Annabel's undies drawer. Why d'ye think it was there?'

'No idea,' I said.

'I hope you left her room in order,' Swift said.

'I made sure it was as it should be,' Mouse answered softly. 'And the gentry are comin' back in now, I saw them in the hall afore we came up here. We'd best be goin', Kipp.' She turned to him.

'Aye, we should,' he spoke gently to her, his eyes soft with a look of something like adoration on his round face. 'Now you let me bring the coal next time. Ye don't need any more shocks like that moonbeam again.'

She giggled, putting her hand over her mouth.

'Come along then.' He put his arm out for her to slip her hand through.

'Yes, Kipp.' She smiled up at him.

They went off together, forgetting to say goodbye.

Swift was engrossed in Wilmslow's will. 'He's worth a very large fortune…whole streets of houses in Manchester, shops and stores…a mansion in Cheshire. It's signed, sealed, and witnessed, there's no doubt it's authentic.'

'Strange that Annabel should have it.'

He raised his eyes. 'Is it?'

I was still holding the gun. 'Where's the fingerprint powder?'

'On the table where Fossett left it.'

The table was fast becoming covered with papers. The tin of powder was under the inky sheet of fingerprints Fossett had taken yesterday. I duly dusted whatever I could; it was a fiddly job and the damn powder drifted about. I had to stop and sneeze twice, which woke Foggy up.

'It's Gilbert's!' I said. 'Here on one of the bullets, a fingerprint and thumbprint.' I pointed at the sheet of inky prints.

'Told you it was likely to be a British Bulldog belonging to him.'

'Yes, well deduced Sherlock,' I replied, carefully removing all the bullets before closing the sidegate. 'It gives us the murder weapon.'

'Probable murder weapon,' he corrected, pedantic as ever. He'd been noting down the details of Wilmslow's will. 'I assume Barbara Boden's prints weren't on there?'

'Not that I could find. All the other prints are smudged.'

'Sir! Sir!' Fossett came in, slightly breathless, but looking very pleased with himself. 'I found stuff among the ashes. You were right, his suitcase was burned up there. Look, here's the remains of the handle, and two clasps and hinges.' He put the bucket on the table for us to peer into. The handle was a warped and shrivelled lump of blackened leather with a metal hoop at each end. The other remnants were burned but easy to make out.

'Buttons,' Swift said.

'Yes, and a tie pin, but it's mostly melted.' Fossett pointed to it. 'And there was a pen but it fell to bits when I picked it up.'

'The killer must have hidden it, then taken it up after the fireworks show at midnight,' I said.

'Yes...' He suddenly noticed the pistol. 'The gun! Where did you find it? Was it used to murder Flyte? Oh, well done, sirs!'

'Mouse found it,' I said.

'And Kibble found Wilmslow's will.' Swift tapped the papers in front of him.

'He never did?' Fossett was astonished. 'What's it say?'

Swift told him in succinct terms.

'That's strange, that is.' Fossett sat down. 'The killer must have had a busy day and a late night, what with drugging Gilbert and shooting Flyte, then throwing Gilbert out the tower and dropping him down the coal hole. Then they'd have had to go to his room and pack his things up–'

'They'd have had to find the gun first,' I cut in. 'In order to shoot Flyte.'

'Aye, you're right, Major Lennox, they would…but it might have been in his pocket when he was drugged and all they had to do was wait.'

Swift waved an impatient hand. 'I've made a list of times and places of the pertinent events. Both of you make a copy in your notebooks, please. It will provide us with a frame on which to pinpoint who was where at the time of each action.'

'Yes, sir!' Fossett hunted for his pencil and notebook.

'All in good time, Swift.' I stood up. 'I'll go and find Annabel Cresswell. Kibble said the guests had returned to the house.'

'Lennox…' he began, then gave up with a frown of irritation. 'Don't be long.'

Fogg followed of course, he knew when I was headed for a quiet walk in the cool fresh air. Swift was in full police mode and I wanted to assimilate some of the information we'd just heard.

I went out by the tower door. There wasn't a sound other than a ripple of breeze among the trees. Foggy snuffled about in the frozen grass. I found the bruised track of footsteps made by the ice skaters and followed it towards the pond.

The day was perfect, so was the setting. I reached the lake. Weeping willow trees, their trailing branches frozen into the ice, along with thorny wild roses and bullrushes lining the bank. The water had turned blue and glazed white, frozen and beautiful, the surface scratched and scored where the skaters had circled in graceful arcs or clipped a submerged log and fallen with a bump.

Foggy wandered off, sniffing out rabbit or fox. I shoved my hands in pockets and gazed with narrowed eyes toward the horizon.

The killer took the gun into the boot room and put it in Barbara Boden's pocket. Why? Everyone must have been jostling in there, hunting for skates, deciding which coats to wear, removing shoes and boots, strapping on skates.

It was a brazen act, or reckless, and Gilbert's body was hardly well hidden, it was only a matter of time before it was found. Not that there was anywhere else to hide it that I could think of.

What was the killer's state of mind? Were they driven by jealousy, or love that had turned to a frenzied hatred? If so, the motive was revenge. But then there was Wilmslow's will hidden by Annabel, but favouring Serafina. Was there something deeper here? Flyte had employed Gilbert as an investigator, or bodyguard, and yet Flyte had voluntarily entered into a duel using live shot. And he'd murdered Wilmslow, so had he done so because he feared Wilmslow was preparing to kill him? If so, he'd never have allowed Wilmslow to carry a loaded gun. So had he woken the man and marched him out to the duelling ground and then shot him?

I mused on that: it would be before dawn, actually it could have been anytime in the night, we were merely assuming it was dawn. And yet the watcher was there, so it must have been light. And I remembered that Lady Rose and Mary both heard the shots…

Had Flyte expected to stroll back indoors and calmly announce he'd shot Wilmslow dead in a duel? Despite the modifications to the pistols that should have prevented any such event? Or had he intended blaming the modification for the death? Stating that he'd aimed at Wilmslow's feet to scare him but the shot had taken its own trajectory? That would only work if no-one else knew that he had been told about the modification.

Maybe the watcher was an accomplice, employed to wing Flyte afterwards, hence the shot to the shoulder? Perhaps it was Gilbert…but that didn't make sense. I shook my head.

Rupert Featherstone said he'd helped carry Flyte into the tower. Why was he up at that hour? Had he heard or seen something?

I turned abruptly back towards the house, following the skaters' footsteps. A single set diverted off towards the tower. Freddie Doggett, why had he come over to see me? He seemed likable, and harmless. I shook my head, I was tying myself in knots.

I made my way round to the front door. Foggy caught up with me, came inside and then dashed off up the stairs. I glanced toward the minstrel gallery, I hadn't been up there yet.

The entrance was from the rear. I went through the servant's arch and trod up the old staircase. Black and rickety, joined with pegs and dowels, I went carefully, testing the treads, which actually held my weight easily.

The gallery smelled old, not of must or dust but something of distilled for centuries. Stale beer, sweat, woodsmoke, tobacco, wax polish, and leather. I could almost hear the music – pipes and drums, lutes, flutes, tambours, fiddles and song.

The floorboards creaked as I moved forward. I walked between worn benches fixed to the floor with black bolts. A few had backs with slots where sheet music would have been held. I reached the heavy rail to lean on it and gaze down into the hall.

In its heyday, the ceiling would have risen two more storeys to the beamed roof and been a far more rudimentary place than it was now.

I imagined the medieval banqueting hall it was designed to be. The minstrels' music aimed at the lord, his lady, and men-at-arms sitting at high table where the main stairs now stood. Two more tables would have ranged down each wall in the form of a horseshoe.

Chimneys hadn't yet been adopted; they'd have kept a huge fire burning in the centre, the smoke filling the room and filtering up to the rafters.

Most of these places had burned to the ground, or rotted away over the eons of human habitation, the only reason this one survived was because it was built of good Cotswold stone.

Life seemed simpler in those days – jousting, feasting, hand to hand combat in heavy armour. War and wenching, drinking and fighting. Actually nothing had really changed at all, the veneer of civilization had simply become more intricately layered over the generations.

Redfern was crossing the floor, a silver tray with teapot, cups, saucers, and some sort of cake.

'Redfern,' I called out. He nearly dropped the tray.

'Sir?' He turned and spotted me, plates and silverware rattling.

'We'd like to interview Miss Annabel Cresswell. Would you send her to the tower, please?'

'Certainly, sir…the ambulance men have taken, the, erm…' He was looking up at me, careworn, with shoulders drooping, his face pale with shadows under his eyes. 'The deceased, sir.'

'So I heard. Don't happen to have seen my wife, have you? And Lady Florence?'

'The ladies are with Lady Rose and Miss Mary in the drawing room, sir. I am taking tea and refreshments.'

'Good…' I was about to ask for the same, but decided things were exciting enough.

'Will that be all, sir?'

'Probably,' I replied.

'Very well, sir.' He went off, cups and saucers still rattling.

I turned for another look about, threading back and forth between the benches. Some had been crudely carved with initials, the letters worn and warped with age. I noticed that there wasn't any dust on the benches, or indeed anywhere – somebody had cleaned the place – probably in readiness for the ball. Actually it wasn't as pristine as I thought, the faint crunch of something underfoot caused me to stop. I knelt down and ran an exploratory hand across the floorboards. Coal dust. It showed black on my fingers. I rubbed it, it was grainy, so it couldn't be gunpowder. I thought of the cellar, and someone looking for a place to hide a body. They'd gone down there, then come here – it was an ideal spot for eavesdropping, or spying. They would have been watching yesterday…waiting for a moment to go to the tower and dispatch Gilbert. I cursed, then swore that I'd find them, and see that justice was done on poor Gilbert's behalf.

I descended the rickety treads and crossed the hall, still simmering with anger.

'Major Lennox.' Barbara Boden was walking stiffly down the wide staircase. 'You should have joined us, a man of your build must be a natural athlete. I was in need of a strong arm to lean on.'

'So I heard.'

She laughed. 'I can feel the bruises forming already.' She arrived at the foot of the stairs. She'd changed into a long black skirt, roll-neck sweater and a peacock blue silk scarf around her neck. Her cheeks were pink from the skating and her eyes bright; she looked quite stunning. 'Rupert Featherstone was sweet, actually.' She flashed speculative eyes at me.

'Your factories and his ten thousand acres would make quite a match,' I said dryly.

'Oh, but can you imagine organising a large estate?

That's what Rupert wants. Someone capable of managing everything for him, just like his dear mama had done. I already have enough people to manage, I think I'd prefer a simple life on a yacht. Somewhere warm with a light breeze filling the sails, and a small but attentive staff to make my life divine.' She spoke with a tease in her voice.

'A life such as Charles Flyte used to lead, before he was shot dead.'

She looked mildly exasperated. 'Major Lennox, must you act the policeman all the time?'

'Who are you wearing mourning for?' I switched tack.

'Nobody. I always wear black. Dress down for business or up for pleasure.'

'The gun that killed Flyte was found in your coat pocket,' I said, watching her as shock glazed her dark eyes, her cherry-red lips parting.

'What?' She stepped sharply backwards as though I'd raised a hand to her.

'I think you heard me.'

'I don't own a gun, why should I?' She was frowning, puzzlement and anger in her voice. 'I don't know what you're talking about.'

'We'll interview you in one hour,' I said, then left her standing as I strode towards the tower.

CHAPTER SEVENTEEN

Annabel Cresswell was already seated; she too looked fresh and bright. The brightness was fading though. Swift was seated opposite her, his back to the wall as she faced him. I didn't know where Fossett was.

Her eyes flicked to me as I came in, and then to the blackboard, where the drawings and list of names were. There was something intimidating, almost threatening about it, as though it were an accusation waiting to be made. I could sense the tension even as I went to sit by Swift.

'How far away is your flat in London from the homes of both victims?' Swift was saying.

'Not far.' Annabel's voice was tight. 'I don't know. Three streets from Bernard, and four from Charles. They lived in opposite directions.'

'You said you've known Bernard Wilmslow since you were quite young?' Swift continued.

'Yes, our mothers thought we were suited.' She wore an opal ring on the index finger of her right hand; she twisted it round. 'We didn't agree. We were at an age where we rebelled against everything…it drew us together actually.'

She'd fixed her dark hair back and changed into beige slacks and a cream sweater. She still wore the same shaded makeup around her eyes, her cupid's bow lips formed into a pout. 'Bernard was spoiled, I suppose I was too. He was terribly wealthy, all his family are. His elder brother inherited the family estate when their father died, and their mother gave Bernard all her properties. She's from an industrial family.' She shifted in her seat. 'She's quite formidable, or was... age has caught her now. Mentally, I mean. She's not with it.' She glanced at me. 'She'd be grief-stricken if she knew he'd died...I'm glad she can't understand, poor soul. Her boy, she used to call him...' Her voice caught and broke, but she cleared her throat and carried on. 'He has two sisters too. Both married Americans, they live in New York. I haven't written to any of them. I assume it's something the authorities will do.' She sniffed, blew her nose on a white handkerchief then sat up with her back straight. 'I didn't love him. He was attractive to look at, but could be awfully mean and petty, and he was jealous of everything. He would question me about where I'd been, who I'd been with, when and where. It was ridiculous and quite exasperating. And he'd come to my flat at any hour wanting to talk, and drink. He drank too much, it made him angry. He would fly into a rage at the smallest thing. I threatened him with the police once, when he was particularly vile.'

Swift had been quietly writing. He hadn't had to ask many questions as she seemed the talkative sort. He looked up. 'Why did you maintain a relationship with him if he was violent?'

'He wasn't physically violent,' Annabel replied. 'Just angry. And he had no reason for it, his life couldn't be more perfect. I think he was simply lacking any sort of…' she sought the word… 'purpose, I suppose. You see, his father had been more than simply a landowner, he was innovative, always seeking new ways to improve the estate, and he was very active in the House of Lords. Particularly in agricultural matters, and his mother's family owned companies that built railways and roads, they were clever and industrious, and Bernard wasn't.' She twisted the opal ring again. 'He was resentful, and controlling, and quite sad. I would never have married him, but I was his friend. He didn't have anyone else.'

'People seemed to think you were on the verge of becoming engaged but then fell out,' I said.

'Bernard told them we may wed, but he didn't want to marry me, he just couldn't bear to lose me.' She let out a loud sigh. 'I should never have agreed to come here.'

'Why did you?' I continued, more intrigued by the girl than I'd expected. She sounded a good friend to the undeserving Wilmslow.

'My mother. She still harbours hopes for us, despite everything.' Her eyes met mine. 'I haven't told her what's happened, she'd be down on the next train and make everything much worse.'

'Why do you think Wilmslow and Flyte fought a duel?' Swift asked. The atmosphere in the room had lulled into something almost peaceful. The fire in the hearth crackled and burned, radiating enough heat to create a warm fug. It was almost congenial.

'I've been thinking about that almost every moment since it happened. Charles was everything Bernard wasn't – tall, masculine, oozing confidence, and terribly popular. He held amazing parties and invited everyone. He'd suddenly declare he was off to the Riviera, ask who wanted to come, and we'd all pile on a train, or a plane if he could arrange it. Or rather his office arranged it, he didn't actually do anything himself.' She gave a wan smile. 'Bernard was terribly jealous of him, really loathed him, actually. Charles was simply contemptuous.'

'Where was Flyte's office?' Swift asked as though running through a list.

'Sloane Square. Serafina ran it.'

We both sat up at that.

'Serafina?' I said in disbelief.

'Yes, why not? She was his Girl Friday.'

'She has an office?' I was incredulous.

'It's very discreet,' she replied. 'She doesn't advertise or anything.'

'Isn't she wealthy?' Swift asked, having forgotten to write in his notebook.

'Not really, no,' she replied. 'Her family are the right sort, but they've fallen on hard times. It's quite common now, what with taxes and the war. Anyway, she has three or four girls working for her and she simply directs them in what to do.'

'Does she have many clients?' Swift began writing more quickly.

'A select few,' she replied. 'I think Charles was the

biggest, he had her running things for him. I don't know who the others might be.'

I was trying to reconcile the remote beauty of Serafina and the idea of a workaday job. 'She hardly seems the type.'

Annabel laughed. 'This is the modern world, Major Lennox. Working means independence and a chance to show what one can do.'

I thought of Persi, who was still working in a way, but not one that led to her travelling to dusty corners of the world without me. I hoped she didn't ever feel the need for that sort of independence.

'Do you have a job, Miss Cresswell?' Swift asked.

She stopped laughing. 'No. I don't need one. I'd love to be an artist but I haven't the talent…unlike Edna,' she said and looked over at the blackboard.

'Are you a close friend of Serafina?' Swift asked.

'No,' she replied with a faint shrug. 'We just know each other socially.'

'What about Felicity Carr?' I added.

'Ha! Hardly, she's a lying little cat.'

'She said you were Flyte's mistress.' Swift spoke bluntly.

'As I said, she's a lying little cat.'

'But you were close to Flyte,' I said. 'You told me he swept you off your feet.'

Her lips opened and closed before she spoke. 'It was true, but then he would blow hot and cold. I realised he was stringing someone else along. Then I heard it was Felicity.' She shrugged. 'I was annoyed, but hardly heartbroken. Charles could be a charmer, and terrific fun. He was pure generosity, never stinting on anything. It was a giddy round of parties in fabulous locations with the "in crowd". Charles was the centre of the bright young things for a while.'

'He didn't remain so?' I asked.

'I think he grew bored of it,' she replied thoughtfully. 'Although the parties continued, he was just more discerning about whom he invited. It was a select few rather than open house.'

'Were you lovers?' Swift asked the direct question.

'You are overstepping the mark, Inspector,' she suddenly snapped, anger sparking in her hazel eyes.

'Answer the question,' Swift replied coldly.

Her colour rose; I waited to see if she would storm out. She didn't. 'Yes,' she hissed through her teeth, her anger unabated. 'And if I weren't so determined to help you find out what happened I would never admit to that.'

Swift merely wrote in his notebook, the consummate policeman.

'Did Flyte buy clothes for you?' I asked, thinking back to Felicity's "confession" to us.

'Sometimes, yes. He loved to go shopping. It was always in the most exclusive stores. Girls would model for us and he'd order something to be tailored for me.'

That fitted with Felicity's description of Flyte's "special girls".

'Was Serafina one of Flyte's lovers too?' I asked at the risk of getting my head bitten off.

Her eyes flashed at me. 'I've no idea…' She bit her lip, smudging her lipstick. 'She may have been in the past.

I've never seen her touch him, or even act affectionately towards him.'

'Does she act affectionately with anyone?' I asked.

She glanced at me. 'No, she's not the tactile sort.'

Swift reached for the stack of papers on the corner of the table. 'Do you recognise this?' He took the top three pages, turned them in his hands then held them up.

She gasped. 'Blast you, you've been through my drawers.'

I refrained from making any sort of risqué response to that.

'Why were you hiding this will?' Swift turned interrogatory.

Her cheeks flushed. 'Bernard asked me to keep it.'

'Why?' I said.

'I…he was being paranoid. It was ridiculous. He said he'd found something out. He wouldn't tell me what it was, he said it would simply put me in danger too.'

'How was his will related to danger?' Swift demanded.

'I have no idea,' she retorted. 'Perhaps you should ask his heiress.'

'Didn't it occur to you that you should have told us this after he was murdered?' Swift suddenly shouted, genuine anger in his voice. 'You just said you wanted to help. How does hiding vital information help?'

She sat back in her chair as though trying to distance herself from him. 'He wasn't murdered. He was shot by Charles in a duel.'

'Wilmslow was murdered by Charles,' I stated.

'That is ridiculous. Duels are just for show – a stupid act of bravado. No-one's supposed to be hurt, not in this day and age. Really, Major Lennox, I would expect you to understand that,' she retorted.

'Charles Flyte wasn't on his mark, he was very close to Bernard when he shot him,' I replied coldly.

I could see doubt growing in her eyes. 'Why would Charles want to murder Bernard?' A tremble in her cut glass voice.

Swift ignored the question. 'Why didn't you give the will to us, or Serafina?'

She stood up. 'Bernard asked me to hold on to it and that is what I have done,' she said, then ran out.

There wasn't much we could do to stop her.

I glanced at Swift. 'Interesting.'

'Yes.' He sat back, relaxed and thoughtful. 'Bernard Wilmslow discovered some sort of secret and was murdered by Charles Flyte. Flyte had already hired an ex-detective. All of them are now dead. And Serafina Deville profits from it.'

'We can't be sure of that, Swift.'

'No, we'd best talk to her.'

'Actually I asked Barbara Boden to come–'

'You did, Major Lennox. And here I am.' She strolled into the room exuding confidence, a seductive allure, and a very expensive perfume.

Swift flipped over the will still lying on the table. 'Please sit down, Miss Boden.'

She didn't sit down, she went over to the blackboard to stare at the two portraits, then the list of suspects. 'I assume you have the experience to resolve this, gentlemen?' She swung on her high heels to face us.

'We do,' Swift replied.

She came and sat opposite us, placed an elbow on the table, rested her chin on her hand and gazed at us. 'You intend interrogating me?'

Swift didn't bat an eyelash. 'I intend questioning you, Miss Boden.'

The corner of her mouth curled up. 'Go right ahead.'

'The gun found in your coat—'

'It isn't mine and I didn't put it there,' she cut him off. 'I assume it was the gun that killed Charles?'

'It was,' he replied.

'Are there any prints on it?' she demanded.

'Only Gilbert's.'

I was watching them back and forth as though it was a fast-paced tennis match.

'Why aren't you out searching for him?' she returned.

'We found him. He's dead,' Swift said.

Which won him the round because she abruptly shut up.

'Do you really have three factories?' I changed tack, thinking to ease the tension.

'Yes,' she replied. 'How did Gilbert die?'

'That's sensitive information,' Swift replied.

She regarded him. There was something about her. Utter determination, but a warmth with it. I doubt much would stop her achieving whatever she set her mind to.

'Boden and Locke,' I said. 'My wife told me you make luxury soap.'

'I do.' Her fine eyes switched to mine. 'Does it surprise you?'

'Yes.'

A smile flickered across her lips. 'I was born in Flamborough, it's a fishing village on the Yorkshire coast. *We oll spake loik thiz,*' she suddenly switched into the local dialect. 'I decided I'd best adopt a neutral accent when I acquired my first factory.'

I tried to hide my astonishment.

'How did you manage to go from living in a fishing village to owning a factory?' Swift asked, as intrigued as I was.

'Yorkshire grit and old-fashioned hard work,' she replied, more animated now. 'My father was a fisherman, my brothers worked with him, and my mother would gut the catch. I helped. We were fishwives,' she laughed. 'Well, I wasn't, but Mam was. Everything stank of fish. We didn't notice it, but then one day a new girl joined my class at school. Beth Locke. She'd come down from Northumberland, the daughter of a farm labourer. I said she stank of cows, she said I stank of fish. We fought. I'm afraid it wasn't unusual, we were terrible tykes. We became best friends. But I hated the idea that we smelled, so I decided to make soap. An old spinster lady at the top of the Head taught us the basics – you'll have heard of Flamborough Head?' she asked.

'Yes, it's said to be beautiful,' Swift answered.

I didn't say anything, but I knew it had a fascinating history of Viking invaders and caves running deep below the high cliffs. I'd ended up there when my compass broke on a trainer flight. I went in entirely the wrong direction in low cloud, ran out of fuel, landed on the hilltop at

Flamborough and had to hitch a lift to a garage. It wasn't my finest moment.

'Beth joined with me and we boiled up pots full of tallow and potash. It was appalling,' she laughed. 'The stench was worse than the fish. Then we decided to use seaweed to make the potash and gathered sea coal to burn it down until it reduced to pearl-ash. And we switched to lard, it was better than tallow, even if it does come from pigs. Our mams were mad at us for taking it just to make soap.' A smile played on her lips as she told her tale, enjoying the memories. 'It took a lot of trial and error, but we finally learned how to make a pure white soap. The perfumes were just as difficult. We'd mither all the neighbours for flowers from their gardens. They'd chunner and moan, but they all saved them up for us and we'd take them to our shed for cooking up,' her perfect English drifted back to dialect as she talked fondly. 'Lavender n' roses were best, but they weren't easy t'grow in a wild place like Flamborough.'

A knock at the door interrupted.

Kibble came in with a tray of tea and cakes. 'Mr Redfern thought you'd be after a brew,' he said. 'An' Chef's just finished a batch of cherry bakewells, so there's a good plateful of them an' all.' He put the tray on the table between us. 'You'll have to help yerselfs 'cos I've got to get back. It's all go around here.' He grinned happily and went off, apparently enjoying himself.

Swift gave an almost imperceptible shake of the head and reached for the pot. 'Miss Boden?'

'Black please, no sugar,' she replied. 'I think I'll have

a cake, I'm starved after the skating.' She reached for the plate of cherry tarts, which had a creamy iced topping, a cherry in the centre, and buttery pastry casing. Nursery fare, but jolly nice.

'How are the bruises?' I asked.

She gave a mock grimace. 'I'll be black and blue tomorrow. My own fault; I've never learned to skate, I've always been too busy.'

I took a bite of cake, it was sweet and sticky and perfect. Barbara picked up her fork and sliced hers in two. Swift made notes while we ate in companionable silence.

I finished first. 'I assume you began selling your soap?' I came back to her story, being very impressed with her pluck.

'We did! Not much at first, Flamborough is hardly prosperous, but we persuaded the grocer to give us lifts to the local markets. He did the rounds and we sat in the back with the spuds and snips. We went to the shops pushing for orders and sold our scented bars on the stalls. We were always skipping school, and ended up with rapped knuckles more than once.' She grinned. 'We didn't care. The shops started buying from us, bit by bit, then the local newspaper took up the story. By then we'd passed fourteen and could leave school altogether. We rented a barn and set up a proper process. *It were freezin'*,' she briefly reverted to her Yorkshire accent once more, laughing. 'When the war came we got a government contract to supply the troops. That was how we ended up with three factories. Now it's lotions, potions, and perfume, as well as soap.'

'What about Beth?' Swift asked.

'She was hit by a car just over three weeks ago.' Her tone dropped; so did her face.

'Was she killed?' Swift asked, sounding as shocked as I was.

'Not yet. She's in a coma. There's no knowing if she'll recover,' she said, anger simmering in her voice.

'I'm sorry,' I said.

'What happened?' Swift was more focused.

She frowned at him. 'She was crossing the road in Cadogan Gardens, and was hit by a vehicle. It was eight o'clock at night, dark and foggy. A proper London pea-souper. The driver didn't stop.'

'Do you know who the driver was?' Swift continued.

'A man called Declan Doyle.' Her expression had turned cold, the hard-nosed businesswoman was now very much in evidence. 'I used a private detective to discover what happened. A bobby had arrived on the scene quite quickly, he called an ambulance. People tried to help…there wasn't much they could do.' She held her cup between both hands, as though to steady them. 'My detective went to the station and questioned the bobby. He told him the witnesses had said it was a van, but they didn't know the make. It had hit her on the front right side and driven off into the fog. My detective made the rounds of all the local garages and eventually found a record in a small workshop south of the river. A vehicle had been repaired on the front right side ten days previously. It was a 1920 Standard Nine commercial van, rented from Brixton commercials. The owner, a bloke called Jimmy Cross, said it had been rented by Declan Doyle the day before Beth was hit. That was January the twenty-fifth. Doyle returned it two days later, sometime in the night, damaged, with fifty pounds in the glove box. Jimmy Cross didn't make a fuss; he had it fixed, made thirty quid profit and forgot about it.'

'Has Doyle been found?' Swift asked.

'No, the address he gave was false,' she replied, her face now stony. 'The man who'd rented it wore a hat and scarf over his face. It was snowing, no one thought much of it.'

'What was the name of your detective?' I asked.

'Godfrey Gilbert,' she replied.

CHAPTER EIGHTEEN

The disclosure upset Swift, though I'd no idea why. I'd anticipated it as soon as she'd said *detective*.

'You knew Gilbert?' He raised his voice. 'Why didn't you tell us?'

'Because I didn't believe it was relevant,' she replied coolly. 'Charles recommended him to me. The man seemed competent. What of it?' She shrugged.

Swift had turned a page in his notebook and banged a hand down on it to flatten it. 'When did he recommend him?'

'Shortly after Beth was hit by the car,' she replied.

'Why had Flyte used a detective?' Swift's voice was clipped in irritation.

'He thought someone was trying to kill him.'

'Who?'

'I've no idea. He wouldn't say.'

The back-and-forth riposte resumed between them.

'And you didn't think this was relevant?' Swift was sarcastic.

'Yesterday you said Gilbert was the killer,' she retorted.

'I thought you must be a bungling idiot to believe that. I had no interest in telling you anything.'

'More information might have given us a better perspective,' he snapped back, his face suffused with anger.

She narrowed her eyes, then sighed. 'He was a nice man, and diligent… He was quite poorly. He hadn't seemed so initially, but I noticed it over the couple of weeks he worked for me. He explained he had a wife in Cork and they were struggling. I think they'd had a dream of living out their days on a little farm, but it was barely sustainable, and his illness was beginning to take a toll. He said he had to come back to England to build up some savings and see his old doctor.'

'Did he continue working for Charles Flyte while he was employed by you?' I asked.

'Yes, he did, but I suspect he wouldn't have done for much longer. He was losing weight, poor man. I think he was going to return to Ireland after this.'

'When did Gilbert discover the name of Doyle?' Swift was making furious notes.

'Ten days ago,' she replied. 'He informed the police. They said they weren't able to find the man either. Gilbert was upset.' She paused. 'More upset than I'd expected really. I paid him well, but he said he wanted to spend some time thinking about the case.' She looked up. 'That's what he called it. A case.'

'What was Flyte to you?' I asked, not wanting to mention the word mistress. She'd probably erupt if I did.

'Not my lover,' she said, the smile playing on her lips as she watched me. 'I am rarely in London, and I'm not interested in the social scene. My work consumes my time, and I enjoy it.' She gave a wry smile. 'Charles would never have interested me. He was far too popular for his own good and I prefer a man who is more discerning. He was keen to spread his attractions among the adoring young things. Sex is becoming quite the rage now, which suited him just fine.'

I shut my mouth firmly to prevent any babbling. She laughed anyway.

'Who here has he had sexual relations with?' Swift had his pen poised over the top of a fresh page.

She shrugged. 'Really Inspector, how would I know?'

'But you said he was keen to spread his attractions,' I reminded her. 'You must have an idea.'

She flashed a dark look at me for that, then shrugged. 'Felicity Carr is gullible enough, and I noticed Annabel was wearing weeds. I assume it was on his behalf, or Wilmslow's. I barely know these people. I took Lady Rose's invitation up on a whim.'

Something about that didn't strike true.

'You haven't been here before?' Swift asked.

'No,' she replied.

'Do you think any of his lovers would be jealous enough to kill?' Swift continued.

'Each other, possibly,' she replied blithely. 'But not Charles. What's the point? He had a reputation for womanising. It would hardly come as a surprise to anyone.'

'But someone hated him enough to kill him,' I stated.

'It would appear so, given that he was shot twice,' she replied dryly then pulled back the cuff of her black sweater to check her rose-gold watch. 'I really must go, I need to call the manager at the Peterlee factory.' She stood up.

A tap on the door sounded and Redfern entered. 'Sirs…' He stopped when he saw Barbara.

She raised her brows. 'Yes?'

'It's…erm…a delicate matter, ma'am.'

'Gilbert's murder?' she guessed.

'Indeed, ma'am. If it is proven to be murder.'

She looked over at us. 'Is there any doubt?'

'There is not,' Swift replied.

'*Well, that's gerrin' t' cause a reet flap,*' she said in a broad Yorkshire accent, then laughed as Redfern's mouth dropped open. '*Ta-ra for now.*' She walked out on high heels.

'She's from Flamborough,' I offered in explanation.

'I…really, sir. Erm, may I ask when you propose announcing the death of Mr Gilbert? The staff are aware of the situation, but Lady Rose and Miss Mary are not. Nor are the other guests. They were out skating when his body was removed.'

'Gather them in the drawing room,' Swift decided. 'I'll come and announce it shortly.'

'Very well, sir.' You'd think he'd just received a death sentence by the tone of his voice. 'Miss Barbara is correct, it will cause considerable consternation.'

'Being in close proximity to a murderer will do that,' I remarked. 'Perhaps a supply of brandy-buttered crumpets would help.'

'Apprehending the murderer would bring more comfort, sir, but I will do what I can.' He eyed the tray and crumb-covered plates on the table, gathered them up and exited, leaving the room to lapse into the soporific peace that only an ancient house built of thick solid stone in the deepest countryside can imbue.

I moved my chair to sit next to the blazing fire. Swift remained at the table to add a few more notes, then came to join me.

'What did you make of Barbara Boden?' he asked.

'Impressive,' I replied.

'Capable of murder?'

'As much as anyone. I doubt she'd do it herself.' I mused on the lady for a moment. 'How relevant is the story of Declan Doyle?'

'I'll ask Billings to run a check on him.'

'Gilbert had already reported him,' I said. 'I imagine they must be on the lookout for him.'

'Hmm.' His mind appeared elsewhere. 'Why would the killer put the gun in Barbara's jacket pocket?'

'To throw suspicion on her…perhaps they knew she had a connection with Gilbert already. Although the action was clumsy. If she were the killer she'd hardly have left the murder weapon in her own pocket.'

'But the killer probably didn't expect it to be found by the maid,' he replied.

'Ah, you're right.' I caught on. 'They'd expect Barbara to find it. Stupid of them – she'd be inclined to use it if necessary.'

'Yes,' he replied. 'Come on. Let's go and see how they react to Gilbert's murder, and the idea that they're sharing the house with a cold-blooded killer.'

Foggy came bounding up when we reached the upstairs corridor and greeted us as though we'd been gone for a month. He trotted happily alongside as we entered the drawing room.

They'd all assembled on the sofas and chairs about the fire. Redfern was serving tea while Kibble was at the tall Elizabethan dresser, placing hot crumpets onto pretty Meissen plates with silver tongs.

'Butter and brandy whisked up,' Kibble said. 'It gets poured on the crumpets to soak in. Chef showed me how it's made, and he let me have a taste. Lovely, it is.'

I had half a mind to stop to sample it myself, but Swift was striding ahead. Fogg followed, weaving between the sofas, heading for the fire.

'Hello, doggie,' Edna called to him, her hand outstretched.

He gave her a sloppy lick then carried on to stop next to Lady Rose, who was sitting with her colourful blanket over her knees.

'We've already heard,' Freddie Doggett blurted out before Swift could speak. 'It was his body lying next to the tower, wasn't it?'

Lord Hector was seated next to Clarissa, his head turned in Doggett's direction. 'Whose else did you imagine it might be?'

'I didn't. I thought it was a scarecrow,' Freddie replied and picked up the cup of tea Redfern had left at his elbow.

'A scarecrow?' Hector said, his voice thick with sarcasm.

'Did he fall from the top of the watchtower?' Rupert Featherstone asked Doggett.

'How would I know?' Freddie sounded rattled as attention focused on him.

'He didn't fall from the tower.' Swift had gone to stand at the front of the room. 'He was murdered.'

Disbelief was their first reaction, followed by a few dropped jaws. They'd no doubt comforted themselves that Gilbert had killed Flyte, and were now absorbing the fact of his murder. The realisation that it was most likely to be someone in this room would be spinning in their minds like a tossed grenade.

'That's it, I'm leaving.' Rupert Featherstone had jumped to his feet.

'Why would you want to leave and miss the finale?' George Lovell said. He'd leaned back in a plump-cushioned chair, one leg crossed over the other, his arms folded and a grin on his face. 'What about you, Barbara?' He caught her eye. 'Are you going to run away?'

'No, I want to stay and see justice done,' she replied. 'And the culprit hang by the neck until dead.'

A ripple of muttering reverberated in response to that.

'I don't think they let anyone watch executions any more,' Edna Kent said. 'But I'd like to come along if they do.' She'd brought a drawing pad and was quietly sketching, sitting with legs curled under her on a well-placed chair.

'This is hardly a time for flippancy.' Felicity glared at her.

'Oh, do shut up, Felicity,' Rupert snapped at her.

'Rupert!' Felicity looked aghast, her irritation draining in an instant. 'I didn't…I mean it wasn't said with any… any ill intention.'

Edna glanced over at her, her brows raised in disbelief.

'Well, we shall all stay here and be comfortable together, my dears.' Lady Rose spoke loudly for all to hear. 'I'm sure the police will root out the murderous monster in no time.'

'The murderous monster who may be sitting here amongst us,' Annabel said.

'No, no,' Freddie spluttered. 'I mean, how can it be one of us?'

'Who else could it be?' Swift said.

'I…well…' Freddie's mouth was opening and closing. 'But that's outrageous.'

'I'd rather go home,' Annabel spoke up again. 'But if Barbara and George can stick it out, so can I.'

'Well, I'm not,' Felicity announced. 'We have rights. There's nothing anyone can do to prevent us from leaving.'

'Oh, yes there is,' Kibble called out, then shut up when Swift glared at him.

'Don't be ridiculous, Felicity,' Serafina spoke in a drawl. She'd been silent until now, her beautiful face impassive. 'All they need to do is set a guard on the gate and none of us will be able to go anywhere.'

'I'll call a cab,' Felicity shot back.

'It will be turned back,' Swift said coldly.

'Do any of you really think you're in danger?' George Lovell spoke out. 'Flyte and his valet were killed for a reason. Unless anyone here is involved, there's no reason to fear for their lives.'

'Exactly,' Swift agreed. 'If you cooperate and work with us, we'll uncover the culprit and you'll be free to go.'

'I can't see any reason to run away,' Serafina said calmly. She'd changed back into the sapphire blue dress.

'Rose.' Mary turned to her. 'It really is the most appalling bad manners to put everyone to such an inconvenience. If this person is here in this room, they must confess.'

'I agree,' Lady Rose said. 'Inspector, you must demand a confession.'

Swift refrained from rolling his eyes.

Redfern came forward and delivered a butter and brandy soaked crumpet to her ladyship, then the same to Miss Mary – who picked up her fork with an unsteady hand.

'Dear Redfern,' she said tremulously. 'And what of Flambert? He will remain with us, won't he?'

'He has sworn allegiance, Miss Mary,' Redfern assured her.

'Oh, thank heavens.' Miss Mary aimed the fork at the crumpet and missed it entirely. Redfern bent over and graciously cut it up into small pieces for her.

'Now, Inspector.' Lady Rose took charge. 'What next?'

Swift's expression had turned hawkish. 'Does anyone here have medical experience?'

The question was unexpected and elicited blank looks.

'Why do you want to know that?' Barbara asked.

'It is related to the investigation,' Swift replied.

'I loathe the sight of blood, it makes me feel queasy,' Annabel said.

'And me,' Felicity said with feeling.

'I have my first aid certificate,' Edna Kent replied.

'Does that include administering medicine?' Swift asked.

'No, but I'm a dab hand with splints and bandages.' Edna grinned at him.

'I have some experience,' Clarissa declared. 'Daddy offered our house as a convalescence home during the war. I doled out pills and such, but I never learned what they were for. I just followed the doctor's instructions.'

I eyed Rupert Featherstone who was seated with legs crossed, his raised foot twitching in agitation. 'What did you do during the war?' I asked him affably.

He frowned at me. 'I was caring for my mother and the estate. We produce wheat and barley. It was part of the war effort.'

'So you didn't join the fighting?' George threw the barb.

Rupert crossed his arms and closed his lips in a tight line.

'What about you?' I turned to George.

'Oh, I was in the thick of it,' he replied. 'Battleships initially, then Q ships hunting German submarines.'

'You were on a Q ship?' Serafina sounded impressed. 'You must have the most remarkable story to tell.'

'Not really.' George appeared relaxed but I'd say he was enjoying the attention. 'We were simply doing our jobs.'

'What is he talking about?' Mary asked loudly.

'Perhaps you could elucidate the purpose and function of Q ships,' Lord Hector said.

'Oh, please do,' Clarissa added. 'My father served with the Admiralty, and was always a great proponent of them.' Her blue eyes were bright with interest. Hector frowned as he watched her lean forward to listen attentively to Sir George.

'Q ships operated out of Queenstown in Ireland,' Sir George began, a smile playing on his handsome face. 'Officially they were SS ships, meaning Special Service vessels; the term Q ship was code. Everything about them was a deception – they were decoys, designed to trap German U-boats and destroy them.'

'Ghost ships,' Clarissa said.

'In a way,' George replied. 'I served initially on HMS Farnborough under Rear Admiral Gordon Campbell. Farnborough had started life as a tramp steamer carrying coal. Once the Q ship tactic was agreed, she was picked up by the navy and fitted out with five 12-pounders, a couple of 6-pounders and a Maxim gun. They were hidden behind dummy dropdown compartments. She'd started life as a collier and to all intents and purposes that's what she still was. We piled on board dressed as stokers and coal trimmers – nothing more than labouring sailors, all bearded, tattered and weatherworn. Campbell played the master and grew a magnificent set of whiskers, I doubt his mother would have recognised him.' He laughed. Redfern filled his teacup then placed a plate of steaming crumpets at his elbow.

'You've never mentioned this before,' Barbara said.

'I said I was in the navy,' he reminded her.

'Not as a decoy.' She smiled.

'I didn't want you to think I was involved in skullduggery,' he replied.

'Ah, is that what you were doing?' she teased.

'Absolutely.' He grinned back, a growing warmth in his eyes.

'Perhaps you'd like to tell us more?' Felicity tried to add an archness, but it sounded false and George barely gave her a glance.

'A U-boat found us off the Irish coast and opened fire with a torpedo across the bow. That was the way they operated, blasting from beneath the waves, hidden from view. A despicable tactic.'

'Which they used on the Lusitania,' Lord Hector interrupted in stern tones.

'Exactly,' George agreed, anger growling in his voice. 'A cruise liner travelling from New York to Liverpool carrying nearly two thousand innocent men, women and children was fired on without warning and sank in minutes.' He was cold and serious, a glimpse of the military man behind the charming veneer. 'Well, we got the beggars back. We spotted their torpedo track and Campbell turned the ship to allow it to hit us. It caused some damage and we were lying low in the water. Campbell sent up a spout of steam and ordered us to stage a panic party – meaning some of the men pretended to flee the ship in rowboats. It fooled the Bosch and they came to the surface to finish us off. Once they were in range, we dropped the dummy sides and let the canons rip. Forty-five shells fired at a hundred yards. We blasted them to smithereens and they sank with all hands, bar two.'

'Bravo,' Clarissa said.

'Well done, old chap,' Freddie Doggett called out.

The ladies all looked suitably impressed.

'Campbell won a VC,' I said, having recalled reading about the exploits.

'Yes, and he was offered another one after a similar escapade – he turned that one down,' George said. 'I'd left to run my own show by then. At one stage we were disguised as a passenger ship and I had half the crew dressed in frocks,' he laughed.

'That must have been rather demeaning,' Annabel said.

'Quite a few of them were more than happy to parade around in dresses,' George replied lightly. 'We were always thinking up new ways to dupe the enemy. We even carried lace parasols and a stuffed parrot in a cage.'

Swift allowed George to run on, it was a useful distraction, calming the nerves of the assembled. Once he was ready, he returned to stand in front of the fire.

'I'd like your attention please,' he spoke out. 'I am reminding you again that this is a murder enquiry. It is imperative you answer our questions truthfully and fully. Who here is familiar with the name Declan Doyle?'

CHAPTER NINETEEN

Silence met Swift's question. They darted looks at each other, as if wondering what it meant and if anyone would speak up. No-one did. Lady Rose's chin had sunk onto her chest and she let out a snore. Mary blinked, then closed her own eyes.

Swift gave it up. 'You are dismissed for the moment.' He turned to Serafina. 'Miss Deville, we'd like to interview you now, please.'

'Why?' she asked, her eyes languid in her beautiful face.

Swift wasn't in the mood to explain. 'Come this way.' He led off towards the tower.

Foggy decided to come along and raced ahead to the stone steps and up to the top floor.

I went at a more leisurely pace, Serafina walking with a cat-like fluidity. Unhurried, though long-legged and flawlessly graceful. I could imagine any number of men falling for such spellbinding beauty. Me included, had I not been wed to the love of my life. My mind flicked to Persi for a moment, wondering what she was doing. Absorbed in some arcane piece of history no doubt, or picking over artefacts with Florence, trying to make sense of evidence left by random chance. As were we.

Fossett was sitting at the table quietly making notes in his notebook. Pen in hand, tip of his tongue in the corner of his mouth, and helmet left on top of the pile of papers we'd managed to accumulate between us.

'Sir.' He jumped to his feet and saluted. 'And, erm… ma'am.' He gazed at Serafina; a look of awe spread over his long face. He had a terrible knack for falling in love at an instant's notice.

'Miss Deville, please sit here.' Swift was businesslike, and pulled out a chair for Serafina to slide onto. Fogg decided he needed a cuddle from the ice maiden and put his soft muzzle on her lap. She smiled and stroked his head, then bent to murmur in his ear. It was the most emotional reaction I'd seen from her.

Fossett was now gazing like a moonstruck hare and shuffled to the other chair without taking his eyes from Serafina.

I went and tossed a few logs on the fire, although the room was more than warm enough, then went to join them facing Serafina.

'You were engaged to Wilmslow,' Swift said.

'I was,' she replied, her hand still resting on Foggy's head in her lap.

'When?' Swift added.

'1915. During the war. It was in France. He announced he loved me and would I marry him? I agreed.'

'Yet you remain unwed,' I stated.

'Ow.' Fossett suddenly jumped, then rubbed his shin.

'Sir.' Swift must have kicked him under the table, he frowned at him then set his pencil to paper.

Serafina smiled. 'Bernard went to war having joined the Royal Sussex. He came back unhappy and haunted. He said he didn't think he'd make a good husband so I returned his ring.'

'Where in France was he fighting?' I asked.

'All over,' she replied. 'It changed us both, but our friendship remained. I have always retained a fondness for him.'

I frowned, trying to comprehend what was behind her beautiful, emotionless face.

'Fond? You'd agreed to marry him because you were *fond* of him?' Swift repeated.

'As he was of me,' she replied, unperturbed.

'Would you have married him?' Swift asked. 'If he hadn't changed his mind.'

'No,' she replied.

'Why?' I asked.

'Because the war was over by then,' she said, which didn't make much sense to me.

'What were you doing in France?' Swift asked her.

'Translating. Je parle un Français parfaitement, und Deustch. My father was from Paris. My mother from Berlin. I was born there.'

'Berlin?' I said in surprise. There was no hint of an accent in her voice.

'We left when I was about five or six, after my mother died. Father and I moved to Aix-en-Provence,' she replied. 'Then to London.'

'And is your father still alive?' I asked, then had to tear

my eyes from her as I realised I had become transfixed. It wasn't simply the beauty, it was the serenity. Her long blonde hair falling down her back, lithe and long-limbed with translucent skin, everything about her was flawless, and utterly self-contained.

She looked down at Fogg, soppily enjoying having his ears rubbed. 'No, he died ten years ago. I have cared for myself since then.'

'Didn't you have any family, or financial support?' Swift asked, forgetting to be a policeman for a moment.

'Father was a gambler. It was stupid of him, he lost everything and shot himself.'

We both looked at her; it was unexpected. 'He left you penniless?'

She gave a gentle smile. 'That was the reason he shot himself.'

'Wouldn't Wilmslow's offer of marriage have secured your future?' Swift asked her.

'It would, but that was not the reason I agreed to marry Bernard.' Contempt curled her lips, her eyes chilled to flint. 'I have long since adapted to fending for myself, Inspector.'

'And yet Flyte was willing to support you financially,' I said.

'He was a client of my firm.' Her voice was now icy. 'He did not support me as a mistress, if that's what you mean.'

'We were told otherwise.' Swift had been observing her, his lean cheeks sharply defined as the room filled with shadows from the gathering dusk. 'The term "special girl" was used.'

'A term he used himself, but do not imagine it applied to me. Charles liked to buy favours, it was his way of controlling people and getting what he wanted. I accepted him as a client for my Girl Friday company. It was business.'

'Was it?' I was sceptical.

'Just because men find me physically attractive, Major, does not mean that I am easy prey. It actually means I can choose my own lovers according to my own desires.'

'Did you ever choose Flyte?' Swift countered.

'No.' She spoke calmly, her voice cool. 'It really is a mistake to mix sex with business.'

Fossett's face suffused red. He leaned in closer to the page he was writing on and abruptly broke the lead in his pencil. 'Sorry, sirs,' he whispered.

Serafina laughed, a light musical laugh.

Swift picked up the will and put it on the table in front of her. 'Wilmslow left you his entire fortune.'

She barely glanced at it. 'He would have made a new one.'

'Can you be sure?' I said.

'No,' she replied. 'But his man of law will settle the question.'

'Would such an inheritance make a difference to your life?' Swift asked.

'Of course,' she admitted.

'A difference worth killing for?' Swift pressed.

'At the risk of ending on the hangman's noose?' she replied.

'Why Did Flyte shoot Wilmslow?' I asked.

Her eyes caught mine. 'Charles was hiding something.'

'What?' Swift asked.

'I cannot say,' she replied. 'Charles was becoming paranoid. It was clear Gilbert wasn't a valet. Charles had any number of servants, he had no need of more.'

'Gilbert wasn't a big man,' I said. 'He wasn't a bodyguard.'

'No,' she agreed. 'He was intelligent and knowledgeable. I assumed he'd been in the military…or the police.' She looked directly at Swift.

He didn't flinch. 'Declan Doyle,' he said.

'It means nothing to me,' she replied.

'Yes, it does,' I said.

'I assure you, Major Lennox, it does not.' Her tone turned icy again.

'Why are you here?' I switched tack.

She didn't answer for a moment. A log cracked and spat bright sparks in the grate. 'I am alone in the world. That is not how I wish to live my life. I've always wanted children, and dogs.' She glanced down at Foggy again, who hadn't moved.

'You're looking for love.' Swift spoke the words that had sprung into my own mind.

'Yes,' she replied.

'Have you found it?' he continued, his tone softened.

'No.' She shook her head. 'Perhaps one day.'

'Doctor Frazer.' The name escaped me before the thought had fully formed.

Her head moved back as if in surprise. 'I think…he hadn't crossed my mind…' she trailed off.

214

'There have been three deaths here,' I tried again. 'We don't know if this killer has reason for their actions, or if they are deranged. It's a dangerous situation for everyone, including Lady Rose and Mary Lovelace. Your help might save a life, Serafina.'

I received the same enigmatic gaze as seconds ticked by, then she gave the slightest nod of the head. 'There was a link between Charles and Declan Doyle.'

Fossett gasped. 'So you did know! That's obstructing the police, that is.'

'Thank you, Constable.' Swift shut him up and focused on Serafina. 'What link?'

'From the past. It was before I knew him,' she replied in her detached manner.

'Why would Doyle be involved in Beth Locke's accident?' Swift continued.

'I do not know,' she replied.

'Beth Locke was badly injured, she's in a coma,' I said, my mind shifting gears quickly. 'Flyte is linked to Doyle. Is he also linked to Beth Locke?'

She glanced up. 'Any information related to my clients is confidential.'

'That's just an excuse for hiding stuff,' Fossett blurted.

'That's enough, Fossett,' Swift rapped.

Fossett picked up the pencil sharpener lying on the desk and began turning his broken pencil in it.

'You organise Flyte's personal life,' Swift continued. 'Have you seen any correspondence between Flyte and Doyle?'

'No. My firm mostly made social arrangements. Charles had a huge staff; I only dealt with a fraction of his life.'

'But you deal with the private fraction,' I said, my voice still harsh with anger.

She nodded.

'How was Flyte's life organised?' Swift asked, leaning back in his chair.

'OceanFlyte own all the properties and the yacht,' Serafina said. 'They supplied his staff, vehicles, everything he could want. They manage and maintain it all. Charles simply made use of whatever he wanted, whenever he wanted. As I said, I arranged the part of his life he preferred to keep private – restaurant bookings, hotels, travel, that type of thing.'

Fossett shook his head as he wrote all of this down. Even Swift seemed surprised by the luxurious privilege of such a life.

'Were you acquainted with Beth Locke?' I asked.

'I met her a couple of times,' she replied. 'She was from Yorkshire; she retained her accent, unlike Barbara. Charles was in love with her…' She paused to push aside a strand of long blonde hair.

'What?' I was astounded. That was a vital piece of information, yet we'd had to drag it out of her…and Barbara hadn't mentioned it either.

She gave the faintest of smiles in response to our astonishment. 'Charles told me one night after he'd had too much to drink. He said he had wanted to marry her. She'd laughed, and said she'd never take a Tomcat like him for a husband. He tried to make an amusing tale of it, but it was clear he was hurt.'

'Does Barbara know this?' Swift asked.

'I have no idea. Barbara isn't part of the London scene. Neither was Beth, but on occasion she'd go out dancing with her friends, or business acquaintants, when she was in London.'

'How long was she in a relationship with Flyte?' Swift asked.

'About a year, from my understanding. I'm not sure she actually considered it a relationship,' Serafina replied. 'Charles played his usual game, throwing out lures, inviting her to parties, the races, his yacht, but she had her own money and her own life. She saw him, and his world, for what it was, and really wasn't entranced by it.'

'I understood Flyte was chasing Clarissa Weston last Valentine's Day?' I said, having recalled being told that.

'Yes, but he dropped her fairly precipitously after he encountered Beth Locke,' Serafina replied.

That was interesting.

'When did Flyte tell you about his love for Beth Locke?' Swift's tone was cold.

'A while ago,' she replied, seemingly indifferent. 'He called me, asking to take me out to dinner. That was when he related his tale of unrequited love. I had no sympathy for him.'

'Was this before Beth was hit?' Swift asked.

'Yes,' she replied.

'So he could have hired Doyle to kill Beth?' I demanded, angry that this had been kept back from us.

She glanced at me, then down at her perfectly polished nails. 'I don't know what Charles was capable of. He was a paradox. He would veer from wild partying to holing up in a blue funk.'

'How long had you worked for him?' Swift asked.

'Since I set my business up,' she replied. 'He was one of my first clients.' She pushed her chair back. 'If you will excuse me gentlemen, I really must leave you. We will have drinks before dinner and I'd like to bathe before that.'

We couldn't stop her. She strolled out, her long hair swaying down the back of her sapphire silk dress. Foggy gazed after with sad spaniel eyes, then sighed and went to curl up by the fire.

CHAPTER TWENTY

We discussed the revelations in a mix of disbelief and exasperation. It lifted a corner of the mystery but hardly shone any light. Somehow the omission by Barbara Boden felt like a betrayal, or perhaps a damning judgement of our abilities.

'I read your notes on what Miss Boden said, sir.' Fossett indicated Swift's notebook. 'This was her first time here, and I don't reckon it's a coincidence.'

'I agree,' Swift said. 'She must know about Beth Locke's and Flyte's relationship.'

'She lied by omission,' I snapped. 'And what the hell was she doing using Gilbert? He was working for Flyte–'

My nascent rant was interrupted by a knock at the door. Redfern came in.

'Sirs.' He seemed flustered. 'I have instructions from Lord Hector Sommerton. He would like to discuss matters with you.'

Swift frowned. It was a summons, and not one we could ignore. 'Right.' He stood up. 'Where is he?'

'He is in the small library, sir.' Redfern waited at the door. 'It was the late Lord Bancroft's private domain.'

'Lead on,' I told him.

'Certainly, sir,' he said and went.

'Fossett, stay here,' Swift told him. 'Put together a case file summary. I want the suspects' movements, a synopsis of their statements, a timeline of events, and the investigation status.'

'Oh, sir.' A beaming smile spread across his face. 'Just like in the detecting manual. I'll do it right away.'

'Process and procedure, Fossett—' Swift launched into his favourite lecture.

'Swift,' I cut in. 'Come on.'

Redfern went ahead of us, walking in leaden steps like a portent of doom heading for judgement day.

'Come,' Sommerton called at Redfern's knock. You'd think the place was his own.

Redfern opened the door, stood aside as we entered, then closed it on himself.

'Sit down.' Sommerton didn't look up. The newly lit fire was failing to dispel the chill and air of disuse. Books lined the walls, a couple of worn leather chairs stood by the hearth, dark red curtains framed tall windows, and a desk was placed in the centre. Lord Hector Sommerton was seated at it.

'I assume you have information for us.' Swift attempted to assert control.

'Patently,' Sommerton replied, then folded his hands on the desk top while we settled on the chairs arranged in front of it.

'Fine.' Swift opened his notebook, then unscrewed his pen in an unhurried manner. 'When you're ready.'

Hector Sommerton remained silent, the clock on the mantelpiece above the fire ticked the seconds away.

'Spit it out, man, we don't have all day,' I said, irritated by his high-handed manner.

That earned me a frown from both of them. I leaned back in my chair and crossed my legs.

'Serafina works for me,' he said. That was a surprise. Neither of us reacted. 'As she did in France during the war.'

'Right,' I said and set my gaze at him.

'I was involved in intelligence gathering, Serafina was my translator. We handled the local resistance, including those working undercover. On occasion we had to interrogate prisoners. Her French and German are flawless…' He paused again, this time to pick up a heavy fountain pen and tap its unopened lid lightly on the desk. 'This information is confidential.'

'We understand,' Swift said. I nodded.

'I am apprising you of this because I want you to understand that Serafina is discretion itself. I trust her implicitly.' He sat back seemingly relieved to have completed an uncomfortable task. 'She remains in my employ, though I am more accurately termed a client, given that she has established her own enterprise.' He paused as though this idea were somehow perplexing. 'My experience in intelligence gathering has led me into journalism. I am now an investigative reporter, amongst other interests. I use the alias, Theodore Grammaticus.'

'You write for *The Times*,' I broke in. The name was highly respected and I made a point of always reading any article written by him.

'I do,' he replied. 'Serafina is one of my top researchers. Either she, or one of her team, verify information for me, or will unearth it if it relates to an investigation I am pursuing.'

Swift was writing quickly; he was using shorthand, long lines of dashes and squiggles that meant nothing to me. 'And the name Declan Doyle is known to you?' he asked.

'It is,' Hector Sommerton replied and firmly closed his lips. We waited once more. He was using silence as a means to control the conversation, and us.

'And what relevance is the name?' Swift prompted as he continued to write, unperturbed by Hector Sommerton's tactics.

'Declan Doyle was hanged in 1917 for the murder of a young woman in Ireland,' Sommerton said. 'He and the woman had worked for the same estate. It was the family seat of the Flyte family. Doyle was a porter.' Sommerton's face fell even graver. 'The woman's name was Aisling O'Connor, seventeen years old and a pretty girl by all accounts. She was a laundry maid working at the Flyte mansion. Charles Flyte had recently returned from Singapore because he wanted to join the British war effort. I assume you know that Singapore is the centre of Ocean-Flyte International.'

'I thought the Flyte family originated in London?' I questioned him.

'They established their business in London and relocated to Singapore in the late eighteen hundreds,' he explained. 'However, the Flytes were an Irish family with landholdings near Ballymacoda. It is a short distance from Cork.'

'How did the girl, Aisling O'Connor, die?' I asked.

'She was found drowned in the lake next to the mansion,' he replied. 'She had been injured, there was bruising to the face and neck.'

'And the case against Doyle?' Swift asked.

'Charles Flyte testified that he was in his bedchamber and observed the man and young woman by the lake; Doyle kissed her, though it appeared she did not welcome his advances. Flyte said he'd intended to reprimand the man at an opportune moment, but when he looked out of his window again fifteen minutes later, he saw her body floating in the water.' His Lordship sat back in his chair. 'Flyte accused Doyle of her murder, Doyle denied it and then took to his heels. They caught him trying to board a ship in Queenstown. He was a foolish boy according to reports, easily influenced and not worldly. He'd been involved in the Easter Rising the previous year. The judge was a staunch Englishman; we were fighting a war, Doyle had previously refused to join the British Army. The judge sentenced him to hang by the neck until dead.'

Swift stopped writing. 'The 1916 Easter Rising was centred in Dublin.'

'Correct, but there was a muster in Cork,' Sommerton acknowledged with a nod. 'Doyle had left his place of work to join the volunteers there. The insurrection failed to overturn British rule and the ringleaders were executed. Doyle was a minor participant and released.'

'Did Doyle admit killing Aisling O'Connor?' I asked.

'He did not,' Sommerton said. 'He swore innocence.

His brother, Liam, worked in the Flyte gardens, and stated under oath that Declan had left the girl alive and come to join him for a cigarette in the gardener's shed.'

'I'm surprised they hanged him on such flimsy evidence,' I remarked.

'If it hadn't been Charles Flyte who'd made the accusation, and had Doyle not volunteered for the Easter Rising, I doubt they would have,' Sommerton replied dryly.

'You think Flyte accused Doyle of something he himself was guilty of?' Swift surmised.

'Possibly.' Sommerton closed the notebook lying open in front of him. 'Serafina uncovered the information I have imparted to you, gentlemen. You know that Beth Locke was Barbara Boden's friend and business partner since childhood. Beth rejected Charles Flyte, and after rejecting him she was hit late at night by a vehicle rented in Doyle's name, a name that had resonance with Flyte. I have offered you this information so that your investigation will not be impeded by lack of it. The chief constable is being kept abreast of your progress, and your oversights. That will be all.'

'Wait,' I said as Swift rose to his feet, his face taut. 'What colour was the girl's hair?'

'I believe it was red, like many of the Irish,' Sommerton replied.

I wanted to ask more questions but Swift was already heading for the door.

Damn it, I muttered under my breath; there was nothing more likely to upset Swift than failing the police force.

'Swift,' I called out as we reached the stairs. 'Will you slow down?'

'Lennox?' Persi called up. She and Florence were down in the great hall. Foggy was with them.

Florence stepped forward as we raced down the stairs. 'Jonathan, is everything alright?' She reached the bottom step at the same time we did.

'Yes, yes,' he replied. His cheeks were pale and tightly drawn. 'Where's Redfern? We have to question Mary Lovelace.'

'She's sound asleep in the drawing room, so is Lady Rose,' Florence replied. 'I don't think you should wake them. Are you sure you are alright, my love?' Her concern was clearly evident.

'Is it urgent?' Persi asked.

'She said something about someone having the luck of the Irish…' Swift said. He shook his head. 'It can wait until later. We'll go back to the tower–'

'No, Swift,' I said. 'We're going home.'

He turned abruptly. 'Lennox, we can't slack off, you heard him.'

'Hector Sommerton is not going to intimidate us, or push us into anything precipitous.' I was adamant. 'We're going home now.'

'We're leaving too,' Persi said. She had come to stand at my side. Florence had placed her hand on Swift's arm.

Fossett came through the door from the direction of the tower. 'Sir? It's dark out, d'you think we should be goin' now?'

'No,' Swift began.

'Yes,' I said. 'Come on.' I headed for the boot room to get our coats. They all followed, bar Swift who stood his ground.

'It's alright, sir,' Fossett told him. The lad must have observed the tension between us. 'I've locked the door to the incident room, the key's in my pocket.' Fossett tapped his jacket. He'd already fixed his helmet on his head and held his satchel under his arm. 'Kibble's staying on, he's going to stick with Mr Redfern and Mouse so as not to get in trouble. And he'll keep an eye on things too.'

'Please come along, Jonathan.' Florence went back to take his hand. 'We've fetched your new trench coat.'

He sighed and took it from her. It didn't take long to don our outdoor togs and file out through the front door. Persi set off before me, speeding along the drive, headlights blazing in the dark, frost already forming in icy droplets swirling in the bright lights.

Neither Swift nor Fossett said a word as we drove the winding lanes home with the hood down, scarves pulled over our mouths and our hands gloved – for all the good it did. We were all clenching our jaws to stop teeth rattling as we climbed from the car and headed for the welcoming warmth of the manor.

'Ah, sir.' Greggs was standing in the doorway, looking rosy-cheeked and plumply comforting as he gathered our ice-glazed togs. 'Miladies are in the drawing room. The fire is lit and Cook has prepared a hot rum punch.'

'Thank you, Greggs,' I said with feeling.

It was some time later, after baths and a change of clothes, that we settled by the fire with a fresh batch of punch in companionable warmth. It had felt like a long day and I'd persuaded Swift not to discuss the case until morning. He was already anxious and talking in circles all evening would hardly help.

'Lady Madeleine left a message in the embroidered flowers,' Florence was explaining about their findings of the day. 'Very few people were literate, and those who were, were often religious leaders or extremely wealthy. Stories were passed through storytellers, or in pictures as complex symbolism. We spent almost all of the afternoon examining the embroidery from the tower.'

Persi smiled and leaned back on the sofa, my arm lying across her shoulders. 'The tapestry in the great hall is about two hundred years old and a faithful replica of Lady Madeleine's embroidery, except for the bottom section. That part hadn't been copied because it was so badly damaged. We've been poring over it with magnifying glasses, but it's still very difficult to decipher.'

'Why does the bottom section matter?' I asked. Fogg lay sprawled at our feet in the warmth of the fire; Tubbs was curled on my lap and we'd all finally relaxed. Greggs pottered about, refilling glasses and offering crackers with slices of cheese and apple on a silver tray.

'It's probably the key to the mystery,' she replied.

'Why?' Swift asked.

'The picture is set as a narrative.' Florence leaned forward to put her glass down. 'The story begins on the left of the embroidery, next to Lady Madeleine's feet. There is holly entwined with ivy, meaning protection, with a snowdrop growing through it. These are symbols of winter. The snowdrop is a sign of hope and the promise of things to come.'

Persi took up the story. 'Higher up, behind the lady is a blooming hawthorn. This is spring. There are other flowers gathered round it: primroses, daisies, violets, and peonies. Hawthorn is another symbol of protection, so is the peony. This repetition implies Lady Madeleine was being kept safe. She was in the shadow of her husband, who is shown much taller than her. We think it means he was protecting her.'

'What about the dog between them?' I asked, recalling the whippet.

'Ah, we'll come to that,' Persi said. 'We should finish the tale first.'

'Daisies, violets, and primroses represent burgeoning love, innocence, and a new life,' Florence added. 'It seems she was telling the story of her love for him and her life at Bancroft.'

'There's another flower amongst them though,' Persi said. 'It is a daffodil, or narcissus, if you prefer. It sometimes can mean a renewal of life, but can also imply vanity, or unrequited love. In Madeleine's embroidery, the flower is at the outer edge of the picture, its stem bending forward, almost hidden among the branches of the hawthorn.'

'We think it could be her French fiancé, Pierre Du Mortier,' Florence said, excitement in her voice. 'It's rather a leap, but it's a matter of reading the narrative that unfolds.'

Swift was listening intently, a smile on his lips, his eyes fixed on Florence's animated face.

'Bancroft Hall is depicted behind the couple,' Florence continued. 'There are honeysuckle and roses shown growing up the walls, and Madeleine is holding a posy of roses.'

'Indicating theirs was a marriage based on love,' I guessed.

'Yes, and passion,' Persi agreed. 'Which was quite rare among the wealthy in those days.'

'The area around and above the hall is shown in summer,' Florence took up. 'The sky is blue, swallows fly above the rooftop and tower, and there are two swans on the lake beyond.'

'Is the lake shown in the actual position of the existing one?' Swift asked.

'Yes,' Florence replied. 'We went to check after the skaters had gone inside.'

'The narrative moves to the area behind Lord Bancroft,' Persi said. 'And it's quite confusing. The theme is autumn. There's a group of tiny lilies on the far horizon. A young oak grows in the meadow next to the tower, its leaves are shown drooping and dark red. Two crows sit among its branches. There are three sunflowers, which portray devotion and abundance, but there are also Michaelmas daisies, which represent a parting, or farewell. There's a mixed group of marigolds and poppies, which shouldn't be there at all. They are associated with death, regret and sorrow, and a hare runs through them, its eyes wide and looking backwards.'

'The hare can mean different things,' Florence said. 'Such as escaping from sin, or evil, or a flight from danger. But whatever it's running from is lost in the rotted section at the bottom.'

'And the whippet between the lord and lady?' I asked again.

'It's watching the hare,' Florence replied. 'Which you'd expect really, but it wears a collar of laurel leaves. The laurel usually represents victory. It's repeated on Lord Bancroft's cap, but we're not sure what it implies.'

We drank our warm punch in quiet contemplation of the puzzle.

'She finished the embroidery,' I said. 'Doesn't that imply she lived to tell the tale?'

'Nor really, and we don't know what the tale truly is,' Persi said.

'If the missing end section completes the story,' I continued, 'then anyone viewing it would surely know what it meant. Assuming they understood the symbolism.'

'It depends where the embroidery was kept,' Florence replied. 'We've been discussing it.'

'Sunlight hasn't affected the colours,' Persi explained. 'They're still very vivid, except for those at the bottom, which have turned dark with mould and rotted away.'

'We think it could have been hidden in the tower,' Florence said. 'Or behind a panel. Propped on a cold stone ledge or a similar type of location. That would cause damp to form and explain why the bottom section had rotted.'

'Doesn't Lady Rose know where it was kept in the past?' I asked.

'Or where it was eventually discovered?' Swift added.

'She said not, although neither she nor Mary were terribly alert after lunch,' Persi laughed.

'Considering how much they'd had to drink, that's hardly a surprise,' I said.

'I think they're enjoying their old age,' Florence said.

'Do you think you can solve the mystery of the Lost Lady?' I returned to the subject, intrigued by the story.

Persi and Florence exchanged glances.

'Whatever we come up with will be mere conjecture,' Persi said. 'I can't imagine there will be any actual proof left after such a long time.'

That didn't stop us speculating on what may have happened, and we continued through dinner in a pleasant, if increasingly weary fashion, until we called it a night.

CHAPTER TWENTY-ONE

'Greggs, what are you doing?'

'I am seated in the car, sir, as you requested.' He was wearing a balaclava under his bowler hat with a scarf wrapped over it and tied under his chin, and his coat, which held a distinct bulge.

'Why are you taking Tubbs?'

'Cook has the day off sir, and Tommy is at school.'

'The cat is perfectly capable of spending the day alone, Greggs.' I was trying to crank the handle, but the Bentley had got cold waiting for Greggs to emerge from the house, clamber into the rear seat and finally settle down with a blanket wrapped around him – and the cat.

'I hesitate to contradict, sir.'

'Then don't–damn it!' The engine suddenly sprung into life, jerking the crank handle from my hands.

'Lennox can we just get on with it,' Swift said through tightly clenched teeth.

'Sir, I'm freezing.' Fossett was shaking next to Greggs in the back. He held Foggy on his knee.

I muttered a curse under my breath and coaxed the

car into gear, then motored along the drive, breaking through a thin crust of snow that had fallen overnight. Persi and Florence were preparing to leave, having decided to follow us after a visit to the Bodleian Library in Oxford.

The route was a glistening delight of white-wreathed countryside under a sky of crisp blue with a cold sun shining. We arrived at the splendour of Bancroft to find it picture-perfect under a light dusting of snow.

'Oh, sir…' Greggs managed as he puffed his way down from the car, Tubbs still tucked tightly inside his coat. 'It's… magnificent…'

'You should see the suit of armour,' Fossett said, his breath misting before him. 'And the flags. It's better than a museum!' His dark blue policeman's cloak was almost white from a covering of tiny crystals of ice.

The front door opened. Redfern stood in upright mode, thumbs aligned with the seam of his trousers. He faced Greggs and proclaimed, 'May I extend a gracious welcome to Bancroft Hall.'

Greggs straightened up too. We had warned him in advance of the elderly factotum. 'Mr Redfern, I believe.' Greggs spoke with a touch of hauteur. 'I am Greggs.'

'Indeed, sir,' Redfern replied. 'I am most pleased to make your acquaintance.'

None of this punctiliousness had been extended to me when I turned up two days ago.

'We would like to speak to Miss Mary Lovelace,' Swift cut through the niceties.

'Certainly, sir.' Redfern gave a stiff bow and wafted us into the great hall. 'May I take your coats?'

Tubbs decided this was the moment to escape his confines and popped his head up from between Greggs' lapels.

Redfern didn't miss a beat. 'And your cat?'

'Indeed. This is Mr Tubbs.' Greggs handed the cat over, who was staring around with great interest, his sooty whiskers twitching. Fogg came to gaze up at him, keen to play.

Once Tubbs was placed on the floor, he and Fogg raced for the stairs. We removed our frosted outer layers and handed them to Redfern. Swift had given his trench coat a quick shake first.

'The ladies have completed breakfast and adjourned to the drawing room,' Redfern informed us. 'Would you care for tea, sirs?'

'No,' Swift responded, then added, 'thank you. We won't take much of their time.'

They were seated just as they were before, each in a chair before a roaring fire, knitted blankets across their laps.

Redfern had escorted us in, introduced Greggs, who was all charm of course, and then they went off for a tour of the place and to meet the staff. The cat and dog were nowhere to be seen.

'You mentioned the luck of the Irish yesterday,' Swift repeated.

'Who are they talking about?' Mary Lovelace quibbled in response to his questions.

'Whom, Mary, dear,' Lady Rose corrected.

'Does he mean the Irish boy?' Mary said.

'Yes,' I said, hoping to jolly her along. 'From Ireland.'

'Ballymacoda.' She nodded. 'Such a nice place. A simple boy, he should never have hanged.'

'They hanged him?' Lady Rose's brows rose with her voice.

'They said he killed her,' Mary continued. 'His aunt, Eileen Doyle, wrote to me. It was quite some time ago… the war, I believe. So much happening at once, and all of it bad. Eileen had been the lady's maid and I was the governess – that was many years before. It was at the Weston mansion in Mayfair.' She turned to Lady Rose with a sweet smile. 'It's where we met, wasn't it?'

'It was, and a kinder friend I could not hope for.' Lady Rose beamed, her double chin quivering. 'You were caring for Clarissa, my dear goddaughter.'

A number of pieces started to drop into place. By Swift's and Fossett's faces, I'd say they'd realised too.

'You were Lady Clarissa's governess?' Fossett said.

'I was,' Mary said. Swift remained tight-lipped waiting for the tale to reveal itself. 'Always such a delightful girl, and fond of Eileen. And then they hanged her poor nephew.' She lifted her hand to her cheek in sadness.

'What was the nephew's name?' I asked, lacking Swift's determined patience.

'Declan Doyle,' she replied. 'Poor boy. Charles Flyte was involved. A charmer, and so handsome.' She shook her head. 'Too rich, too spoiled. And lonely. His mother and father left him in school, or at the Irish estate. They lived such a distance away. Foreign, you know, somewhere in the

Far East. So many servants, but none who truly cared for him. A lost and lonely boy, with too much of everything, bar love. That's the only thing that really matters.' She looked over at me, where I'd perched on the arm of a sofa. 'Eileen met a nice man in London and married him, but she missed her home and went back to Ballymacoda. He joined her when he could, then he retired. But there was no money from the farm. They had a hard time of it, poor souls.'

'What was the name of the man Eileen married?' Swift asked.

We both knew the answer before she replied. 'I believe it was Godfrey, or perhaps, Gilbert.' Mary smiled. 'Something like that.'

'Did Clarissa and Eileen stay in touch?' I asked.

'Not really,' Mary said. 'You know how young girls are. And she is the age to marry now. She brought young Flyte here last year, she was quite keen I think. Hector had come too, and he was jealous. We hadn't thought of him as a match for Clarissa at the time. So silly of us to miss that. Well I told Clarissa later that Flyte really wasn't the reliable sort, and of course, there was the question of the girl who drowned, and the boy they hanged. After that she saw more of Lord Hector. He is so much more suitable.'

'Did Eileen Doyle ever work at the Flyte estate in Ireland?' I asked.

'No, it was her sister's boy. And after the girl was killed, the estate was shut up and the servants sent to other houses. A few of them are in London now, I believe.'

'Working for Flyte?' I asked.

'I imagine so,' Mary said.

'Did you write Valentine's notes for the men to give to the ladies?' I asked, thinking of the note found in Flyte's jacket.

'Yes.' Mary smiled. 'I do so each year. You can't rely on them to do it themselves. They are supposed to give them to their Valentine, but the duel…' she broke off.

'What did you do with the notes?' Swift asked.

'They were slipped under each man's door the night before St Valentine's Day,' Lady Rose explained. 'I do not know if the gentlemen passed them on or not.'

Swift stood up. 'Thank you, ladies.'

'Oh, are you going?' Mary asked.

'Yes, but not far, we'll be in the house,' I told her.

'There,' Lady Rose said. 'Such nice young men. And so handsome. One's a Lennox, you know.'

'The Melrose family.' Mary nodded. 'A long lineage, and very little scandal.'

'The other is married to a Braeburn,' Lady Rose said. 'Do you recall Craig-Dunbar? Now he was a dasher. A Highlander of course. Nothing dour about him, I can tell you. Not that I mentioned a word to his dear granddaughter.'

Swift gave me a sideways look as we left.

'Hector Sommerton has had more than a hand in this,' I said. We were striding for the tower, aiming for the incident room.

'I'm going to move him and Lady Clarissa higher up the suspect list,' Fossett said.

'I don't think they're the type to shoot Flyte,' I replied.

Despite having agreed to not discuss the case last evening, I'd been giving it a great deal of thought, and I was sure Swift and Fossett had too.

We arrived at the top chamber of the tower and unlocked the door. The fire was out and it was freezing. Fossett went to set about lighting it.

'They're just the sort to have manoeuvred this gathering,' Swift said. 'Clarissa is Lady Rose's goddaughter. I guarantee she had a hand in choosing the guests.'

'At Lord Hector's direction,' I added, wondering what else he'd manipulated.

'Devious, that's what it is,' Fossett said as he piled more sticks onto the fire. 'And them proper toffs with titles and all.'

'Hello!' Kibble walked in. Mouse was with him. 'We've been spyin', haven't we Mouse?'

She nodded, her eyes large in her face. She looked over at Fossett, whose cheeks instantly flushed pink. 'Now don't you fret. I've got brothers,' she said quietly. 'It wasn't that I haven't seen such-like before.'

Fossett straightened up. 'I'm proper police. You're not s'posed to see me like that.'

'Moonbeamin',' Kibble said with a chuckle.

'That's enough.' Swift brought an end to the joshing. 'Did you discover anything, Kibble?'

'Not exactly,' Kibble replied. 'But Mr Doggett knows Miss Barbara better than either of 'em lets on. He went an' knocked on her door last night at nine o'clock. Talking they was. I went and put my ear against the door, but I couldn't make out a word. Then Miss Felicity came along, so I had to go off. Then I sent Mouse to ask if Miss Barbara wanted tea or 'owt, but she barely opened the door, did she, Mouse?'

'No,' Mouse took up. 'She was careful not to let me see in. She said she'd have cocoa with a drop of cognac at ten. So I took it up to her as the clock struck the hour and she opened the door wide to let me in. I could see she was all on her own.'

'Good,' Swift said. He'd sat down at the table and was shifting papers into neat piles. 'Kibble, go and find Mr Doggett and tell him we'd like to interview him.'

'Eee, it's all go today, innit,' Kibble said.

'Attend to your duties, Constable,' Fossett ordered him.

'Right ye are, sir.' Kibble straightened his back, and made a salute. 'An' I'm sorry for laughin' and larkin' about.'

'Well, don't you forget you're an officer of the law,' Fossett reminded him sternly.

'I won't, sir.' He went off, Mouse quietly following him.

'Fossett,' I said.

'Sir?' He'd gone over to the blackboard and was carefully rubbing out names and rewriting them in a new order.

'Add the old ladies to the list.'

Even Swift looked up at that. 'Why?'

'Because there's more we don't know about,' I replied. 'Mary has just told us she knew Gilbert's wife from when they both worked in London at Clarissa's family home. She told Clarissa about Flyte and I'm damn sure Clarissa told

Hector. If he is behind the gathering of these people, then any of them could have connections we don't know about.'

'You think it's all about Declan Doyle, sir?' Fossett asked.

'I think it started as revenge, but once Beth Locke was injured it became retribution,' I replied.

'You're assuming Flyte lied about Doyle in Ireland,' Swift said. 'And that he was the one to rent the vehicle that hit Beth Locke.'

'There's more to it than that,' I said.

'Somethin' went wrong, because Bernard Wilmslow got himself killed,' Fossett added. 'I wouldn't think Lady Clarissa, nor Lord Hector, would have expected that to happen.'

'No,' Swift said. 'They wouldn't, would they.'

'And I think they were the ones to ask Mr Gilbert to spy on Mr Flyte,' Fossett said. 'Just like Kibble's supposed to be spyin' here. Not that he's much use at it.'

I didn't say anything because the connotations were spinning around too fast in my brain to take them all in.

'That new footman practically ordered me to come up here.' Freddie Doggett came in without knocking. 'Really, I don't want to complain but it's a bit rum.'

'Sit down.' Swift was less than friendly.

'Look,' Doggett said as he plonked down on a chair. 'I object to this high-handed manner–'

'What were you doing in Barbara Boden's room last evening?' Swift had his hands on the table in front of him and Doggett in his sights.

'I…well, talking, of course…and how the devil do you know what I was doing?' Doggett's usual amiable manner had now evaporated. He was prickly and trying to assert himself, in which he failed entirely.

'What does the name Declan Doyle mean to you?' Swift was in full interrogatory mode. Fossett had sat on the other chair, penciling notes.

Doggett let out a long sigh. 'That was the name of the man who almost killed Beth.' His face fell, suddenly downcast. 'I was trying to court her in the weeks before she was hit by the car. She'd agreed to allow me to escort her out to dinner, and the cinema. We even went to a funfair. It was quite wonderful, and I had high hopes.' He stopped to blow his nose on a pristine handkerchief. 'I don't think she's going to make it. I'd be with her now, but her parents are there. Not that she'd even know me. I've been to the hospital most days; she's plugged into a machine…just wasting away. It's awful, it's as though she's dead, but not dead. I came here to see if there are any answers to it all.'

'And are there?' Swift was watching him closely. I was leaning back in my chair.

'I haven't the foggiest. I was convinced Flyte was involved…but now he's dead, and Bernard…and Gilbert. Why?' He looked at us, almost in despair.

'We were told you'd been asking to come here for some time,' I said, wanting to divert him back to his tale.

'I had.' He nodded. 'Beth had already accepted an invitation and I'd done the same. I'd mentioned it ages ago to Clarissa. I didn't know Beth back then, but I'd decided it's time to settle down and all that. A man can't go rattling around town his whole life. Clarissa is Lady Rose's goddaughter–'

'We know,' Swift rapped, which further ruffled Doggett.

'Yes, yes, I suppose you would,' he stammered then pulled himself together. 'I'm not very good with girls. I'm trying to learn how to act around them. It's not going terribly well, really.' He pushed a hand against his sandy hair. I had some sympathy, I'd never understood how to talk to women either. 'Anyway, I'd met Beth late last summer, at one of those balls in London the old dames like to throw. Beth was utterly different than anyone I'd ever met. She had a really broad northern accent; some people were making fun of her behind her back, and she didn't care in the slightest. She just laughed at them.' He looked at Swift. 'She and Barbara have built themselves up from scratch. Poor as church mice to start with and now they make bundles of money. And they're women.' He shook his head. 'I really admire her – both of them.'

'Hadn't Beth been seeing Charles Flyte?' Swift asked.

'He'd been running after her.' He was staring at his hands. 'But she wasn't interested. She saw him for what he was, a philanderer, and not to be trusted. She said he was fun, an amusement, but there was nothing behind the charm.'

'What was she like?' I asked.

He swallowed. 'Dazzling. Always laughing, clever and sharp, not as intense as Barbara, but the same acumen. Nouse, she called it. Common sense. It wasn't very common, she'd say. Hard work and never ever let anyone tell you what you can't do.' He smiled. 'She was so vibrant, fizzing with life…and now it's all slipping away.' His voice broke and he blinked away tears.

'What do you think happened?' I asked him quietly.

He shook his head. 'I don't know. Barbara told you she'd employed Gilbert to find out who was driving the car. Gilbert was supposed to be working for Charles, but we don't think he was. Barbara and I spoke about it last night. She cornered him after dinner and demanded the truth from him. He's been pulling strings behind the scenes. Everyone here is connected somehow to Doyle or Charles, or Beth. Now we think Gilbert was actually investigating Charles about the hanging of Declan Doyle. It makes sense doesn't it? Barbara's been suspicious right from the start.'

'With Charles Flyte being the common denominator,' I said.

'Yes,' Freddie agreed. 'If Charles had set Doyle up for the murder of that girl in the lake, and used his name to hire the van that hit Beth, then I think he deserved what he got. It was vile and using the dead man's name is like making some sort of sick joke out of it.' He sniffed again, took his handkerchief out, then shoved it back in his pocket. 'Anyway, I didn't know what relevance the name Declan Doyle actually had until Barbara explained it last night, and she didn't know until Hector told her after dinner. She was pretty mad, and really tore a strip off him. I wish I'd been there to see it.'

Swift grinned at that, then switched back to the dogged policeman.

'Flyte asked Beth to marry him, that implies a more serious relationship than you've suggested,' Swift stated.

'Yes, she told me he had,' Freddie retorted in a rare flash of irritation. 'That was typical of Charles. He'd go after any girl just to spite a chap. He made a point of it. But it didn't do him any good with Beth, she told him to shove off. When he asked her to marry him, she laughed at him. It was a ploy, that's what she told me. He'd stop at nothing to get someone, then drop them when the next conquest came along.'

'When you say he'd go after any girl just to spite a chap,' Swift picked up the relevance, 'is that what he did to Bernard Wilmslow? Steal his girlfriends?'

'Yes, I thought that was pretty obvious,' Freddie said, then stood up. 'Do you need to know anything else because I'd like to go out for a walk. I'm finding things quite claustrophobic, if you must know.'

'You can go,' Swift told him, which surprised me.

We waited until the door closed behind him.

'That Lord Hector's playing his own game, isn't he sir?' Fossett said.

'Yes.' Swift closed his eyes for a moment.

'He's trying to get to the truth,' I said. 'Just as we are.'

'Do you think Mr Gilbert was going to kill Mr Flyte if he found out he really did set up Declan Doyle?' Fossett asked earnestly. 'Cos it makes sense with him being near the end himself.'

'He was a detective,' Swift replied. 'If he had proof he'd have turned it over to the authorities.'

'But that was the trouble, wasn't it?' Fossett continued. 'There wasn't any proof. Nor was there over who hit Miss Barbara's friend. If it was Flyte, he was goin' to get away with it, and he might even have got away with killing Mr Wilmslow. Blaming it on a duel, even though we know he must have been closer than he was supposed to be. No-one could prove that neither.'

'Ballistics could prove the likelihood,' I countered.

'That's not enough to convict a man of murder, Lennox,' Swift said. He was in pensive mood. 'It's nothing more than conjecture.'

'Which is why someone just got fed up of waiting for justice and shot him,' Fossett said.

Which made a lot of sense to me.

CHAPTER TWENTY-TWO

'Hello.' The door had opened unnoticed and Edna Kent had walked in. 'You've thrown a real damper on the place today. It's like being at a temperance wake.'

'Lady Rose and Mary Lovelace seemed perfectly fine this morning,' I said.

She grinned. 'True, but their world is cocooned in a rosy glow, liberally doused in some jolly fine spirits.' She sat down. 'I'd quite like to know what's going on.'

'So would we,' I replied.

She laughed. She'd dressed in corduroy slacks today with a simple aran sweater, her brown hair tied in a ponytail. It looked like she was ready for a cross-country ramble.

'You had an affair with Charles Flyte.' Swift killed the laughter in an instant.

'Why do you say that?' she replied, all animation draining from her plain face.

'The drawing you made.' Swift indicated it on the blackboard with a nod of the head. 'He was sitting for you.'

'I can assure you, Inspector,' her tone became stonily controlled, 'I do not sleep with all the men I sketch.'

Swift stood up and strode to the blackboard, pulled the picture of Flyte from it and returned to bang it on the table in front of her. 'His self-satisfied smirk gives you away.'

Fossett and I craned forward to take another look at the drawing, then sat up again when Swift frowned at us. I had no idea how he could interpret any such thing.

Edna's eyes were now blazing. 'You're letting your imagination run away–'

'This is a murder enquiry,' Swift snapped. 'Three men are dead. Answer the question.'

She swallowed, then nodded stiffly, conceding without defeat. 'Yes. Alright. It took Charles months of flowers, books, expensive trips and a lot of fun before I fell for his charms.'

Fossett studiously wrote in his notebook though I couldn't see what he was writing.

'Were you one of his "special girls"?' Swift continued.

'For a while,' she admitted. 'I never expected anything from him. I didn't bargain, or demand. I knew him for what he was, and that he was running around with other women while he was seeing me.'

'When was this?' Swift moderated his tone to marginally more friendly.

'Last year,' she said. 'He'd been chasing me on and off all spring and I let him catch me in June. By Midsummer Eve I told him I didn't like the arrangement; he said it was all he could offer so I said goodbye. He'd lost interest by then anyway.' She looked Swift in the eye. 'But he promised to arrange an art exhibition for my work this spring. It was to be a thank-you gift. That's how he termed it. *Thanks for the company, ma'am.'* She shrugged. 'I don't regret it. It added a spark to my life and I've done some of my best work since.' She leaned forward. 'Maybe you'd like to answer my question now. What is going on?' she repeated.

I didn't think he was likely to answer that, and I was right. 'What does the name Declan Doyle mean to you?' he asked.

'Nothing,' she replied.

'What about Beth Locke?' I asked.

She blinked. 'Beth Locke was the reason Charles lost interest in me, and every other woman he was stringing along.'

'Until she was hit by a van and put into a coma,' I said.

'Yes,' she said, more subdued now.

'Um, can I ask a question, miss?' Fossett said, his hand held up.

Edna smiled. 'Please do.'

'Did you think Mr Flyte was dangerous? Artists are supposed to be able to really look at people, aren't they, and understand them on the inside.'

'That's a bit of a myth,' she replied. 'Although I think Charles could be dangerous. There was nothing specific, it was just an aura about him. He was so absolutely a man. He projected masculinity: assertive, challenging, utterly confident in himself. If you add handsome and immensely rich to the mix, you can see why he was so successful with women.'

'Were you ever scared of him?' Fossett persisted.

'No, not at all,' she replied firmly. 'He was assertive

but not bullying, or at least not towards women as far as I could see.'

'What about men?' Fossett asked, pencil poised above the page.

She nodded at that; a shaft of sunlight through the misted window caught the angle of her cheek, and jutting jaw. Determined, funny, and brave, I thought, but not a match for a man like Charles Flyte.

'I'd say yes, he could be a danger to other men,' she said. 'He told me that he'd come back home to Ireland to fight. It was early 1917 and we were losing the war. He joined the Household Cavalry and enjoyed it, or so he said. The filth, the blood, the killing…' She joined her hands, long fingers with short nails showing patches of paint. 'I don't think he was boasting. He said life felt richer once you'd let the beast loose.' She glanced up. 'He meant the beast within.'

'Beth Locke was hit by a vehicle on January twenty-fifth.' Swift asked formally, 'Do you know where Charles Flyte was that evening?'

'Shouldn't you have found that out already?' she countered. Then grinned when Swift looked piqued.

'Mr Gilbert would have known where he was,' Fossett said, which I agreed with. She was right though, we should have checked ourselves.

'Well, I was in Wales with my parents, it was my mother's birthday. So you can count me out of that one. And now I am going to join your wives in the drawing room. They've just arrived and I said I'd help them with their quest to find the Lost Lady. Bye, bye.' She got up and left.

None of us said anything until Swift sighed a long exasperated sigh.

'I'm going to call Billings.' He pushed back his chair. 'The local Garda promised to send someone to talk to Gilbert's widow. She must know what his intentions were.'

'Sir?' Fossett said to me after Swift had closed the door behind him.

I eyed him. 'What?'

'Yesterday, the inspector asked me to make a case file summary, and I spent hours doing it last night. I've written pages an' pages.' He looked at me, his eyes bright with enthusiasm. 'Can I practice it with you before I show it to him?'

It was the sort of request that made me want to bang my head against the wall, but the lad was keen and I couldn't say no. Greggs broke into Fossett's eager explanations fifteen minutes later.

'Ah, sir,' Greggs began. He was brimming with news, his chins raised high, chest puffed out. 'I have uncovered a secret.'

'Excellent!' This sounded more like it.

'Should I await the inspector's return?' He was milking the moment.

'No, Greggs, just get on with it.'

'Very well, sir.' He straightened up.

Swift walked in. 'Everything is confirmed. Patterson finally told Billings that Gilbert was in London to investigate Flyte and the Declan Doyle case. Hector Sommerton was behind it all.'

'That's hardly a revelation,' I spoke dryly.

'Typical bloody toffs, playing their own damn game and leaving us hamstrung and floundering.' He sat down, anger in his eyes.

'Greggs has made his own discovery,' I told him.

All eyes now turned to him.

'It is Monsieur Flambert, sir.' Greggs let the moment extend before proclaiming. 'He is not French. He is from Brighton.'

'He never is!' Fossett exclaimed. 'But he's got a moustache and everything. An' he speaks French all the time.'

'Speaking with a fake French accent does not a Frenchman make,' Greggs said with a suitable degree of drama. 'I have asked Kibble to bring him here, sirs,' he continued, now thoroughly enjoying his role as star turn. 'So that he may account for himself.'

'Is he bringing coffee and cake?' I asked because I was really feeling in need of coffee.

Greggs huffed at that. I don't know what he expected, a round of applause, I suppose.

'Ere we are, sirs!' Kibble came in, armed with a tray rattling with cups, plates, and the like. 'And Monsieur Flambert has summat he wants to say to you.'

A short rotund chap shuffled in. Fossett was right about the moustache. It was a magnificent white affair curling around a rosy red nose, and covered half the man's face. Bushy eyebrows took up much of the rest of it. He wore the usual chef's whites, complete with toque blanche hat and flour-covered apron.

'Bonjour, messieurs,' Flambert began in a florid French accent. 'Ay 'ave been ask'd to come 'ere et –'

'Enough, Chef! Act no longer,' Greggs told him. 'You are exposed as an army cook and imposter.'

Flambert wilted. 'Oh blimey, you've found me out 'ave you? I knew I were on a sticky wicket once there was police in the 'ouse. It was a good act, though, weren't it?'

I almost burst out laughing.

Kibble's jaw dropped. 'You mean…you're not French?'

'That's enough, Kibble,' Swift said, then demanded from the chef, 'What's your real name?'

'Alfie Brooks, sir.' The chef hung his head. 'I didn't mean nothin' by it. It were just a lark to start with, but then the toffs really thought I was French, and I like cooking fancy grub, so I carried on.'

'Well, knock me down with a feather,' Kibble uttered. Fossett hissed something to him, so he started arranging cups and a plate of enticing fancies, each covered with different-coloured icing.

'How did you come to be here?' Swift continued his interrogation.

'Lady Clarissa asked me.' He looked worried, or the bits that could be seen between the overhanging brows and bushy moustache did. He was reminiscent of an overgrown garden gnome. 'I'd cooked for a weekend party at her parents' place an' she mentioned it to Lady Rose. An' I'm glad she did, 'cos I really like it 'ere. Them ladies is the nicest you'd hope t'find. Real quality they are.' He suddenly grinned, or I think he did because the moustache shifted further up his nose.

'Have you ever worked for Charles Flyte or Bernard Wilmslow?' Swift wasn't giving up.

'Them blokes what's shot each other?' he said. 'Nah. Never heard of neither of 'em afore now.'

'Where did you learn to cook?' I'd picked up a blue-iced cake that Kibble had put in front of me, along with a large cup of creamy coffee.

'In the army t' start with,' he replied. 'Officer's mess for the 49th, then headquarters for a bit, this was in the war, o' course.' He sniffed. 'Then when it were all over, I started working with a French lady in her restaurant. Did really well for a bit, but I 'ad to come back to Blighty.'

'Why's that?' I asked, having polished off the cake in two bites.

''Er husband came back. We thought he'd copped it at Mons but turned out he'd been taken prisoner. Anyways, that were that. I come back to England and turned meself into a Frenchman. Worked a treat until Mr Greggs here recognised me.' He nodded in my butler's direction. 'What gave me away then?' He looked up at Greggs who was taller than him by at least a foot.

'The French fancies.' He indicated the small squares of iced cakes. 'I'd only ever encountered them at Headquarters when Major Lennox was called in, and I attended. I wished to express my appreciation and the steward took me to the kitchens and pointed you out. You were roasting a suckling pig at the time.'

'Ah, well, there y'are. I did them porkies real crisp, with the meat just tender an' pink so's it were fallin' off the bone.

Nice sauce too, orange an' apple with a touch of ginger, red currant jelly and a good dollop of port. Can't beat it,' he said, then looked at us in hope, his pudgy hands clasped over his tummy. 'I din't mean no 'arm, guv.'

'Don't worry, we'll not say a word.' I assured him. Swift looked about to contradict that so I changed tack. 'Tell us what happened over the bombe surprise.'

'Just a bit 'o nonsense,' he replied. 'Weren't nothin' to get riled up over. I'd made it 'cos 'er ladyship said she'd like it. Then that little bloke got all bolshy and the big one needled 'im. I came up after Miss Meg the housekeeper said they was upsettin' Lady Rose. I made a bit of a show, stamped on me 'at and shouted some French. It was just to divert them away from 'er Ladyship – an' it worked. They shut up, ate their food and I thought that were that till they went an' shot each other next mornin'.'

'Was that all there was to the argument?' Swift asked, apparently mollified.

'Yeah, well that an' that Rupert bloke gettin' all hot under the collar. Seems he wanted to have a go at the big guy, an' the little 'un hissed at 'im to let it go.'

'By the big guy, you mean Mr Flyte?' Fossett asked. He was fast becoming as pedantic as Swift.

'Ay. I reckoned there were summat between the little guy and the Rupert bloke. Dunno if anyone else noticed cos they were more interested in bein' polite and not arguin'.'

I glanced at Swift, whose face had sharpened.

'Thank you, Flambert, you may go,' I said. 'And excellent food, by the way.'

'Mais wee, monsieur, I am wishing to be only of serveece.' Flambert bowed, then cleared off.

CHAPTER TWENTY-THREE

'Go and get Featherstone, Fossett,' Swift ordered. 'Kibble, return to your duties.'

'Will do, sir,' Fossett replied. Kibble seemed inclined to hang about asking questions but Greggs herded him out before he had a chance.

'Rupert Featherstone helped Redfern carry Flyte from the duelling ground,' Swift said. He'd grabbed the statements from the little cabinet by the window and was shuffling through them. 'Damn it, we should have interviewed him before now.'

I finished my coffee then went over to the blackboard to peruse it with hands in pockets. 'Why?'

He didn't answer, just went and sat down again, papers in hand.

Featherstone was a long way down the list of suspects Fossett had written and rewritten in his cramped handwriting. He'd put Barbara Boden at the top for reasons I understood but didn't agree with.

'I object to this authoritarian diktat. Just because you're wearing a uniform does not give you the right to order me about.' Rupert Featherstone's peeved voice announced him before he and Fossett entered the chamber.

'Please sit down.' Swift didn't get up.

'I have been marched over here like a common criminal,' Featherstone complained.

'You might be for all we know,' Fossett retaliated, red-faced.

'That's enough, thank you, Constable.' Swift was the calm and collected detective.

'You were a friend of Bernard Wilmslow,' I said from my position by the easel.

'What do you mean by that?' Featherstone demanded.

'May I remind you that this is a formal police interview, Mr Featherstone,' Swift said.

'You and Redfern carried Flyte from the duelling field,' I said. 'You know what happened.'

Rupert Featherstone glanced at the door as though wanting to escape through it.

'You shot Flyte, didn't you?' I said quietly.

'I did not,' he replied vehemently.

There was something about his response that was convincing. 'But you were there, weren't you?'

'I'm going to talk to Hector, you can't treat me like this.' He stood up.

Fossett ran to the door to stand in front of it, feet firmly on the ground, hands behind his back and chin raised. 'You'll be assaultin' a police officer if you barge me out the way,' he warned.

I hid a grin as Featherstone sank down onto a chair. He

wore another very smart suit although he didn't look quite as natty today; he was probably missing his valet and the comforts of a fully staffed home. 'I didn't shoot anyone. I never have,' he spoke wearily.

'Did you see what happened?' I asked in amiable tone.

He stared at the flames of the blazing fire, then nodded. 'Bernard wasn't all that bad, you know. Charles brought out the worst in him. He'd formed a loathing for him. God knows why, or what he thought he'd achieve. I told Bernard to just stay out of his way.' He sighed, resistance melting away. 'Charles was a bully, a womaniser, and a charmer when he wanted to be. He thought it was all highly amusing when chumps like us tried to woo ladies with old-fashioned courtesy.' He looked at me. 'Why wouldn't one treat a lady with due respect if one were hoping to find a wife? That's my view of it, and I think most decent chaps think the same way. Yet there was Charles just giving them the glad eye and finding them practically falling into his arms…' He sighed again. 'I don't understand women, not even my mother. She was terrifying. She'd have made mincemeat of Charles. I'd quite like a wife like that.'

I opened my mouth to say something, then closed it again because the implications were verging on the Greek.

'You saw Flyte shoot Wilmslow.' Swift brought him back to the point.

'Yes,' he admitted. 'Bernard was inflamed by the non-sense at dinner, and nobody except me had taken his side in the argument. That's what truly upset him. Most of them agreed with Charles, even Felicity, and she was supposed to be Bernard's Valentine. I was pretty riled up too. Annabel had let Flyte flirt with her. I snapped at Charles, and Bernard told me to leave be, he had it in hand. He came up to my room after we'd broken up for the night and told me he'd called Charles out, who had instantly agreed. That talk about the pistols by Redfern had given him the idea. He was deadly serious, he truly wanted to kill Charles. I told him not to be ridiculous, Charles was far too dangerous, but he just ranted on, getting himself more and more enraged, and then he left. I didn't know what to think, but I decided I'd best keep an eye on things next morning, so I got up at the crack of dawn and came in here to take a look out of the window. I had to melt the ice off first with my sleeve. I was still in my dressing gown and slippers and felt like a bit of a twit, worrying over nothing. Then I heard the door on the ground floor bang open. I could just make out Bernard, then Charles. I could barely believe it. I tried to open the window and shout out. It was frozen shut and I rattled it to make it come loose.

'And you saw Flyte shoot Wilmslow?' Swift demanded.

'Yes,' he admitted. 'Charles didn't pace across the field like he was supposed to. Bernard did. Charles cheated, he just stayed by the stump and shot Bernard when he stopped and turned around. I got the damned window open just as it happened. I couldn't do anything to stop it. I ran downstairs and out of the door. Bernard was lying on the ground, blood all over his face, and Barbara was there. She had a pistol, it was Bernard's, and she was aiming it at Charles. He was backing away. She was shouting at him, asking if he'd run Beth over. He was telling her to calm down, and said he'd never harmed Beth and never would. And she shot him.'

He'd stopped abruptly. The admission took us all by surprise. No-one spoke, then Fossett did.

'It was Miss Boden?' He sounded stunned.

'Yes and she was blazing mad,' Rupert continued. 'She went to stand over him. I ran over and bent down. He was still breathing. She swore and threw the pistol on the ground, then she stalked off. Redfern came out after that and we carried Charles into the tower between us.'

'You saw Flyte murder Wilmslow,' I snapped. 'A man who was supposed to be your friend, and you didn't say a damned word.'

'I was going to, but then someone shot Charles anyway, and I wanted to protect Barbara,' he retorted.

'Did you know the pistols had been modified?' Swift asked.

'Yes,' he replied, beginning to sound sulky now. 'Lady Rose let me in on it; some of the others must know too.'

Which shouldn't have come as any surprise really.

'You saw Flyte murder Wilmslow and Barbara Boden shoot Flyte, and said nothing to the police,' Swift accused him.

'Yes, I did. I didn't want to tell you.' Featherstone's voice began to shake. 'I talked it over with Hector, he's the most senior man here. We didn't know how you'd turn out and we decided not to say a word. Redfern was terribly worried, poor chap, but he promised to keep the secret.'

'You've all been lying to us.' Swift could barely believe it. 'Including Hector Sommerton.'

'Not everyone. The old dears didn't know, nor did Freddie, or George or the girls, as far as I know. It was just me, Hector, and Redfern,' Rupert admitted. 'And Barbara, of course.'

'This is a murder enquiry,' Swift shouted. 'You've obstructed justice.'

I don't know why he was upset, it was pretty obvious they must have known more than they were letting on. 'Who shot Flyte the second time?' I asked Featherstone the more pertinent question.

'None of us knows,' he said. 'We were waiting to see if you found out. Nobody wants Barbara to be put away, and I know she didn't shoot Flyte later because she stormed upstairs and locked herself in her room until lunch.'

'She was in the hall when I arrived on the day Flyte was murdered,' I said.

'Yes, I think she'd calmed down by then. We'd set Mouse to follow her around, and Mouse said Barbara never went near the tower after that,' Featherstone admitted.

'You mean even Mouse knew!' Fossett was incredulous. I suspected his faith in human nature was rather dented. 'This is just…just wicked this is. You made Mouse lie.'

'We didn't *make* her,' Featherstone muttered. 'We just thought it would complicate things, and I didn't want to end up in court and…well, all that sort of thing. And we wanted to protect Barbara.'

'Who you've just betrayed,' I said.

'And I feel bad about that, but she shouldn't have shot him. Now it's all getting out of hand and it's not going to be long before the newspapers get hold of it. Flyte was always in the society pages. The mud will start flying as soon as they hear he's been murdered and we'll all be hit by the accusations. Things like this stick, you know, and my family name will be dragged into it.'

I doubted that. Hector Sommerton, in the guise of Theodore Grammaticus, would hardly allow any such mud to fly, but I didn't say so. It did reveal his true motive though, he simply didn't want any notoriety affecting him.

Featherstone fidgeted in his seat. 'Can I go now?'

'No.' Swift banged a piece of paper in front of him. 'Sit there and write a full statement while Constable Fossett watches you. Then sign it.' He turned to Fossett. 'Read every word and don't let him leave until he's included every detail.'

'Yes, sir.' Fossett saluted, then aimed an angry glare at Featherstone. 'You heard the inspector. We don't want no more lies.'

'Lennox.' Swift was already heading for the door. 'Come on.'

I knew where he was going: to confront Lord Hector Sommerton.

'Swift, I'll talk to Barbara Boden.'

He was rattling down the stone steps of the tower. 'We can both do that after we've spoken to his bloody Lordship.'

'You won't learn anything from him.'

'He's obstructed our inquiry, Lennox.'

'Fine, you go and lambaste him, I'll go and corner the Yorkshire wildcat.'

He glanced at me, then stopped. 'Bring her up to the tower in twenty minutes. Fossett should be finished with Featherstone by then.'

I had no idea where her room might be so I went to the great hall and picked up the brass bell from the oval table and gave it a hearty ring.

'Hello?' a voice called out. I recognised it as Mouse. She came to the rail of the minstrel's gallery, a broom in hand. 'Oh, it's you, sir. Do you be needing something?'

'Yes, just wait there,' I called back then strode across the hall to take the rickety stairs up to join her.

'I'm havin' a good clean up,' she said as I arrived. 'I haven't had a moment since those men shot each other. There's black coal dust on the boards.' She'd started to sweep the ancient floor, the dust and dirt falling through the cracks between the warped boards. 'I'll brush below when I'm done.'

'Mouse, you didn't tell us that Miss Barbara shot Mr Flyte.'

She stopped sweeping to gaze up at me with large innocent eyes. 'I was asked not to, and I didn't see her do it, so it wouldn't be right for me to say anything anyhow. They did want me to watch where Miss Barbara went though.'

'And did she go anywhere?' I asked.

'Not until lunch, and then she was with the others all through before going back to her room.'

I rather hoped that was the case. 'Surely you must have

been quite busy that morning and couldn't have watched her all the time.'

'Oh it was frantic. We were all ready for the ball, but I just wanted to make sure there wasn't anything missing. It takes most of the year to prepare and then it was all for nothing in the end. Such a shame. I hung a bell on her door handle while I was in the ballroom. I'd have heard it ring if she'd opened her door, but it didn't, and she'd have had to pass me by to go to the stairs and I'd have seen her go if she had.' Tresses of honey-brown hair had escaped her cap and were curling around her pretty face.

'Did anyone else go by the ballroom?'

'A few of them. Sir George came and went, and that Rupert. Miss Serafina went down to the telephone. Miss Carr was around, and Miss Annabel came back from a walk.'

None of that really helped pin anyone down. 'Who do you think left coal dust up here?' I indicated the floor.

'Oh, I've no idea, sir.' She smiled sweetly. 'But whoever it was trailed it all the way across the hall floor and through to the tower. Miss Meg was already mad about the mess made by the police and ambulance, and then after all that, more ambulance men came and you'd think they'd know to wipe their feet clean, wouldn't you!' She smiled again and moved to begin brushing once more.

'What time did you sweep the coal dust from the hall?' I asked, realising the significance of it.

'Oh, now.' She stopped mid-sweep. 'It was after you had gone up to see Mr Flyte. You can ask Mr Redfern. He told me that one of the guests had mentioned it and he said I'd best be quick or Miss Meg would be on the warpath again.'

I left her to it and strolled down the rickety steps to the hall, my hands in pockets. That snippet of information may well be the last lever I needed to force the truth out of the person who murdered Charles Flyte and the man who died trying to find the truth, Detective Sergeant Gregory Gilbert.

CHAPTER TWENTY-FOUR

'Why didn't you interview Barbara?' Swift asked when I arrived back at the tower.

Fossett was sitting at the table, his long face subdued, much as Swift's had been. I assumed Swift's encounter with Lord Hector Sommerton had been less than cordial.

'It can wait. I want to prise out the real culprit.' I'd gone to stand by the fire and face Swift who was trying to chalk something on the overcrowded blackboard. 'What did Hector Sommerton say?'

'He said why has it taken us so long to find that out. He reminded me that the guests are due to leave tomorrow and there isn't anything we could do to stop them. He's been testing us, Lennox, and withholding information. He doesn't like dabblers, those were his words. Policing should be left to the professionals. I told him I am a professional, but he said if that were the case I wouldn't have left the force.'

'Did he admit Gilbert was with Flyte at his direction?'

'Not in so many words, but I'm sure he was.' He put the piece of chalk on the easel. 'I said that if he'd have trusted us, and given us more information, we might have averted Gilbert's death. That stung him and the argument escalated.' He went to slump in a chair. 'I walked out.'

'I'd have done the same,' I said

He glanced up, then down again. Swift was never anything other than his own man, but I knew he found members of the establishment unnerving. The power of the men who ran the country from the shadows would always be a mystery to those outside the bounds of ancient lineage.

'Gilbert's death is the only one that will allow us to catch the killer.' I shifted back to practicalities.

'But what about all the rest, sir?' Fossett asked.

'There's no real evidence of anything,' I said.

Swift frowned. 'Billings is trying to pin down Flyte's movements the night Beth Locke was hit.'

'As Fossett said, Gilbert would have already done that,' I said. 'I've no doubt Flyte was in London, but I don't think he did it.'

'What? Why not?' Swift demanded.

I sat down and told them, and who I thought did it, and why, and that it was all conjecture.

We discussed it for an hour, swapping ideas, bringing up evidence, trying to determine the facts among the subterfuge and lies.

'Sounds like you're going to have to finagle it out of them, sir,' Fossett said.

'Quite possibly,' I agreed. 'But we're not there yet.'

'What do we need to do?' Swift was containing his excitement though I knew he was burning to prove himself to Hector Sommerton.

'We need to put the sequence of events together, and have lunch.'

'Oh! We need to make up a strategy, sirs.' Fossett jumped to his feet. 'Shall I clear the blackboard?'

'No, we can turn it around and use the back,' I told him.

'Oh that's a corking idea!' He moved to grab one end and we helped flip it about. 'This is going to be a doozy!'

'A what?' Swift asked.

'It's from the movies, sir,' he replied with a beaming grin. 'It means right good.'

Which was hardly decent English either. We gathered around the board, a piece of chalk each in hand, and drew and wrote and rubbed out and finally established what and who and why.

Then we sent Fossett off to bring back a simple lunch and make our excuses to Lady Rose, Miss Mary, and those guests who had gathered down in the dining room for the official version.

Greggs arrived shortly after, along with Kibble, Foggy and Tubbs, followed by Persi and Florence. It was rather crowded, and we didn't explain why we were in good spirits, but we all shared chicken mayonnaise sandwiches, a choice of cheese, sliced apples, pickles, and bread rolls fresh from the oven. Flambert also sent up a tray of exquisite pastries, which we took with a fine Darjeeling tea.

And then we were ready.

'Drawing room in fifteen minutes,' I told them. 'Fossett, inform Redfern and then gather the household. Including the staff.'

'Does that include Chef, too, sir?' Fossett asked.

'Don't think ye should ask him, sir,' Kibble countered. 'He's roasting a fat capon. It's a tradition on the last night of the Valentine's do. Stuffed with chestnuts, shallots and sage and everythin'. Goin' to be fabulous it is.'

'I said everyone, Constable.' I spoke firmly.

'Oh, well righty-o.' Kibble seemed nonplussed. 'What about Dr Frazer, d'ye want him too?'

'Yes, you'd best telephone him,' I said.

'It must be important then.' Kibble replied.

'Course it is,' Fossett told him. 'Come on.' They went off, Tubbs and Foggy bounded out with them.

'Lennox.' Persi put her hand through my arm. 'Are you going to corner the killer?'

'Yes.'

She smiled up at me. 'You have your hunter's look.'

I didn't know what to say to that.

'We've made some interesting discoveries about the mystery of the lost lady ourselves.' Florence was ready to walk out with Swift. 'Haven't we Greggs?' She turned to my old butler.

'Indeed we have, m'lady,' he twittered. 'I believe our findings may shed considerable light on the story.'

'We'll tell you all about it later,' Persi said as we headed for the stairs. 'We didn't want to cause a distraction.'

The hall was vacant and we walked across it in a small procession, with Greggs and Fossett bringing up the rear. Visions of the medieval past ran through my mind. The Lord in his rich robes, his ermine-trimmed cloak flowing from broad shoulders, his pretty French wife on his arm, just as Persi was on mine.

I glanced again at the minstrel gallery where brightly coloured musicians would have gathered. I wondered if they'd had a jester in their midst, and hoped they did.

The drawing room fire was blazing; Lady Rose and Mary were sitting before it, colourful blankets around their knees, just as they had been when I'd arrived. Tubbs was on Mary's lap and Fogg was lying across Lady Rose's feet. Neither bothered to greet us.

'Oh, our investigators!' Lady Rose called out. 'We have your adorable little dog and cat, they have just arrived to sit with us. Such charming souls and so friendly.'

'We had a cat,' Mary said. 'He was our Timmy, but we lost him last year, didn't we, Rose?'

'Black, with a white bib, and a moustache. He was our baby. Twenty-one years old and never a day's illness until the last.' Her lips trembled.

Greggs stepped forward. 'May I offer a handkerchief, m'lady?'

'Oh, you dear man,' she sniffed. 'I have one, thank you.'

'You know, Rose,' Mary continued. 'Perhaps it is time for a new baby?'

Lady Rose blew her nose very loudly into a large cotton square. 'I do believe you are right, Mary. We shall set Redfern on the quest.'

Swift had been standing in stiff patience until now. 'I'm afraid we are going to disturb your peace.'

They looked up.

'More questions?' Mary said.

'No, we are going to arrest the killer of Charles Flyte and Godfrey Gilbert,' he announced then went to follow Fossett, who was placing the cardboard box he was carrying on the Elizabethan dresser.

'Just keep to the relevant evidence,' I told him.

'That's what I'm doing, Lennox,' he said, then he and Fossett began rummaging through the box.

Hector Sommerton came in and walked purposefully to the front and sat on an upright sofa. He had a presence; a self-appointed adjudicator weighing everyone around him, waiting to be impressed, or not, as the case may be.

Clarissa had come in his wake. She slipped next to him and neatly crossed her ankles. She'd dressed in sombre tweeds, her blonde hair behind a simple brown velvet Alice band. She caught his eye and smiled. He gave the faintest smile in return.

Freddie Doggett arrived with Felicity Carr. He waited to help her find a seat; she fussed about the sun being in her eyes and he offered to pull a curtain. She moved to another chair and sat primly upright. He slid down onto the chair she'd rejected.

Annabel Cresswell trailed in wearing the same black dress, her string of long white pearls swinging slightly with her movements. Her short hair was held down by a black sequinned band in the flapper style, her eyes smudged with shades of charcoal and grey, her cupid's bow lips painted pink. She sat down quietly at the edge of the group and began fingering the knot in her necklace.

Sir George Lovell arrived with Barbara Boden, chatting and laughing, both animated and a welcome contrast to the glum faces of the others. They sat on a sofa together, still in close conversation, unconcerned by the situation.

Rupert Featherstone came in, or rather sidled in, cast an anxious eye at Barbara then skirted the room to sit on the sidelines, near Felicity.

They must have all been aware something was about to happen, and yet no-one had asked. Edna Kent arrived, still wearing the cream sweater and slacks, a big smile lighting up her plain face. She spotted Persi and Florence at the front and strode straight up to them and sat down. They began a huddled discussion, their heads close together.

Serafina was the last of the guests, just ahead of Fossett and Kibble. She walked in unhurried style to the front, her cream silk dress flowing with her movements. She could have been strolling along a catwalk, long slim neck gracefully holding her head high. She stopped to sit on a sofa placed dead centre at the front and gazed with an impassive expression at the box on the dresser.

'Ladies and gentlemen.' Kibble came bustling up to the front. 'Tea will be served after an announcement by Major Lennox an' Inspector Swift. It's official police stuff, so ye'd best be listening carefully to them.'

'Kibble go to the back of the room,' Swift told him.

'Righty-o, sir.' Kibble beamed and went off.

Mouse had come in with Meg, the housekeeper. Redfern came to stand near the ladies at the front, and Flambert remained at the rear, his short plump form enveloped in chef's whites with whiskers, brows and round ruddy nose visible below the toque blanche.

I bit back a smile.

Greggs had closed the door but it opened again now and Dr Frazer slipped in.

'I was asked to attend, but couldn't find a soul in the house,' he explained.

'Sit down, please,' I told him.

Puzzlement creased his brow but he came forward. Serafina looked up, then patted the cushion next to her on the sofa. He gave her a warm smile and sat down.

I took a breath. 'Charles Flyte was murdered by someone sitting in this room, and so was Godfrey Gilbert.'

CHAPTER TWENTY-FIVE

'It is a disgrace,' Mary called out. She seemed quite with it this morning. 'You shall hang for your deeds.'

'Quite right,' Lady Rose agreed.

I ignored the interruptions. 'On the morning of St Valentine's Day, Charles Flyte and Bernard Wilmslow held a duel in the old duelling grounds. We were lied to about what happened, and the cause was covered up–'

'The cause was never clear,' Sir George Lovell interrupted. 'It was just some stupid squabble over dessert.'

'You didn't socialise very much with Flyte's group of friends,' I stated.

'No,' he replied. He was finely turned out, thick hair combed back, the grey at the temples adding to his good looks. He wore the same light grey suit and blue silk naval officer tie. 'I'm not keen on jazz or the modern scene.'

'You must have been aware of the animosity between Bernard Wilmslow and Charles Flyte, though.'

'To a degree, but I hadn't thought they were at the point of killing each other,' he replied in a relaxed fashion.

'I doubt it had been deadly until Beth Locke was

deliberately hit by a van and put in a coma,' I replied. 'That event turned everything malign.'

'I'm afraid I never knew Beth Locke,' he replied. Murmurs rose at the mention of her name.

'But you knew Declan Doyle, didn't you?' I said.

He had sat with legs crossed, leaning back on a sofa, but now tipped his head slightly to one side, his focus narrowing on my face. 'How would you know that?'

I hadn't but Hector had been manoeuvring behind the scenes and George Lovell had to be here for a reason. 'Queenstown, Ireland, the home of the Q-ships during the war,' I said. 'Doyle was captured in Queenstown trying to escape.'

He nodded. 'An alert was put out for him. We were in dock at the time and my crew was involved in the manhunt. They were the ones who caught him and they dragged him onto the ship I commanded.' Regret pulled at his lips. 'He was terrified, crying and pleading to be released. He said they'd hang him for sure and he hadn't done anything wrong.'

'Did you believe him?' I noticed Hector Sommerton shift forward in his seat.

'I did, actually,' George said. 'It didn't make any difference. The army came and took him before anyone could intervene.'

'Did you know that Flyte was the one to accuse him?' I asked.

'The name was mentioned,' he replied, his tone becoming more military, as it would have been when he'd captained a ship. 'I didn't know who he was at the time, although I'd heard of OceanFlyte International. They'd contributed ships to help the war effort and held a lot of sway in government.'

'Did you hear Doyle say anything significant?' Hector joined in.

'He used the word "Gombeen" which could mean either a scapegoat or someone shady,' George replied quietly. 'When you're stuck with a bunch of men, day in day out, sometimes in extremes of fear, or danger, you become proficient at reading the nuances. A ship in wartime can be a dangerous place. We couldn't have the weak or wily on board. I spent a short time with Doyle after they'd caught him. We sat him down and gave him tea. He was jabbering, and shaking with fear. Only just eighteen and not much flesh on his bones. He said he'd been keen on a girl on the estate, but then the master had come home and she'd had her eyes dazzled by him, according to Doyle. But then the girl decided nothing good would come of it and she was being played for a fool. The next day she was found dead in the lake with bruises around her neck. Flyte had accused him, so he'd run away, hoping his nationalist friends would help him escape. They tried, but they were being watched. They were in a local house they thought safe when the Constabulary arrived. Doyle squeezed out of a window and ran for the docks. My men caught him in one of the storehouses…I wish they hadn't.'

'I assume you testified in court,' I said. The room had been very quiet, apart from a rumbling purr from Mr Tubbs on Mary Lovelace's lap. I think very few people would have heard much about the story of Declan Doyle.

'I did, it was the next day,' he replied. 'There was a trial, the country was under martial law at the time. The commander-in-chief was away and his stand-in was keen to make a name for himself.'

'Do you think an injustice was done?' I asked the question that had probably been a long time coming.

'Yes, I do, and that is what I testified in court for all the good it did,' he said, a frown now furrowed deep between his brows. 'I hadn't known Flyte, but some years later we were introduced at some official do. I had a drink with him and after a while I brought the matter up. I asked him what he thought happened to the girl, Aisling O'Conner. He gave a smirk, and said, "She was out of her depth." He seemed to think it amusing.'

'Why didn't you report this?' Hector demanded.

'To whom?' George replied with irony in his voice. 'The man who sentenced Declan Doyle is now the under-secretary of state with ambitions to climb higher. How much support do you suppose I would have had in trying to open up that particular can of worms?'

'More than you'd expect,' Hector replied and folded his arms as though satisfied. 'Although it is all academic now.'

I glanced at Swift who gave a faint nod. The picture was falling into focus and so was the method. Hector Sommerton was deeply immersed in the establishment and had acted as a form of spymaster in France. Now he was an investigative journalist, and I was certain he was more than that. He was one of the equalisers, rooting out corruption in high places, cleaning out the house to keep the establishment in order. Whoever the current under-secretary of state was, I doubted he would keep his position for very much longer.

'Declan Doyle is the reason Gilbert was hired by Charles Flyte, although Flyte didn't know it at the time.' I turned to Mary Lovelace, watching me. 'You knew Gilbert's wife, she came from Ireland. You worked together in London.'

'Dear Eileen, yes.' Mary nodded. 'We have spoken of it. You were talking about her nephew, weren't you?'

'I was.'

'A scapegoat. I said so to Clarissa only last year, didn't I, my dear girl?' She smiled sweetly at Clarissa, who smiled back.

'You did, Miss Lovelace,' she replied. 'And we agreed it was an injustice that had lain too long.'

'Well there has been a reckoning and I am glad of it,' Mary said, not sounding in the least addled.

There were a lot of confused glances being exchanged in the room.

'Miss Lovelace was Clarissa's governess in London, and Eileen Doyle was lady's maid to Lady Weston,' I explained. 'Eileen Doyle was aunt to Declan Doyle. Eileen married Godfrey Gilbert, who retired from the Met some years ago. Gilbert was struggling financially and with his health, but he was as keen as anyone to see justice done for his wife's nephew.' I swung on my heel to regard Hector. 'Someone wanted justice and was prepared to pay for it. It was you,' I said, to which I received an enigmatic smile.

'And you were involved, Clarissa.' I turned to her.

She, too, smiled.

'One or both of you triggered this.' Actually, the trigger was Flyte himself when he'd dropped Clarissa almost a year ago, and turned his attention to Beth Locke, but it would gain me nothing by saying so. 'Someone told Charles Flyte that his life was in danger, and he believed them,' I continued speaking into a very quiet room. They were listening as though mesmerised, nothing to be heard but the purr of my cat and the occasional crackle and hiss of the fire. Dr Frazer looked mystified. I carried on. 'Flyte accepted the suggestion to take Gilbert on as a valet, or rather an investigator, to help discover the apparent plot against him. Ironically Flyte himself was the one being investigated. I cannot imagine Gilbert would have had an easy time proving anything. After all, why would Flyte retain anything that would point to his guilt? The best he could hope for was some information from the servants and I'm sure he set about inveigling himself into their confidence. A number had come from the Flyte estate in Ireland and may very well have had secrets to impart. But, partway through Gilbert's investigation, Beth Locke was hit by a van supposedly driven by a man named Declan Doyle.'

There had been quite a lot of fidgeting, and the level of muttering had grown louder. I stopped to allow their questions to fly. 'Swift will give what answers he can.'

He didn't, of course, he merely turned the questions

back onto them while I wandered to the window to stare out at the wide expanse of the front gardens.

'Coffee, or a glass of good burgundy, sir?' Greggs had come to my side offering much-needed fortification.

'The red,' I replied with a grin of thanks.

He must have prepared it already because he returned from the Elizabethan dresser within an instant. 'I have made a tour of the wine cellars, sir. There are some excellent vintages laid down. I perceive the late Lord Bancroft to have had an excellent nose.'

'Apparently so,' I said as I sipped the fine wine in appreciation.

Greggs cleared his throat. 'I…um… I rather hope this incident will not affect Lady Rose, or Miss Mary.' His gaze had wandered in their direction as he spoke.

'You mean the incident of three people all murdered in their house on St Valentine's day?'

'But the press, sir.' His chins wobbled in distress. 'The ladies have held the day in celebration of romance. It would be quite devastating if their gatherings were sullied by murder.'

I finished the glass of red nectar and felt ready for the next session. 'Lord Hector is Theodore Grammaticus of *The Times*. I'm pretty certain he can spin a story any way he chooses.'

'Ah, really sir?' His brows rose. 'Perhaps he would also appreciate a glass of burgundy?'

'I'm sure he would, and so would the old ladies,' I told him.

He bimbled off, a look of intent on his phiz.

Swift and Fossett had joined forces in front of the fire.

'It serves you right for not tellin' us the truth in the first place,' Fossett was responding to something Rupert Featherstone had said. 'If you'd have said you was there when Miss Boden shot Mr Flyte, it wouldn't have taken so long for us to find out what's what!'

'You told them that?' Barbara Boden was on her feet, her dark eyes flashing fire at the chinless wonder.

Rupert shrank against the cushions. 'I had to, it would come out sooner or later.'

'He's right,' I said, and strode back in front of the fire. 'And you've lied by omission, Miss Boden.'

She turned blazing eyes at me, then gave an angry sigh. 'I know, I was furious. I was convinced he'd tried to kill Beth…but I didn't shoot him the second time. That was someone else.'

'Ha, that's what you say!' Kibble called out from the back of the room.

'Who is that man?' Mary turned to Lady Rose.

'He's the local police constable in disguise,' Lady Rose whispered loudly to her.

Mary formed a silent 'O', then giggled.

'Would you please tell us what happened on Valentine's Day morning, Miss Boden?' I asked her in an amicable tone.

She sat down again, anger abating although I could see she was still simmering. 'It was obvious something was brewing, Flyte had been needling Bernard Wilmslow since he arrived. Demonstrating the pistols was idiotic, you might as well have handed them one each where they sat,' she spoke bluntly. 'You all know what happened to Beth. I was convinced Flyte was behind it somehow, so I was watching him. I was up early next morning, wanting to see what they were about–'

'Were you hiding in the minstrel gallery?' I interrupted her.

'No, I was in the ballroom with the door open a snatch. Once they went past, I followed. They went out through the tower door leaving it open, typical men.' She shrugged.

'Would you please give a full account of events,' Swift reminded her.

Dr Frazer leaned forward to see her more clearly. Serafina turned her gaze to him, and calmly put her hand out. He frowned, then took it, and held it in his.

Nobody else noticed, all eyes were on Barbara as she continued. 'I watched from the open doorway. They went to the old stump in the duelling ground, both of them had got dressed but neither wore coats. They stood back to back and Wilmslow started walking, counting as he went. When he got to twenty, he turned around and stopped and stared. Flyte hadn't moved an inch, he just stood in the same place. He had the gun already raised and he shot Wilmslow dead.' Fury rose again in her voice. 'It was cold-blooded murder. The man didn't stand a chance. I was raging. I ran and picked up Wilmslow's pistol and aimed it at Flyte. He backed away. I was yelling, wanting him to tell me the truth about Beth. He said it wasn't him, he ordered me to put the gun down. Then he stopped and said I didn't have the guts to shoot. So I shot him.'

'Good for you,' Freddie Doggett said.

I was inclined to agree.

'Rupert Featherstone came running out?' I prompted her.

'Yes.' She glanced over at him. 'I told him to call an ambulance, but he was shaking too much to listen. Redfern arrived; we talked about what to do. Flyte was still alive. I'd have left him there to freeze but Redfern wanted to move him indoors and he asked Rupert to help. They carried him into the tower.'

'Did you go with them?' I asked her.

She'd calmed down, the anger quickly dissipating. 'No, I stayed and spoke to Gilbert, he'd been watching from a distance.'

I nodded. I'd come to think it must have been him hiding in the bushes. He would have been aware of the storm brewing between the two men.

'What?' Fossett was riled by that. 'You didn't put none of this in your statement. I'm goin' to make sure you're charged with wasting police time, as well as tryin' to murder Mr Flyte.'

'I'm hardly the only liar here, Constable.' Barbara was insouciant.

Fossett hadn't finished. 'Who put the pistols back in the men's hands then?' he demanded.

'No-one,' she replied, a smile beginning to flicker across her cherry-red lips. 'It was another lie.'

'It was Mr Redfern as told us that!' Fossett turned to him; the poor factotum turned puce.

'Thank you, Constable. Redfern was only carrying out orders. There will be no consequences,' I said then turned to Barbara. 'He's quite right, Miss Boden. You will be charged. Please, tell us why Gilbert hadn't stopped the duel?'

'Because he wanted the truth out of Flyte, just as I did,' she said.

'How the devil did you think a duel was going to force the truth out of him?' I demanded, also irritated by the lies we'd been told.

'There wasn't a plan.' She shrugged. 'Everything just happened. You could have cut the atmosphere in the house with a knife. It felt like everyone was on a tightrope. Gilbert wanted to know about Doyle, and the girl. He'd told me about it. He even kept a lock of the girl's hair in an envelope in his suitcase. He thought maybe he could have Flyte arrested for fighting the duel, and then he could be questioned. He was as shocked as I was when he saw Flyte kill Wilmslow.'

'Did you learn anything from Flyte?' Swift asked her.

'Yes, that he hadn't been the one who'd tried to kill Beth,' she replied. 'I asked him at the point of the pistol if he had. I believed him when he said he hadn't.'

'And you shot him anyway?' Fossett said, incredulous.

'I shot at his feet,' she replied. 'I wanted to scare him. He deserved that at least. He'd just killed a man in front of me. The gun fired high and the ball hit him in the shoulder. I didn't hit him on purpose.'

'Flyte would have lied to you about Beth. He had every reason to,' Swift continued.

'I know, but I'm no fool, Inspector. I'd have seen it in his face,' she replied firmly.

'I agree with Barbara,' Serafina spoke out. 'I don't believe Charles wanted to harm Beth. He was upset by what happened to her. When Gilbert told him the name of the driver he was puzzled at first, and then he was enraged. He swore he'd avenge her.'

'Which is why he shot Wilmslow, wasn't it?' I said.

'Yes,' she replied, as serenely calm as ever.

CHAPTER TWENTY-SIX

There were shouts of outrage when she said that, mostly from Fossett and Kibble, but also from others, including Freddie Doggett.

There was no point in asking why the hell she hadn't told us, because not telling us was part of their damn tactics. Serafina and Hector must have made a formidable team during the war, I'm glad I'd never had cause to cross them.

'Typical of you, Serafina, always playing games,' Annabel practically spat the words at her. She'd been quietly watching until now. 'I know how you manipulate men. I hope you've got what you wanted now.'

That sudden explosion of venom instantly shut everyone else up.

'What do you imagine I would want?' Serafina asked coolly.

'Bernard's money,' Annabel spat back. 'Charles had been gunning for Bernard, and I think you've been behind it.'

Serafina's lips parted to reply but Felicity broke in.

'What money?' she demanded.

'Bernard left everything to her in his will,' Annabel told

her, her face animated with anger. 'He never changed it, and now she'll have everything.'

'So she thinks,' Felicity said. 'But he'd already rewritten it.'

'In favour of whom?' I asked, being pretty sure of the answer.

'Me, actually,' Felicity replied. 'We were talking about marriage. We thought it might suit us both.'

'And who said romance was dead,' Serafina said mockingly.

'Don't you speak like that. You broke his heart,' Annabel launched another attack. 'He never got over you, that's why he and I were only ever friends,' she yelled, then turned her wrath toward Felicity. 'And he wouldn't have wed you either. I told him you were a gold-digger looking to live off a rich husband. He wouldn't have written a will for you.'

'Well what the hell do you know,' Felicity retorted.

'Nothing, but you won't get a penny,' Annabel spat back.

'Which serves you right,' Edna said to Felicity. 'You admitted it yourself that you didn't want to demean yourself with work.'

'And you think drawing is work!' Felicity snapped back.

I took a step backwards towards the fire, it seemed like a nasty catfight was breaking out. Even Swift looked alarmed. I glanced over at Persi, who widened her eyes in mock horror. Nothing ever seemed to worry my brave girl.

'Wait a minute.' Freddie Doggett stood up. 'Major Lennox, are you saying Bernard rented the van that ran over Beth?'

That shut them up and they all looked at me.

'Yes,' I lied.

'But why would he do that?' Freddie's lips trembled, he seemed close to tears.

'To hurt Charles Flyte,' I replied.

'Bernard deliberately ran over Beth just to spite Charles?' Barbara's voice held venom and she reverted to her native Yorkshire. 'Well I'm right glad Flyte shot him, and I just wish it was me.'

'I wish you had too, Barbara,' Freddie stuttered. 'I can't believe Bernard was so vindictive.'

'I bet he was put up to it,' Barbara said. 'Don't you worry, Freddie, these men will find out the beggar who did it.'

There were a few raised brows at her language but the focus was on the revelation. Wilmslow had deliberately driven into Beth in an attempt to kill her, or that was how it appeared.

My focus switched from Felicity to Edna to Annabel, and then Serafina. 'Bernard loved you, Serafina.'

'He worshipped her,' Felicity hissed. 'He'd do anything she asked.'

'Why would she ask him to kill Beth Locke?' I replied.

'For his money, of course.' Felicity's lip curled. 'Charles would have killed him when he found out.'

'And yet you thought Bernard's money would come to you,' I replied, then turned to Edna before she could think of a response. 'What would you have gained from Wilmslow's or Flyte's death?'

'Nothing,' she said. Her large eyes in her plain face regarded me steadily. 'Nor would I have wished for it.'

'Annabel?' I turned to her last.

'Why would I play such nasty games?' she replied, a sulkiness in her tone. 'Besides, I've never heard of Declan Doyle until now.'

And that, of course, was the crux. 'Who had heard of him?' I turned again to Serafina.

'Bernard had found the story out,' she replied.

'Bernard didn't "find the story out",' I retorted. 'Did you, or Hector, feed the information to him to inflame the antagonism between him and Flyte?'

'I did not.' She gazed back, her beautiful face impassive.

'Nor I,' Hector said, equally basilisk.

'And yet you had been investigating him?' I wanted them to admit their role in all this.

'Yes,' Hector said. 'You know my background. I wanted the truth about Doyle, and do not forget, the Flyte family had been very generous in donating shipping during the war. That fact could have influenced the man judging Declan Doyle in Ireland that day.'

'All of which will make a very good story,' I snapped back.

'There's more to this than a mere story and you know it, Lennox.' He stabbed a finger at me. 'People who wield power must have clean hands. The judgement of Declan Doyle was biased and a man without veracity cannot be allowed to wield power in the land.'

'High words for noble deeds,' I said with sarcasm. 'So you manipulated events around Flyte to prove that some ambitious politician could be revealed for what he was.'

'And to expose Flyte, and to find justice for Declan Doyle,' he replied.

'You haven't found justice though, have you?' I retorted. 'Nothing was proved and three men are now dead.'

He took a breath and let it out slowly. 'I did not foresee this outcome. But each player has acted according to their own nature.'

'Even poor Gilbert?' I said.

He nodded. I turned on my heel.

'Redfern,' I called over to him. He had moved back to join the staff at the rear of the room.

'Sir?' He came forward, worry etched deep in the lines on his face.

'Who told you about the coal dust on the hall floor?'

'It was Miss Felicity, sir. She showed it to me, saying someone had left a mess.'

That resulted in blank looks. I turned to fix my eyes on Felicity Carr. Her jaw tightened.

'I saw it, why wouldn't I mention it,' she said through gritted teeth.

I glanced over at the box on the dresser, containing the gun, the lock of red hair, the Valentine's letter, bits of Gilbert's suitcase, and all the papers, but decided against using any of it. This would be down to the hunter's logic and I had my prey in my sights. 'Bernard Wilmslow hadn't plotted to kill Beth Locke, someone was playing their own game. Someone with a lot to gain and very little to lose. Isn't that right, Felicity?' I turned on her. 'You told me Serafina was one of Flyte's "special girls", I've no doubt you'd told Bernard Wilmslow the same.'

I waited for an answer. It didn't come. She glowered at me.

'Wilmslow had never stopped loving her. He'd had a series of platonic relationships, with Annabel, with you, who else? Edna?' I turned to ask her.

'Yes.' Edna nodded agreement. 'He was terribly good looking but never seemed to want to be more than friends. If he hadn't been so waspish, he might have had more.'

'A lonely and vindictive man,' I said. 'And very wealthy. You returned to your "friendship" with Wilmslow after your humiliation at Flyte's hands, didn't you?' I said to Felicity.

'Oh for heaven's sake,' she muttered. 'I wish you would just go away,' she yelled those last two words.

'You wanted to know everything about Charles Flyte, and his life. You'd stayed at his house, his yacht and wherever else, during your brief fling with him. And you knew Gilbert from your time there. Gilbert made notes, he was a detective. Detectives are obsessive about notes.' I didn't look at Swift, but this is what we'd been discussing before lunch and were pretty sure that it had to be how it was done. 'You uncovered the name and the facts pertaining to Declan Doyle from Gilbert's notes…' I paused for a response. It didn't come. 'And when things didn't go your way, you decided to profit from it.'

'Don't you dare talk to me like that,' she shrieked. 'I am so sick of you men. Everything in life is yours to take. You think you can treat me like dirt just because I am a woman?'

'No,' I replied. 'Because you're a murderer. You wanted

to kill Flyte because he didn't offer you what you wanted. Those letters you sent were deadly serious. But then you thought of a better plan.'

She threw her chin up in defiance. The curl to her lip destroyed the prettiness of her face, which was now contemptuous.

'Bernard Wilmslow didn't rent that van,' I continued. 'You did. You wore his coat, his hat, maybe even his scarf. You gave Declan Doyle's name to put Flyte in the frame. Once you had the van you drove it into Beth Locke to spite Flyte. Wilmslow didn't suddenly turn into a murderer just because you told him Serafina was Flyte's mistress. You were behind it all, and you told Flyte that Wilmslow had tried to kill Beth. And that's why he killed him. Just as you knew he would.'

There were a few gasps at that revelation, but my focus was on her.

'You think I could force a duel?' she was mocking.

'No, although you'd have known there was a possibility. Wilmslow had talked about changing his will, or rather you had probably persuaded him. Did he actually do it?' I held my hand up to quieten Annabel, who was about to reiterate what she'd told me already.

'Yes, and I have the copy of it,' Felicity hissed back at me. 'You can't take that away from me.'

'You had anticipated the duel hadn't you? Or some sort of fight. Flyte was a very dangerous man. But had you worked out all the probable consequences? I doubt it, you don't strike me as particularly intelligent, you're merely venal,' I threw that barb to gain a reaction. It failed, so I continued. 'Things began to go awry. People were already on the scene. I've no doubt you were watching. Where were you? The top of the tower? You could have gone down and finished Flyte off with Wilmslow's pistol if it hadn't been for the others. Featherstone was there, and Barbara Boden. Redfern appeared, even Gilbert was hiding in the bushes. Flyte was still alive and Gilbert had seen it all. Which of them would figure out what you'd done? Gilbert most likely. You panicked. You decided to kill Flyte with Gilbert's gun and make it look as though he'd run away. But where to hide the body?' I asked, then answered the question. 'Where else but deep in the dark. You went down to the cellar because there was nowhere else. His body would have been found eventually, but not until you'd long escaped.'

'Are you sure about this, Lennox?' Sir George interrupted, 'because it seems poorly thought-out to me.'

'I agree,' I replied. 'It was improvised. What did you do, Felicity, in your guise as the helpful little woman?' I goaded her. 'Offer to help Gilbert by running up to get his medicine for him? You gave Gilbert an overdose in a tot of whisky and waited for the medication to take effect. You knew the phenobarbital was a sedative from your time working in a chemist. You emptied the bottle, and shot Flyte once Gilbert was dopy. Then you went up to clear his room, and his notes, and gather all his belongings into his cardboard suitcase, hide it away, then return to the minstrel gallery to watch and wait. Once the coast was clear, you went back to push Gilbert out of the window and roll his body down through the coal hatch.' I stopped at that point, letting the words seep into her mind and the inevitable outcome of uncovering her actions.

She'd pushed herself deeper into the sofa where she was sitting alone; her fingers had curled into claws, her long brown hair falling around her face, which had taken on the snarl of a cornered animal. 'I hate you. I hate you all. Everyone has been given everything, you've done nothing but be born, and you've lived lives of idleness and luxury.'

'That couldn't be further from the truth,' Barbara Boden spoke out.

'Well you were just lucky,' Felicity shouted. 'You and your stupid partner. Charles treated me like a third-rate tart, but he couldn't do enough for Beth bloody Locke. And she couldn't even talk properly. She was from nowhere, and he thought she was better than me. I was only good enough to be his whore but she was good enough to be his wife,' her voice rose to a shriek. 'My family is aristocracy, and hers were stinking peasants,' she yelled.

Barbara Boden was on her feet with rage in her eyes. 'You tried to kill Beth, you slattern.'

'She deserved it,' Felicity screamed back.

'And you put the gun in my pocket to implicate me,' Barbara yelled, moving towards her.

'Sit down,' I ordered her.

George had grabbed her arm. 'Come on Barbara, let the law deal with it.' He practically dragged her onto the seat next to him.

Swift and Fossett now moved in to take Felicity prisoner, but she suddenly sprang up and raced to the door. Kibble attempted a flying tackle to stop her but missed and fell with a thump to the floor.

'Get her,' Swift yelled as he raced out on her heels, Fossett with him. Rupert Featherstone leapt up, dithered for a moment, then ran after them. Freddie Doggett did the same.

'I hope you're satisfied with what you've done,' I spoke to Hector Sommerton, who hadn't moved.

'Justice, Lennox,' he replied.

'You've manoeuvred people like pawns on a chess board.'

'Do you think those who kill would not kill again? Flyte proved himself for what he was.'

'And Gilbert and Wilmslow paid the price for it,' I snapped the retort and went to sit next to my wife, who had remained stoically silent along with Florence throughout the process.

Greggs came to stand behind us, then Foggy came wagging his tail and curled up by my feet.

'Please don't be despondent, dear Major Lennox,' Lady Rose called over. 'It will turn out for the best, I am quite sure of it.'

'Dear Hector will smooth it all over,' Mary said. 'Perhaps we should ask Redfern to prepare tea and brandy-buttered crumpets?'

'Oh, no dear,' Lady Rose said. 'We must wait until it is finished.'

Swift stalked in a few tense minutes later, followed by

295

Fossett and the others. 'She climbed to the top of the tower and then jumped.' He sounded dejected.

Somehow it seemed inevitable.

'Ah, Inspector Swift, that is a great shame,' Lady Rose told him. 'But it brings to mind Proverbs 1:31. *So you will get what you deserve; you will get what you planned for others.*'

CHAPTER TWENTY-SEVEN

I was in no mood for tea. Felicity Carr may have deserved her death, but it was a tragedy nonetheless. Dr Frazer attended the body, Swift and Fossett stayed with him to await the ambulance and the Stratford-upon-Avon police. Billings had insisted on it when Swift had called him and informed him of the outcome.

Persi decided we should retire to the incident room and led me off. Florence came too, so did Greggs and Foggy. Tubbs remained in the drawing room to be cooed over and petted while everyone sat in wide-eyed shock at the terrible turn of events. Redfern organised Kibble, Mouse, and Flambert to whip up brandy-butter crumpets and tea for the old ladies and their surviving guests.

'The ambulance and police have gone,' Swift said some time later when he and Fossett came in. 'Dr Frazer is going with them. We've made statements. I questioned Barbara again, and Redfern. There will be an inquiry; it will help that Frazer was there as a witness.' He sounded subdued.

'Shame about how it happened,' Fossett said. He was

more prosaic. 'But it was awful what she did. Trying to kill Miss Barbara's business partner was evil.'

'She said she hated everyone,' Persi added.

'Yes, but hating is an emotion,' Fossett said. 'And emotions are something that you just have for a while. Like when you get mad at something, or embarrassed, or something, but she planned all this for weeks. That's more than just hate.'

We all looked at him.

'I read about it,' Fossett explained. 'In the *Times Literary Supplement*. Mrs Summerour at Tommy's school saves them for me.'

'I too read the supplement,' Greggs said. 'There was a most excellent review by Mr Tolkien on the thirteenth-century treatise, the Holy Maidenhood. The treatise discusses female sanctity during the mediaeval period.'

'I read that!' Fossett said. 'It's about instructing young ladies to resist temptation and be virtuous. Just goes to show that they thought a lot about chivalry and chastity back then.'

'It was actually trying to encourage noblewomen to live lives of spiritual devotion,' Persi said. 'And dedicate themselves to God.'

'Indeed, milady,' Greggs enjoined. 'But the moral aspect was aimed at the wider readership.'

'Those at the time who could actually read,' Florence added. 'Such texts would only be available to a very small number of extremely wealthy families.'

'But the ideas would be spread about, books were like

gospel in them days,' Fossett added, and so they began an unlikely debate about morals, the mediaeval romantic movement and the chivalric code, which Swift and I let ring about our ears without feeling the need to contribute. It was comforting in an abstruse way.

Kibble arrived with tea and crumpets to break up the discussion.

'Mr Flambert not only covered 'em with brandy butter, he's put a dab of cream on top too,' Kibble said. 'We thought you might be needin' a bit of cheering up.'

Mouse came in behind him. 'And when you're feeling up to it, Lady Rose said would you like to come and join them all in the drawing room.'

'How are they?' Florence asked.

'Her Ladyship and Miss Mary are fine,' Kibble explained. 'But everyone else is a bit glum.'

'Lord Hector wasn't,' Mouse said.

'How can you tell?' Kibble asked her.

'He was talking to people,' she replied. 'He doesn't usually talk to anyone unless he has to.'

'Oh, well I never met him afore now,' Kibble said and poured the tea. Greggs handed out the crumpets.

Mouse turned to Persi. 'Miss Edna wanted to know if she could say anything about the Lost Lady?'

Persi looked at me. 'Actually, Lennox, we would rather like to explain our findings.'

Swift had been sitting quietly next to Florence. 'You've discovered something about the mystery?'

'Yes.' Florence smiled. 'We wanted to tell you, but there

wasn't a good moment. Edna and Sir George helped us after our trip to the Bodleian this morning. We think we have made some sense of it.'

'Lennox, we should listen to what they've learned,' Swift said

'It's quite exciting,' Persi added.

I could hardly say no. 'Right, Mouse, tell Lady Rose we'll join everyone in the drawing room shortly.'

'I will, sir.' She smiled and went off.

Twenty minutes later we all trailed into the great hall, and then up the stairs and into the comforting embrace of the drawing room.

There was a fair amount of chatter as we entered. Redfern was wandering about with a decanter of sherry and pouring liberal amounts into people's glasses. It felt as though a cloud was beginning to lift, and a sense of relief forming after the terrible tension in the house. The warm welcome we received buoyed us further.

'So, the intrepid detectives return,' Barbara Boden called out.

'Pleased you've come to join us,' George Lovell said.

'Do come and sit near the fire,' Lady Rose insisted.

'Yes and we could explain what we've learned about the Lost Lady.' Edna Kent jumped up from her seat and went to Persi and Florence. 'I've been dying to tell, but I couldn't do it without you!'

'You've discovered something new about the Lost Lady Madeleine?' Clarissa said.

'Yes,' Persi said. 'It's quite intriguing.'

'We do have a question, Lady Rose.' Florence turned to her. 'Do you recall where the old embroidery was found?'

'Oh, I've been racking my brain over that,' Lady Rose replied. 'It was quite a few centuries ago, dear. Every piece of art and furniture here has a history, it's really quite difficult to keep up with it all. I think I recall the late dowager saying it was discovered in the same room where it was hung up. That was the ladies' chamber when the tower was used as the family's private quarters. The old bed had fallen apart and I believe they found it in one of the panels.'

'That would be consistent with the state of it,' Persi said.

'And the copy made for the great hall is around three hundred years old,' Hector said. 'Judging by the dyes.'

'You've studied dyes?' Barbara asked him.

'I collect antique tapestries and rugs,' Hector replied, slightly abashed. 'I admire the skill of the craftsmen and women who created them.'

That was an unexpected side of him.

Persi nodded and she and Florence joined Edna in front of the fire.

Edna was holding the embroidery in its frame. 'I've been keeping it under my chair, hoping we could present our ideas.' A big smile lit up her face.

'You begin,' Florence said to Persi.

'Right.' Persi took a breath. 'This tableau runs backwards.' She indicated the embroidery in Edna's hands. 'It appears to begin in winter and end in autumn.' She briefly explained the seasons depicted around the two figures in the centre. 'But it doesn't truly make sense. The year does not begin in winter, that is when it ends. We found a few other books showing a similar design in the Bodleian earlier today and none are like this. As you know, Edna is an artist and also an excellent needlewoman. She suggested we make a lightbox and examine the embroidery with the help of modern technology. We constructed a raised box and fitted a glass top then placed an electric bulb under it.' She smiled at the other two. 'This helped us decipher the bottom section. Edna, perhaps you could explain.'

'I could.' Edna held the embroidery up. 'We took it from its frame and draped it over the glass above the light. This has never been done to our knowledge, as electricity hasn't been available until relatively recently. The rotted section was very difficult to decipher, but we are pretty certain it is a sequence of squares showing the change of seasons. They're all in short form. Snow for winter, wheat sheaves for autumn, flowers for spring and a blazing sun for summer. There are eight seasons, or two years, if you prefer.' She stopped and looked at Persi.

'And so,' Persi explained, 'if we reinterpret the picture, we see the opening scene running right to left, and the hare running through a meadow of marigolds, poppies, and daisies, its eyes wide with fear and looking behind it. Florence?' Persi turned to her.

'When we lifted the embroidery from the frame,' Florence began. 'We realised there were raised areas under the stitching. There is such an area within this young tree.' She pointed to the tree that had blood-red leaves hanging from it. When we looked at it on the light box, we could make out a wolf, staring at the hare. It had been sewn very carefully into the bark of the tree, but couldn't be seen by the naked eye. The wolf symbolises danger; it is also one of the heraldic symbols of Pierre Du Mortier's family. Which we discovered today in the library.'

'Pierre du Mortier was a member of an ancient French aristocratic family,' Persi took up the tale. 'We believe the hare is Lady Madeleine running in terror from her old lover. The hare is running through flowers that represent grief, sorrow, and regret. There are two crows in the tree, watching the hare, they are harbingers of death. If we look next at the little whippet seated between Lord Bancroft and his lady, you can see laurels on its collar and also in its master's hat. This implies the dog somehow represents its master or its master's deeds. In other words, the dog has enacted a noble feat.'

'You think it alerted the Lady to Pierre Du Mortier's presence?' George Lovell said.

'Yes,' Persi replied. 'And your help with the translations has made this much clearer. Pierre Du Mortier was released from prison after a ransom was paid. We discovered a reference to this today in the library. There are some copies of the Agincourt rolls kept in the reference section. Du Mortier is not listed anywhere after that though, or at least that we could find. We think he came to England vowing to reclaim his lost bride from the Englishman who had stolen her away.'

'But you said her and Bancroft's marriage was a love match,' Lady Rose reminded her.

'And I think it was, everything in the embroidery indicates that,' Persi agreed. 'There isn't a church or chapel here at the house, is there?' she asked Lady Rose.

'There is a little house chapel but I'm afraid we rarely use it.' She sounded puzzled. 'The parish church is over the hill some four miles away. It has always been rather an inconvenience.'

'It's far from the house because it was once a convent,' Persi said. 'And we think the lilies on the horizon signify the convent. Which we believe is where Lady Madeleine fled to.' She pointed to the tiny lilies on a distant hill beyond the house. 'Is that where the church is?'

'Yes, it is.' Lady Rose leaned forward to squint at it. 'But it cannot be seen from the house at all.'

'Because the nuns wouldn't want none of the men-at-arms from the house going over there,' Fossett said.

'Exactly,' Edna said to him.

Mouse raised her hand. 'If Lady Madeleine ran away to a convent, and there's the crows that means death, did she kill the wolf?'

'Yes,' Persi said. 'We think she did, and Edna was the reason we found the proof.' She looked at Edna.

'It was because of the light box,' Edna said. 'We could see the wolf in the tree, but we also found it again. Its corpse is lying below Lady Madeleine's feet, there is a dagger in its heart.' She pointed to the area. 'It's dark with mould, and it's sewn in shades of dark grey and brown and appears to be simply a shadow or bare earth. The only light is from this shape here.' She ran a finger over a sliver of paler grey.

'It appears to be a fallen flower, but hidden beneath the stitching is a dagger.'

'The embroidery is a confession.' Rupert Featherstone had been sitting quietly alone, but now spoke out. 'She killed him then ran to hide herself in the convent.'

'We agree,' Persi said. 'And she remained there for two years until Lord Bancroft persuaded her to return to him.'

'But everyone would know what happened,' Kibble said. 'All them in the village and in the house. They'd all have talked about it.'

'They may have whispered it,' Florence agreed. 'But none would dare speak out against the lord or lady.'

'So why is there a story of her disappearing one night and never being seen again?' Freddie Doggett asked. He too had been sitting subdued and quiet.

'That would have been the official story put about by Lord Bancroft,' Hector said.

'Yes, it would,' Persi agreed. 'It wasn't only minstrels who travelled from one great estate to the next. Mummers, players, and storytellers did too. The story would have been told to groups passing through, they would have been well paid to spread the story until it quickly became the accepted version of the truth.'

Florence added, 'And Lady Madeleine became known as Lord Bancroft's second wife to protect her and her family from any revenge sought by the Du Mortier's.'

'Which is why she is surrounded by so many flowers and plants representing safety and protection,' George said.

'Where do you think Du Mortier's body was buried?' Swift asked.

'Under the tree stump in the duelling field,' Persi replied. 'We counted the rings, it's about the right date. The sapling in the embroidery is the old oak, and the stump is of an ash, which symbolises penance. There's a weeping willow by the lake, which represents remorse and the seeking of forgiveness of sins. Lady Madeleine and Lord Bancroft may have planted them all.'

'Oh,' Mary exclaimed. 'What a wonderful story.'

'Is there any proof?' Swift asked.

'Not unless anyone wants to dig up the stump,' Persi said. 'And assuming Du Mortier's bones have survived.'

'So the lady didn't vanish, after all?' Barbara said.

'No, she was hiding in plain sight,' Persi answered.

'I am so pleased to hear that.' Lady Rose beamed.

'And now we have a lovely new story to tell,' Mary said, smiling in contentment.

'And much nicer than the events of today,' Edna added. To which we all murmured agreement.

***

It was some weeks later when life had returned to our comfortable country rhythm that Persi came to sit with me in my library. She'd collected the eggs, discussed the week's meals with cook, opened and read the post and all her usual morning activities.

'Lennox.'

'What?' I was reading an article in *The Times*, Theodore Grammaticus, or rather Lord Hector Sommerton, was commenting on the entirely unexpected early retirement of the current under-secretary of state. Nothing was said of his time in Ireland, or his brief period sitting in judgement of men such as Declan Doyle.

'I have to tell you something.'

I lowered the paper. 'You're going away on a dig?'

'No, of course not.'

That was a relief. 'You've pranged the car?'

'No.' she laughed.

'What then?'

'You may have noticed I haven't been feeling terribly well.'

'Um…' I hadn't, apart from her refusing breakfast a few times. 'Should we call Dr Fletcher?'

'No, it's fine.'

'Oh.' I twitched my newspaper, thinking to commence reading it.

'Lennox.'

'Yes?'

'We're going to have a baby.'

I looked at her. She was serious. Then she laughed at the expression on my face.

'Don't look so horrified. It'll be really rather fun.'

'Will it…I mean…a baby. We're going to…have a…a baby…' I babbled because it was totally unexpected, and terrifying, and…

She leaned forward and kissed me. 'You will make a marvellous father.'

'Will I?'

'Yes, and we will be a family. Our very own family.'

I thought about that, and what it meant, and my own parents, who I dearly wish had lived to see this day. I dropped the paper and took her in my arms and kissed her tenderly. It might be terrifying but it would be fine, because I had Persi, and we would have our very own family, and there was nothing more important than that.

EPILOGUE

Braeburn Castle, April 1924

Lennox,

The inquiry was held in closed court and we were thanked for our efforts in uncovering the culprit responsible for the unfortunate deaths. You should have attended, although I'm aware that you were concerned about Persi's condition. Florence said she hopes the morning sickness passes quickly.

Wilmslow had made out a new will in Felicity Carr's favour. It nullified all previous wills, so Serafina will not inherit. It's likely his estate will go to his elder brother.

According to Florence, who has maintained a correspondence with Lady Rose and Mary Lovelace, Dr Frazer might yet win Serafina's hand. They were at the court but I didn't have a chance to speak to them.

The gloves found in Felicity Carr's room have been analysed and they're fairly certain that it's human blood on them. They used the Kastle-Meyer test. It's not definite proof, but her words and actions had already condemned her.

Beth Locke has made some progress. Freddie Doggett and Barbara Boden were both at the inquiry, they said things were much more positive and Beth might one day recover. Doggett was dedicating his time to her.

Miss Boden was severely reprimanded. We saw her in close conversation afterwards with Lord Hector Sommerton. It seemed to Florence and I that he had some sort of demands to make of her.

Redfern's acts were deemed to be light and he was merely given a lecture on cooperating with the police. He admitted to me afterwards that he had left the Valentine's note in Flyte's jacket as a clue for us to find. He wasn't aware of the whole story but he did want to aid us as far as he was able.

Poor Gilbert's widow was unable to attend. She has been granted a generous widow's pension, which I believe Hector Sommerton was responsible for. She asked for the lock of red hair to be returned. It was Aisling O'Connor's, as we'd thought. It must have fallen from Gilbert's suitcase when Felicity Carr pulled it down from the top of the wardrobe.

I assume you heard that an American corporation has bought out Boden & Locke for a very large sum. Miss Boden will be able to retire in luxury, if it appeals to her.

Edna Kent was there. She and Sir George were sitting together. Florence spoke to them at length, she said there is a burgeoning romance, although it seemed unlikely to me. Edna is holding an art exhibition in London, Hector Sommerton is sponsoring it.

And I've no doubt you will have seen the announcement of Lord Hector and Lady Clarissa's engagement. Florence thinks they are a well-matched pair. I agree, though not for the same reasons.

Persi wrote to say you were coming up to Braeburn shortly. We will all look forward to it. Miss Fairchild is visiting and she and Florence are knitting together.

The laird and clan are as usual.

Best wishes to you all,
Swift

I would have carried the missive to Persi but she was in the garden organising the planting of roses and the like. Greggs and Tommy were with her.

Since the announcement that she was in the family way, Greggs had followed her around like a mother hen. She'd been queasy for a while, and I'd put my foot down about trailing to London for the inquiry; we'd both made sworn statements and there was nothing more we could add by being there in person.

I hadn't quite adjusted to the idea of a baby yet, and had spent quite a lot of time at the lake with Foggy, fishing. Well, I was fishing, he was chasing rabbits.

Spring had sprung and with it new life and a sense of renewal.

Fossett was about to sit his sergeant's exam. He and Mouse were due to wed in June, it had come almost as big a surprise to me as the baby. Kibble had decided to become an assistant cook and was working at Bancroft Hall, where Flambert had also decided to remain.

I tossed Swift's letter onto the pile of correspondence on my desk. What would it be like with a baby in the house? I tried to imagine it. A tiny vulnerable child to protect and care for. All the dangers…and responsibility…and the joy.

Foggy was snoozing at my feet, Tubbs was on my lap. I was wearing my shooting jacket, he could still fit into my poacher's pocket, so I slipped him gently in. I whistled to wake Foggy up, then I went to join my wife in the garden to plant roses and perhaps an oak, for our own future legacy.

I do hope you have enjoyed this book and if you'd like to leave a review, I will be eternally grateful!

Would you like to take a look at the Heathcliff Lennox website? As a member of the Readers Club, you'll receive the FREE audio short story, including the ebook itself, 'Heathcliff Lennox – France 1918' and access to the 'World of Lennox' page, where you can view portraits of Lennox, Swift, Greggs, Foggy, Tubbs, Persi and Tommy Jenkins. There are also 'inspirations' for the books, plus occasional newsletters with updates and free giveaways.

You can find the Heathcliff Lennox Readers Club, and more, at karenmenuhin.com

You can also follow me on Amazon for immediate updates on new releases, plus special deals, sales and free giveaways.

* * *

Here's the full Heathcliff Lennox series list. All the ebooks are on Amazon. Print books can be found on Amazon and online through your favourite book stores.

Book 1: Murder at Melrose Court
Book 2: The Black Cat Murders
Book 3: The Curse of Braeburn Castle
Book 4: Death in Damascus
Book 5: The Monks Hood Murders

There are Audio versions of the Heathcliff Lennox series read by Sam Dewhurst-Phillips, who is superb. He 'acts' all the voices – it's just as if listening to a radio play.

The audio versions of Miss Busby Investigates are narrated by the amazing Corrie James and extremely popular.

These can be found on Amazon, Audible and Apple Books.

Here's the list so far of the Miss Busby series.

A little about Karen Baugh Menuhin

1920s, Cozy crime, Traditional Detectives, Downton Abbey – I love them! Along with my family, my dog and my cat.

At 60 I decided to write, I don't know why but suddenly the stories came pouring out, along with the characters. Eccentric Uncles, stalwart butlers, idiosyncratic servants, machinating Countesses, and the hapless Major Heathcliff Lennox. A whole world built itself upon the page and I just followed along.

Now, some years later I have reached number 1 in USA and sold over a million books. It's been a huge surprise, and goes to show that it's never too late to try something new.

I grew up in the military, often on RAF bases but preferring to be in the countryside when we could. I adore whodunnits, art and history of any description.

I have two amazing sons – Jonathan and Sam Baugh, and his wife, Wendy, and five grandchildren, Charlie, Joshua, Isabella-Rose, Scarlett and Hugo.

My wonderful husband is Krov Menuhin, a retired film maker, US special forces veteran and eldest son of the violinist, Yehudi Menuhin.

We live in the Cotswolds.

For more information you can contact me via my email address, karenmenuhinauthor@littledogpublishing.com

Karen Baugh Menuhin is a member of The Crime Writers Association, The Author's Guild, The Alliance of Independent Authors and The Society of Authors.

Printed in Great Britain
by Amazon

55688086R00178